THEY
THEM
WOLF
by Jaydell

ISBN: 978-1-7640237-0-2 (Paperback)

Any references to historical events, real people, or real places are used fictitiously. Names, characters, and places are products of the author's imagination.

Front cover image by Jaydell.
Book design by Jaydell.
Edited by Rebecca Scharpf at Scrollwork Edits.

Instagram: @jaydell_writes
Email: jaydell.writes@gmail.com

In the shadows of identity, where the moonlight reveals the fluidity of existence, this book is a testament to the unyielding spirits of all queer, trans, and non-binary individuals. As a howl echoes through these pages, may it resonate with the courage to embrace one's true self, much like the wolves within.

Moon's genderless glow,

Shifting spirits, unbound, free,

A pack of true selves.

CONTENT WARNING

This book contains themes that may be sensitive or triggering for some readers, including acts of violence, explicit language, gender dysphoria, police brutality, gore, and mental health issues. These elements are integral to the narrative and are presented within the context of the story. While every effort has been made to handle these themes with care and respect, individual reactions may vary.

Readers are encouraged to assess their comfort levels and choose books that align with their preferences and sensitivities. If certain content causes distress, we recommend seeking support from relevant networks or professionals. Your well-being is important to us, and we appreciate your understanding as you navigate the pages of *They Them Wolf*.

This book is written in Australian English.

ACKNOWLEDGMENT OF COUNTRY

In the heart of ancient sands, where dreaming spirits dance,
Beneath the Southern Cross's tender, watchful glance,
A land of ochre, rich and deep, where stories ebb and flow,
This tale unfolds on sacred ground, where ancient breezes blow.

Upon the earth, where footsteps trace a lineage untold,
I pay respects to elders, all, their wisdom manifold.
The gum trees whisper tales of old, the rivers sing in tune,
In this fictional Australia, under same Southern moon.

Custodians of this dreaming land, the First Nations strong,
I acknowledge your sovereignty, your culture's sacred song.
May this tale serve as a bridge, uniting past and now,
In this imaginary landscape, where sacred footprints plough.

The spirit of this earth, resilient, timeless, and grand,
Guides the words upon this page, like shifting grains of sand.
In respect and gratitude, I stand on ancient ground,
This acknowledgment of country, in a whispered vow, is found.

PROLOGUE

12 YEARS AGO

The air was thick and heavy, the moon's rays cutting through the stagnant night, casting strange shadows on the bedroom walls like twisted monsters lurking in the darkness. The eerie glow spilled through the window, illuminating the dust and cobwebs in a sinister dance.

"We just need to give them some space to talk," the man's low and urgent voice sliced through the tension as he slammed a backpack into the woman's chest, knocking the air from her lungs.

"He gives me the creeps," Aasta huffed.

"Why do you think I wanna get out of here?"

"What about Winnie? She's fast asleep. We can't –" Aasta began to protest, her voice silenced as her partner's fingers gently covered her mouth.

Footsteps, heavy and booted, crunched against the gravel driveway at the front of the cabin.

"Winnie will be fine. Her room is hidden," the man whispered in Aasta's ear, releasing his hand. "And anyway" – he paused, collecting a small canvas satchel, the contents rattling softly – "he's not after her. You know who he wants to see."

Turning, Aasta took the satchel and opened it. The rune-stones inside glistened in the dull light of the bedroom. "Connor, we at least need to let them know he's here. *Early*, of course," she scoffed. "Wasn't he meant to come tomorrow?" Her fingers delicately drew a stone from the bag, the sigil glowing golden at her touch. "Maybe we should warn them, or something," she said, her thoughts on the sleeping couple in the bedroom down the hall. "Quickly sneak in, wake up Mal."

Connor shook his head and sighed. "He's here already. You heard him. Anyways, the old man won't hurt Mal."

Aasta's gaze lingered on Connor, her brows furrowed. A heavy unease settled in her chest, as if a subtle whisper of doubt tugged at her. She bit her lip, unable to shake the feeling that something was wrong.

In the distance, a door creaked open, and light footsteps padded over the carpeted floor, down the hall, stopping just outside the bedroom door. The smell of mould and rot leeched through the cracks. Aasta slowly stepped back, her eyes finding Connor's.

"That's not him." Aasta's voice trembled.

The shadow of the creature on the other side seemed to creep under the door like a silent thief, searching for lives to steal.

Aasta and Connor held their breath, the shadow shifting,

edging from the room, the sound of boots receding.

Connor moved towards the opened window. "Now, Aasta. We have to go, now!"

Aasta stood, her back to her husband, gaze fixed on the opposite wall, locked on the hidden room where their daughter slept.

As if knowing her thoughts, Connor whispered, "We'll be back in the morning. Winnie will be okay. The room is soundproofed; it's warded."

"Against *that*?" Aasta hissed.

"Even against that." Connor's jaw twitched, his eyes shimmering golden before subsiding.

"You don't think it's…" Aasta's voice trailed off.

"It's probably some pathetic attempt to win Mal over." Connor rolled his eyes, hefting his bag out the open window.

The room around Aasta suddenly felt small, the darkness closing in. Aasta breathed heavily through her nose and placed the bag of runes on the windowsill before following her husband out into the night.

The air outside was crisp compared to the thick soup of dread that lingered inside the cabin. Aasta turned, her eyes wide, looking back at the house, her heart heavy with hesitation.

"Winnie's hidden. She's safe." Connor's voice was soft, yet Aasta noticed it hitched at the end. She knew he was worried, too, but he was right. Even the monster lurking in the shadows wouldn't find Winnie's secret space. But where was the other, where was the old man?

Aasta's gaze lifted to the full moon, suspended like a glowing pearl in the dark velvet of the night sky. Closing her eyes, she whispered a prayer; her words, like magic, sealed the house.

"Shield her from harm."

The sigil Aasta had seen on her runestone, the crude shape of a trident, swirled in the air, radiating a golden glow before disappearing. As the last traces of the sigil faded, a manic scream shot through the house.

"Run!" It was all Aasta could say, the only word she could force past her lips.

Dodging hanging branches and billowing leaves, their hearts pounded heavily in their chests until they reached the lake, its water lapping at their feet, the moon's reflection lighting up the island ahead.

"Quickly," Connor barked. "We have to swim across. We must —"

The crack of a gunshot echoed through the trees, birds once roosting for the night scattering into the darkness. Connor fell, heavily, blood pooling at his neck, trickling down his forehead from the still-sizzling entry wound.

"Silver..." Aasta growled. In that harrowing moment, a

surge of sorrow gripped her heart, threatening to drown her in a sea of grief. Yet she knew there was no time for such indulgence, no room for the luxury of sadness. She had to transform that pain into anger and rage.

She screamed, howling at the moon – a primal, guttural cry. Bones cracked; skin slithered from her muscles as fur bristled along her back. She knew she was no match for the monster that made its way through the trees, rifle in hand, standing before her. But she had to try. For her daughter. For her Winnifred.

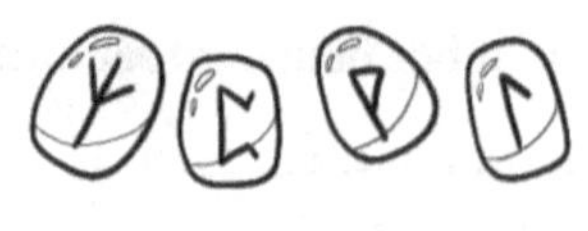

CHAPTER ONE

PRESENT DAY

"Sorrow… what rhymes with sorrow…"

A chip of plastic peels off in my mouth as I bite the end of the pen. It's one of those cheap pens you get for free at school – unreliable, and probably highly carcinogenic. But when inspiration strikes, you'll use whatever's within reach. Toxicity and all.

Borrow, follow… "Tomorrow!"

My words scrawl across the page, the notebook slipping against my thigh, and I swear as black ink smudges the paper. A cockatoo flies overhead, screaming loudly, its wings casting a fleeting shadow over the sun-drenched backyard. By the sounds of that squawk, it's clearly equally annoyed about this ridiculous pen. However, determined as I am to continue, to chase down these elusive rhymes and rhythms that dance through my mind, I persist, pulling another Biro from my bag.

Writing has always been a means of escape for me, a way to slip into new worlds and forget about the troubles of the present, the past. It's been this way for as long as I can remember, ever since I was a small child scribbling stories at recess. I pick up a pen, and the world falls away, replaced by a blank page waiting to be filled with my thoughts and dreams.

Of course, it's not always easy to make time for writing. There are days when life takes over. But even then, I find myself stealing moments here and there, jotting down a few sentences on my arm during class or staying up late to finish that perfect line.

Writing is the compass that guides me through the maze of life, helping me make sense of the world. Without it, I wouldn't be the person I am today.

The side of my hand smudges against the paper once more, the ink still not dry. I can't help but chuckle at the familiar chaos I've created on the page. My handwriting an intricate code known only to me and a few unwitting teachers who've tried to decipher it. It's as if my pen and paper share a secret pact to thwart all readability. Yet, amid the ink-blots and wayward strokes, my words take shape, my stories emerge, and that's what truly matters.

My fingers trace the drying ink, and I feel as if a weight has been lifted from my shoulders, even just a little, by placing these roiling thoughts on the page.

I let out a heavy breath and read over the words…

Anxiety steals,

our precious moments, lost.

A hollow feeling buried deep inside

of spinning shadows, churn...

But at what cost?

The air is thick with the scent of memory.

Echoes of yester – day, week, month, year –

like ghosts, haunt me.

I try to outrun the shadows that follow,

but they wrap around me,

like a cloak of sorrow.

Sorrow.

    Hollow.

      No tomorrow.

Breathe in, breathe out...

It's okay. It's just today.

"Winnifred…" Jocelyn's voice coos from the kitchen window. The sound of dishes and cutlery clatter in the sink. I gently cap my pen, close my notepad, and slip them into my backpack between a recently *liberated* book of Sappho's poetry, and an open packet of beef jerky.

Jocelyn calls again, her voice singsongy and sweet. Up until the fourth call.

"WINNIFRED!"

Flip-flopping thongs clap from the kitchen, echoing up the hallway to the front door. The flimsy laminate squawks open with such force the reverberating sound of it banging against the brick wall makes me wince.

"This bloody door!" Jocelyn swears a rainbow of curses before stomping back inside. "It's fallen off the bloody hinge again, Terrence!"

Sitting on the rusty swing set that stands lonely in the backyard, I ignore the tirade of expletives coming from inside the house, focusing instead on the cicadas buzzing in rhythm to the squeaking metal. Dragging my shoes through the dirt, dust drifts into the thick summer air. Watching the brown specks, I idly swipe the screen of my phone until I find the song I'm looking for and feel my body sigh. A long, extended breath where I feel my soul sink into the deep, husky voice of Amy Winehouse, her contralto tones drowning out the cursing, the cicadas…

drowning out life.

Her songs, and a stack of old school music, fill my phone. They're some of the only memories I have of my parents. I remember all the CDs of theirs Aunt Sofia had, and after years of lugging them around, I'm oh so grateful for the cloud. My parents' eclectic taste, spanning from the grunge of Nirvana to the haunting melodies of The Cure and even the pop nostalgia of the Spice Girls, makes it feel as if they're still here with me.

I have a few other trinkets, too, like Mum's locket necklace and moonstone runes. The smooth stones sit snug in their little canvas bag, wedged into my jeans pocket. The weight of them is always reassuring.

Jocelyn and Terrence are the latest foster carers to take me in. This has been my fourth house in just as many years. But lately, no matter where I end up, no one takes the effort to get to know me. They all reckon I'm cursed. And to Jocelyn, especially, I'm just a paycheque, and paycheques don't get a voice.

I watch as one of the other foster kids jumps out a window and runs for the street, laughing.

Even over the music, I can still hear Jocelyn carrying on. And hearing *that* name shouted through the house? *Winnifred…* sets me on edge. What were my parents thinking? Winnifred? Clearly they had hated me from the start, especially considering they'd abandoned me. Gave me a shit name, then pissed off.

That name is dead to me.

A long, heavy sigh filled with years of anger and sadness slides from me. I slip my hand into my pocket, into the canvas bag nestled within, and roll the runestones in my fingers.

"They didn't piss off, you idiot…" I find myself breathing, the words edging past my lips, the sounds drowned out by the birds in the trees.

They died.

Like everyone else. Like Aunt Sofia. The Donaldsons.

I turn the music up some more. A new song, a heavier song, full of drums and bass, to push back that tightening, burning feeling curling up my stomach.

I've met with a bunch of school-appointed counsellors over the years – social workers, therapists… each with their own theories and assumptions about why I hated my name so much. They suggested that maybe I preferred to go by Fred because Winnifred reminded me of something unpleasant. Because *Winnifred* reminded me of all those people I'd lost.

I can feel my eyes rolling even thinking about it. No shit, Patricia, for sure, but did you ever think it's also because I identify as non-binary and Winnifred is an epically femme name? It wasn't until I met this last social worker who moved me out here that someone finally understood the truth and accepted me for who I was, and that my being non-binary wasn't a faze or a fad, just like me liking girls isn't a faze or a fad. It's not because of *trauma*. Oh, how head shrinks *love* that word. I reckon they get paid by big pharma every time they say it.

I turn the volume up some more with a tap of my thumb.

And now, here I am. Another house. Another town. Another life. A life that I'll no doubt be kicked out of again. Maybe that's why no one bothers with me; I'm just a temporary resident.

Admittedly, I don't exactly make the time to let anyone give a shit about me. The walls I've built around me are so formidable, even Atilla himself would struggle.

There's a lull in my music, and I hear the back door creak open. It's the type of sound a door makes when the person opening it is trying extra hard to *not* make a sound. In other words, it was loud. A long, drawn-out wail of a creak. The door jangles shut as smaller, lighter footsteps run across the back deck and over the dusty grass. And who pops their head out from the overgrown oleander? Cassie – another foster kid from this foster farm. There are about five of us now. Cassie's the one I can tolerate the most.

She smiles at me, a giant, toothy grin full of mischief, and throws her hands on her hips.

"Shit, Jocelyn's pissed," she breathes heavily, holding back a laugh. "We've all done a runner. She's been on the drink again." The waif of a girl sits on the swing next to me, her orange braid winding down her back. "You alright?"

I keep quiet, as always. As much as the concept of *friends* sounds like a nice idea, there's no point. I'll be shipped off soon enough. Jocelyn will get tired of me, figure the money isn't worth the hassle. Either that or the *curse* will catch up with me. Either way, it's just a matter of time.

I offer Cassie a shrug.

"Suit yourself. I'm off down the road to a party." Cassie swings off the seat, landing on a skip. She twirls around, her hands zipping up her silky blue jacket before popping the collar. "The party's at Randy's place." She grins, shaking her shoulders in the oversized piece of clothing. I bite my lip, holding back my laughter.

"Really?" I finally speak, staring at the giant, sweat-stained jacket. "Randy?"

"Yeah, Randy."

I can't hold back the laughter anymore, the chuckle forcing its way out of my nose in a snort as I buckle over and pretend to vomit into the garden bed.

Cassie scoffs, but a smirk soon twitches on her cheeks and she's giggling. "He's not that bad…"

"If you like a guy that looks like chicken bones wrapped in papier-mâché."

Cassie snorts a laugh before flipping me the bird and leaving the yard through a gap in the back fence, her voice sounding in the distance. "Come hang later!"

I scrunch my face at the idea, despite *The Great Wall of Fred* crumbling, just the slightest.

Thanks, but no thanks.

Randy and his crew aren't exactly my style. A small town like Acacia Hills breeds small-minded people. Hence why I don't exactly fit in. I think I'm the only queer kid around.

The dulcet tones of free-to-air television hum from inside the house, followed by the familiar *crack* and *fizz* of Jocelyn opening another beer. I close my eyes and focus instead on the other sounds of the evening; kookaburras cackle in the distance, their laughs overshadowed by the screeching chatter of the lorikeets, high in the blossoming gum above, squabbling over a place to roost. One lone lorikeet flits down and rests on the slide, its tiny feet tapping against the metal before it gains purchase and flies back up into the branches, finding the best place, the safest spot, to spend the night.

"Guess it's time for me to do the same."

In one swift motion, I pick up my backpack and swing it over my shoulders. Sliding my phone into the front pocket of my hoodie, my fingers find the volume button once more, pushing down as the angsty, emo sounds of nineties punk blast through the headphones hanging around my neck. Just like the locket that hangs there, nestled beneath my binder.

Walking the cracked concrete path that clings to the wooden fence at the side of Jocelyn's house, I soon find myself at the driveway and step out onto the sidewalk and onto the street. The afternoon sun, setting on another shitty Sunday, is at least something I can enjoy. Golden clouds like tufts of freshly spun cotton fill the lilac sky – a storm rumbling in the distance. The smattering of late Victorian houses, with their chipped cladding and rolling tin roofs, sit hidden behind tractors, trolleys, and scuffed up couches.

As the pounding music from Randy's house grows louder with each step, I can't help but let my mind wander back to the fragments of my past, like faded photographs in the attic of my memories.

My parents, gone when I was just five years old, have left me with a void that no amount of music, writing, or reading can ever truly fill.

Aunt Sofia tried. She was my beacon of hope during those shitty years. She gave me stability until, well… I was ten when she died, thrusting me into another dark chapter of my life. Greg, her loser husband, turned into an absolute prick, blaming me for her death. Didn't want me around anymore.

The foster system soon followed, and it wasn't so bad. Glyness and Martin Donaldson were great. *Were* being the operative word there. That's when people started to think I was cursed. Just dumb luck, really. After the car crash, it was just one shitty home after the other. I've gotten used to leaving behind fragments of my life. Tragedy seems to follow me.

And now, here I am. Going to Randy's party in this bumfuck nowhere town. I still remember the hope I'd felt when the social worker had said they'd found some distant relative here. But hope's a lie.

Startled from my thoughts, a stray dog's growl comes from behind a garbage bin, its snarling snout poking out from the corner. I freeze, slowly removing my headphones as I back away. The dog steps out, its growling silenced as it locks eyes with me.

"You look a little worse for wear, buddy…" I offer, stooping gently. I remember the jerky in my bag and reach for it, tossing it towards the mangy thing. Its nose twitches, and it quickly snatches the beef scraps before darting off down a laneway to the campground.

"Pfft. Righto. Bye, then."

The smell of sizzling snags wafts through the air, and my stomach growls in response. I reach into my pocket and pull out a runestone, feeling the smooth, cool surface of the pearlescent stone under my fingertips.

"Perthro," I muse, tracing the carved sigil that resembles a pointy capital C. "Good luck or bad luck, huh? And which are you going to be?" The opaline colouring shines in my hand. "A free feed sounds like pretty good luck to me." I stare down the road towards the sound of the music. "Maybe I'll just duck in, grab a bite to eat, and bugger off."

If this really is *good luck*, then why is my stomach twisting with something other than hunger…

CHAPTER TWO

The sun has dipped behind the mountains now, pulling with it a blanket of rain clouds covering the valley. The worst of the sweltering heat has subsided, and a coolness fills the air. I'm grateful I decided to put my hoodie on before leaving.

Randy's place is absolutely packed. Loads of sweaty teens spill out into the front yard like a drunken river of hormones – swearing, grinding, fighting. I begin to wonder whether a free feed is worth the hassle, but the smell of the barbeque pulls me in.

The house is cramped. It feels like half the school is here, including teachers. I spy the math teacher, Mr Croft, upside down with a plastic tube in his mouth, beer frothing over his cheeks. Randy and the rest of the guys chant as Croft performs the testosterone-fuelled challenge of the keg stand. Hip-hop blares over the speakers. Even the goth kids have come out to play, the group huddled in the far corner smoking clove ciga-rettes.

Winding my way through the house, avoiding the drunken laughter and make-out sessions, I find the kitchen, my prize for this social outing spread across the bench. Plates of snags, piles of bread, and the caramelly deliciousness of fried onions.

"Jackpot."

An esky of beer glistens in the corner of my eye.

"One won't hurt." I smile, grabbing an unlabelled brown bottle, sliding it into the pocket of my hoodie. "And another, because why not."

With my bounty made, I make a beeline for the backdoor. It's just a jump over the fence and a few blocks' walk until the river. Fresh air sounds good right about now. Way better than this sweaty cesspit.

"Y'made it!" the voice cuts through the music.

I feel my cheeks puff, filling with air. I turn, blowing out the bullshit and replace my frustration with a half-arsed smile. I am so not in the mood to *people*.

"Cassie!" I grimace.

Cassie's face lights up. "You're here!" she says, the words a little less slurred this time around. Hobbling towards me, her red plastic cup tips slightly, the liquid pouring out. "Oops…"

"Drunk already, I see?" I take the cup from her and empty what remains into the sink, filling it with water. "Look, *vodka*." I smile. Cassie greedily chugs. I roll my eyes. *That's one way to sober her up.* I fill another cup from the sink and hand it to her.

"This vodka tastes weird," she grumbles, but chugs the

contents again, all the same. She throws the cup in the sink, rubbing her face, her eyes finding mine. "Fred!" Cassie squeals, lunging for a hug.

Really? A hug? We've lived under the same roof for how long now, and we've never been *huggers*. Alcohol does crazy things.

"Nope," I say, sidestepping the flailing drunken embrace.

Her arms fall to her side. "Wai…" she slurs, the letter *'t'* at the end of the word nowhere to be found. "What d'you mean, *nope*?"

"I'm not here," I mutter, trying to escape the noise and chaos of the party.

"Piss off, you are!" Cassie teases, her eyes squinting playfully.

"I'm just a figment of your drunken imagination."

"I'm not *that* drunk."

I sigh, pulling my hoodie tighter around me, ready to leave, when I see her. Strawberry blonde hair that frames a face of dancing freckles. And her eyes? Even in the dull light of this party, they shine so blue. I watch as she effortlessly smiles and laughs, weaving through the crowd. That smile… heart-melting. The kind that could turn even the iciest soul into a puddle of mush.

It's me. I'm mush.

It's as if time has folded in on itself, and I'm transported to one of those movie moments where everything else fades into the background. I can't tear my gaze away from her, even if I tried, and a few more bricks are dislodged from my emotional barricade.

"Hoo'da?" I mumble, mentally facepalming. My stomach roils with embarrassment. Wow. That's as good as a Neanderthal grunt. Clearly my mouth hasn't caught up with the fireworks of thoughts popping off in my brain.

Fred, get a grip!

That's when I realise the biggest mistake I've made since moving here. My eyes shift towards Cassie, her face alight with excitement, her eyes on me. She's been asking and asking, ever since I moved into Jocelyn's, "*Do you have a boyfriend? Girlfriend? Joyfriend?*" Over and over. And here I am, standing like a complete wall of jelly, about to squelch down into a puddle of goo.

"Genevieve Chase." Cassie grins. "Or, just Ginny," she continues. "She left right about the time you rocked up. Went overseas. Her grandad had to go away for work, or something – Amsterdam! How cool's that?"

Finally I can feel myself gaining some sort of control over my body, and I stand tall, my shoulders squared.

"Cool." I nod, as if this information is completely

uninteresting and nothing I care about at all. Because it's not.

Cassie eyes me sideways. "Want me to introduce you?"

"Rack off," I grunt, pushing my way through the throng of sweaty people, away from that moment, through the backdoor and out to the fresh air. Spying a lone chair under the back veranda, I throw my body down, stuffing the remnants of sausage sandwich in my mouth, and chew hard.

"Genevieve," I groan, spitting crumbs. "What kind of name is that?" Not that I can talk. *Winnifred.*

"It's Old Germanic," a voice croons from the shadows. The man steps forward, his face an eerie canvas, etched in shadows cast by the ember of his cigarette. The dim, orange glow traces the contours of his features as he inhales, releasing tendrils of spicy, woody smoke that twist up into the night. "French origins. Family name, I believe," he continues, all black crewneck and swept-back blonde curls. I'm beginning to wonder which goth brought their dad along.

"Righto," I scoff, adjusting in my seat.

The man pops the top of his pack of cigs, sitting at the table over. "Smoke?"

I can feel my face scrunch before I even answer. "Yeah, nah, thanks."

"Next time." He shrugs, and stands, gliding down the back steps and around the side of the house.

Creep.

Screwing the top off the beer, I take a swig, my attention back on Ginny. The way she moves, you'd think she runs the place. She's short and curvy, all romantic looking, like one of those old renaissance paintings.

A masterpiece in pink, with cheeks blushing like roses.

I feel a smile creeping up, but I drown those thoughts with another gulp of hoppy homebrew. Who's the creep now?

She's standing in the kitchen with Cassie, all rosy cheeks. Even her plaid jacket is bloody pink.

Before I know it, I've downed the first bottle of booze and crack open the second.

Leaning back in the chair, I imagine what Ginny's voice sounds like.

"Bet it's like a squawking cockatoo," I laugh out loud.

Then comes that golden glow once more, that fuzzy, warm feeling…

I reckon she sounds like honey tastes. Sugary sweet.

"Pfft," I spit. "More like rancid and dumb."

Wow, Fred. You're a wordsmith tonight.

Spying a half-empty bottle of tequila on the table across from me, I stand, grabbing the liquor, and leg it for the back fence. The porch light barely throws any light, but whatever, I've got this. Stumbling in the dark, my shins collide with a rusty old fridge, and I fall face first into the sodden grass. Ugh, could this get any more embarrassing?

The glass sliding door rattles open behind me.

"You alright?"

Ginny. Her voice *is* sweet like honey.

Clambering, I stumble to the fence and manage to jump over it before Ginny makes it to the crash zone. With ragged breath, I lean my back against the wooden slats, my bum hitting hard against the concrete below.

A warm, pleasant smell drifts on the wind.

She even smells like honey…

I listen and wait. Ginny's footsteps recede; the door slides shut.

A lone raindrop falls, sizzling on the still warm pavement. Following the droplet, I realise two of Mum's runes have fallen from my pocket, the stones shining in the dark; *Wunjo* and *Laguz.*

"Come on…" I groan, picking them up. The stones slip from my hand, rolling back into the grass, landing in the exact same position, as if desperately trying to show me something.

"Love. Really?" I say, picking up the 'P'-looking *Wunjo.* Sighing, I slide it into my pocket and reach for the second stone. "And what am I meant to be paying attention to, hm?" The sigil's paint is slowly rubbing away along the backwards '1'-

looking *Laguz*.

Dusting off the grass and dirt and ensuring the runes are safely stowed, I make my way to the street, the earthy smell of the river calling me.

Swigging the bottle of tequila, I follow the eucalypt lined road towards the campground on the outskirts of town. I've set up a nice little spot by the river – an old, torn sofa, a tarp for shade, and a nifty DIY fire pit made with an old metal drum.

The streets, the campground, the river… anywhere is better than this shitty party. Better than any shitty foster home. Nature never promises more than what it is.

I'm better off out here. Alone.

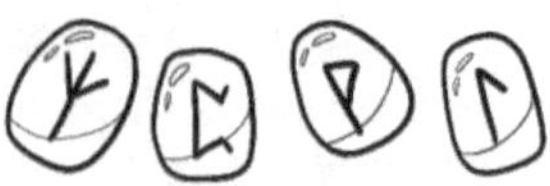

CHAPTER THREE

It's been raining on and off throughout the night, and the campground's already thick with mud. Ribbons of moonlight cut through the canopy above, and I spy the glowing source in the velvet night. It's not quite full, but she's still so bright, even when the rainclouds dance in front of her.

Trudging through the scrub to my little makeshift oasis, the trees all start to blur together as I down the last bitter dregs of tequila. I stop, willing my eyes to focus, muscle memory alone setting my drunken legs on their path.

At the edge of the river, the sound of a flapping tarpaulin calls my name, and in no time, my body has found the old sofa. I drag a tattered blanket from the esky and drape it over me. The rain has slowed now, save a few random drops against the tarp, and I find my world drifting away, replaced with the warmth that only a bottle of booze can bring. My eyes close, the heaviness of my lids overwhelming, and I let my mind wander, rooting around in the cold darkness of my thoughts.

Besides the snuffle of a random wombat and the thudding bounce of a 'roo, the bush is quiet.

Until it's not. Until the screaming starts. My screaming – the sound erupting from my throat, thick with pain.

I howl in frustration, anger, and self-loathing. Why can't I be normal? Why do I always shut myself out?

The birds in the surrounding trees scatter, my wailing subsides, and I feel my lungs empty of all that anger and hurt.

I think back to the party, the normalness of all those people enjoying themselves. Of Genevieve fucking Chase. Why can't I have that? Why can't you let yourself have that, Fred? Just be fucking normal!

As the bush settles back into its tranquil silence, the sound of bare feet crunching on loose gravel echoes through the empty campground just beyond the tree line behind me, and I freeze. Peering over the back of the couch, a running shadow makes its way into the underbrush.

Throwing the blanket to the corner of the couch, I force myself to stand. Fear washes over me. Did someone follow me? That cigarette creep from the party?

My vision blurs – stupid fucking tequila – and my thoughts fade as the shape darts between two trees… and I follow, heart pounding in my chest.

Branches whip past my face, scratching at my skin as I push forward. Before I can question why I'm running into the night, chasing shadows, my feet become a steady thump, each stride fuelled by adrenaline. My body slams against a scribbling gumtree, the rough bark scraping against my cheek, my knees buckling as a twisting, tearing pain in my head takes over, momentarily halting my pursuit.

The figure ahead of me stumbles and falls, letting out a deep cry. "Stop, please!" The voice, a boy's, cracks on the edge of puberty. "Please!" he begs.

That's when I see it, a looming darkness from the corner of my eye. The second heavy thud of running stops, replaced by the towering shadow's low, chesty growl.

The boy tries to escape, but there's nowhere for him to run. His jacket, blue silk all tattered and shredded, clings to him with blood and filth as he crawls along the muddied ground.

The snarling grows louder, the sound reverberating in my chest. The world around me blurs once more; the stabbing pain in my head, overwhelming now, rings in my ears, my body slumping into the thick spinifex.

A southerly wind sweeps through the undergrowth, forcefully snatching away every known sound in its retreat. In its wake, silence lingers in the air, tangible and heavy. The rustle of grass is all I hear before the vicious shadow lunges from the bracken, tackling the boy, pinning him to the ground. More scratches and scrapes are added to the ones on his arms and legs as the boy desperately fights back.

He pleads once more, his eyes widening, begging in terror.

The reflection of the beast stares back, its eyes glowing red.

The boy's scream pierces the night as the creature ruthlessly slams its knuckled fist into his face with brutal force. The sickening crunch of bone cracks through the surroundings, his nose shattering under the merciless impact.

Raging fists keep pummelling, fuelled by bloodlust, beating until the boy's screams are silenced, replaced by a sickening gurgle.

Standing, blood dripping from its hands, the creature looks down at the twitching body before retreating into the darkness.

The shadows weave their inky tendrils, growing tighter, squeezing me until the darkness is all I see, and I succumb.

CHAPTER FOUR

Waking from a deep sleep is an odd sensation. That feeling of your mind crawling back from its dark slumber, with your body in slow pursuit, not knowing what's reality and what's still a dream.

I can feel my mind waking, but my eyes aren't quite ready to follow. My body feels like a dead weight on the mattress, the quilt a forcefield holding me down. I lie in this daze for some time, as if between worlds. Awake, asleep. Dream, reality. I can sense the space around me, the scratchy sheets against my skin, but it's all just a fuzzy memory of what bedding is meant to feel like. As my eyes slowly open, eyelashes stuck with sleep, I wriggle my toes beneath the blanket.

After another night of roaming the streets, I still ended up in the bedroom I had left behind. I vaguely remember making my way to the campground, to the little spot I'd set up by the water. I must have drunkenly stumbled back to Jocelyn's at some point, Dad's torn and tattered Nine Inch Nails shirt hanging loosely over my shoulders. I hold the fabric up to my nose – I don't know how, but it still smells like him.

How much did I drink last night? The taste of alcohol is bitter in my mouth.

The morning sun takes on an orange glow as the light streams into the room. Yawning, inhaling the damp morning air, I can feel the weight on my chest. A surge of discomfort courses through me, and I instinctively recoil. It's a reminder, an insidious presence that sneaks into my consciousness every day. The conflicting emotions swirl within me, a bittersweet cocktail of frustration and resignation. I know the importance of not wearing a binder during sleep, allowing my body to breathe and recuperate, but the consequences of that action greet me every morning. It's like a sudden jolt, a cruel awakening, a mockery of who I really am. In these moments, I find myself grappling with the disheartening truth: despite my fervent yearning, society still insists on labelling me as a girl.

I instinctively grab the rolled-up stretch of fabric from the bedside table, whip off my shirt, and curl the material over my head and arms, down over my chest. Tight, snug, familiar. A necessary armour, a shield against a body that seems determined to contradict me. I pull Mum's golden heart locket out from the bindings, the chain hanging loose around my neck. Popping the shell open, I say good morning to the parents staring back at me. Despite being told they had abandoned me. Despite being told they'd chosen their crippling drug habit over their own child… I miss them. The real them. The memories I have of them, not the stories told and retold.

Making my way towards the mirror, pulling the ratty NIN shirt back over my head, a smile sneaks into the corner of my eyes and every crappy thought fades, my attention drawn instead to my chest, and how wonderfully flat is. My fingers trace over the smooth lines the binder makes. It's a daily ritual, seeking solace and validation in my own reflection. I long for a reflection that aligns with the person I know myself to be – a person who transcends the constraints of societal expectations. But I guess this will do. For now.

My smiling eyes shift to the black-and-white clock ticking on the wall.

"Shit, the time!"

Pulling on a pair of ripped black jeans and the hoodie from the night before, I slip my feet into my high-tops, though I am greeted with a soft squelch. Was it raining last night? I shake my head, as if the motion will shed the sleep and help me remember, but instead I'm left with a strange sense of worry. And hunger.

Kicking my shoes off, I rummage under the bed and find my old Doc Martens boots, hurriedly shoving them on before grabbing my bag and running down the hall, out through the broken front door, and into the morning sun.

Even with this sense of unease, this tightness in my chest, I feel myself calm as I catch a glimpse of my reflection in a busted car window. The music in my ears, the heart around my neck, stones in my pocket, this shirt… they're all I have left of my parents. And today, I feel like they're here with me.

Mondays at Acacia High unfold like a never-ending déjà vu, where teachers stumble in late, students stumble in later, and today, I'm honestly shocked there's anyone here at all given the epic shindig Randy threw last night.

Acacia High, well, it's the kind of place you wind up when all other options have vanished. Picture it as a bit like a school-shaped babysitting service – except, I'm not quite sure who's babysitting whom.

Acacia Hills, like the school, is a last resort kind of place. Typical rural town in the middle of nowhere – at least 120kms to Outwash, the nearest city. *City* is a generous name for it. They only really call it a city because it has an airport. Well, an air-strip. An airstrip that has to be booked in advance to ensure the local sheep are moved.

Ambling up the steps and through the grimy double doors, I make my way to the homeroom. Walking past the teachers' lounge, I spy Mr Croft, minus the dribbles of beer, but he's too busy rolling a cigarette to notice me. The unmistakable pungent blend of herbs and cat piss wafts from the lounge – tobacco, my arse. It's just another reminder of how little they seem to care.

"Only one more year," I mumble under my breath. "This is it – last year. Then graduation, shortly followed by *see you never*."

Soon I'll be able to leave this shithole. Leave the foster system. Be my own person. Away from Acacia Hills. Away from all of this. I'll be eighteen then. My grades have been great this past year. I smashed my preliminaries, and I can apply for a creative writing scholarship already at Outwash's Capitol University. All I have to do is keep to myself – easy.

Turning the corner, I enter the classroom, my eyes glancing at the clock on the far wall. 8:58 AM. Still beat the teacher. Making my way to my desk past the gossiping girls and the testosterone-fuelled boys, I can feel my lips crease into a smile as I see Cassie in the back corner, minus the gross jacket.

"What happened to that magnificent piece of fashion, Cass?" The words are out before I even think. *Keep to yourself, Fred.*

Cassie rolls her eyes. "Bastard can keep it. He took off without me last night."

Shit. There's a part of me that wants to console Cassie, say *screw Randy – his loss*. But I know it's easier to just nod and smile. Nothing good comes from making friends.

With a shrug, I sit at my desk.

Mrs Rochester, in her dowdy floral tunic, waddles through

the door towards the shabby table at the front of the classroom. The old aluminium chair buckles as she sits heavily on the cushioned seat. Shuffling the papers on her desk, she searches for the list of names for roll call.

"Randy? Is Randy Anderson present today?" Mrs Rochester's nasal voice repeats. "Not today…" she says, her pen scratching at the paper on her clipboard. She continues with names on the list, when eventually…

"Winnifred McTire?" the teacher's voice twangs.

I groan and raise my hand. "Present."

"Oh, aren't you a polite young lady. Hand raised and all."

Young *lady*. The word grates in my ears, making me sick. I can feel my chest tighten.

I guess today is going to be a very dysphoric day.

I cough, clearing my throat, wanting to respond, to say something. Instead, the corner of my mouth curls into a weak smile and I simply nod.

The teacher speaks at length about absences and upcoming events, her voice a mere whisper amongst the chaos of the room. Stella and Tiffany are gossiping about some new reality TV show. Steven and Tyson are cracking jokes until it's one mum joke too far, and punches are thrown. Cassie sits up the back at the open window, smoking a durry she clearly pinched off Croft. My eyes glance around once more, and it's then I see her.

Ginny, the honeybee herself, all freckle-faced and adorable. Said adorable face is buried in a book, and I squint to read the title: *Falling for Her Rainbow*. My heart quickens as I take in the vivid cover art – two women, their arms wrapped around each other, their lips meeting in a sweet, longing kiss, painted in hues of deep purples and bright pinks, like a swirl of emotions captured on canvas. I can almost feel the softness of their touch, taste the anticipation in that kiss.

For a moment, I can't help but feel a surge of excitement, a flutter in my chest at the thought that maybe, just maybe, Ginny might be queer, too.

I flick my septum piercing, the pinch sending a tingle through my sinus – *no, Fred* – and cover my face with my hand, pulling my hoodie close.

The bell rings, and as slow as everyone rolled in, they're out twice as fast – with few heading to any sort of class, I'm sure. I manage to shuffle past Cassie, past the bigots, and especially past Ginny, out into the foyer to get this day over with.

First class of the day: English. Not a bad way to start the second week of school term. I like English. The written word is my friend – not so much the spoken. That I struggle with. But writing? Yes please.

"Morning Miss," I nod, gliding through the doors towards

the back of the room.

Ms Robinson eagerly smiles, her hot pink lipstick matching her hot pink shoes. Not to mention her hot pink handbag, her hot pink blouse… Ms Robinson likes colour and likes her colours to match. Today is *I'm going to puke* pink.

"Okay, class. As promised, you had over the weekend to finish your poetry work from last week, and your words of wisdom are due today!" her voice bounces around the room, a groan from every student following. Ms Robinson claps. "Glad you're all so excited! You'll also be excited to know this is an oral exam…"

A wave of laughter spreads through the classroom.

"Yes, yes, *oral*. Get your giggles out now, and get ready to share your poetry," Ms Robinson says, sitting in her chair.

Pulling the piece of printed paper from my bag, words typed across the page, I find myself wilting into the seat. I hadn't realised we'd have to read it out loud. In front of people. I feel my body puddling to the floor, my chair letting out a loud *squeak* as I sink.

Ms Robinson's eyes jolt at the sound, falling on my withering corpse.

"Fred," her voice beams. She's the only teacher in this dump of a school to get my name right. "Sounds like you're ready to start us off."

"Am I, though?" I grimace.

Ms Robinson stares at me, one perfectly shaped eyebrow arching.

I groan, grab my paper, and plonk down the aisle towards the front of the class where I make the mistake of looking up. Sure, the class is close to empty. Maybe five kids? But sitting all pretty, front and centre – with that ridiculous smile on her face – is Ginny.

My throat tightens.

"Go ahead." Ms Robinson nods.

I clear my throat and suddenly become very aware how warm I am. Swallowing hard, I begin to read. My voice wavers at first, betraying the nervousness that grips me. Each word feels like a stone in my mouth, heavy and difficult to utter. But as I continue, the sweet, honeyed smell of Ginny seems to call to me, coax my words, and something shifts.

I take a deep breath, and continue…

A Gendered Woe

To rise from rest, a lull as dreaming moors,

though fog of sleep obscures, I cannot think;

my eyes do hang like heavy leaden doors,

and mem'ries crawl back slow from darkest brink.

Soon dreams turn cruel, and waking in despair;

the truth sits pert beneath the crumpled sheet,

while whisp'ring lies of sleep now fill the air;

dysphoric thoughts have come to take a seat.

Oppressive heft commands a woman's worth;

chest tight, air thin, breasts sway, my mind a blur;

The fresh morn' dew had promised a rebirth,

A dream of dreams where, please, I was not her.

    It is in dreams our hearts and souls do soar;

    The sweetest slumber is a hope for more.

The sound of the teacher's fervent clapping brings me back, the knot in my stomach easing, slightly.

"Well done, Fred! A Shakespearean sonnet!" Ms Robinson guffaws, smiling widely. She pats me on the back, ushering me to my seat as she talks in depth about how stories surrounding love and loss are essential in a Shakespearean sonnet, and that they're a perfect mode for the poetic exploration of gender and sexuality.

Ginny's smiling eyes find mine as I walk past her desk and I feel as though my cheeks are as pink as Ms Robinson's everything.

"Alright you lot, before I pick my next victim," Ms Robinson chuckles, "I want to remind you to select your poet to study for the remainder of the term."

A groan rolls through the classroom.

"Some of you have already chosen," the pink popsicle says, looking at me with a wink. I'd chosen my *poetess* months ago – Sappho. I've been a bit obsessed with her work lately. I feel a connection to her words. Her writing was criticised and destroyed by the patriarchy, by the church – too queer. We're both outcasts, and I like that.

"Now, next up..." Ms Robinson's voice invades my thoughts. "Cassie!"

As Cassie begins to read, I find my attention drifting away from her dodgy limerick and towards Ginny. The morning sun seems to catch in her hair like golden threads woven by the hands of dawn itself, casting a radiant glow that illuminates the classroom with a warmth that eclipses even the brightest of stars.

Wow. That's good.

As my pen surrenders to the page, Ginny emerges as my muse, her presence igniting the flames of inspiration within me. In the tradition of Sappho, who found inspiration in the beauty of her beloved, I weave Ginny's essence into my words, each syllable sparking a fire within me, a fire I struggle to contain as it blazes with the intensity of unspoken desire.

Shit, rein it in, Fred. I scrunch up the paper. No point pining over something I can't have.

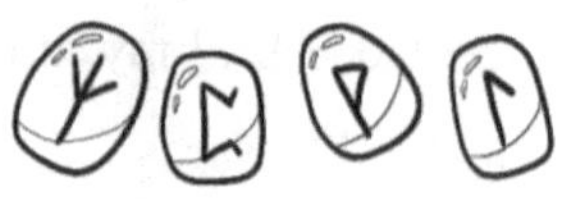

CHAPTER FIVE

"Hey, Fred!"

I hear my name coming from the throng of adolescents when I see Ginny Chase, her short crop bob bouncing as she makes her way down the steps. She's all smiles and pink plaid.

"Wanna walk to bio?" she asks, tucking a stray hair behind her ear.

"Not really," I grunt, and walk in the opposite direction.

"I saw you last night."

Ginny's words crash into my back, anchoring my feet in place.

"At the party," she continues.

I can feel my cheeks warm.

"You were talking to Cassie."

Oh good, she didn't see me faceplant the ground.

"Cassie told me about you."

Screw you, Cassie…

"I loved your sonnet."

"Good for you," I finally say, the words edging over my shoulder as I keep walking. I'm halfway down the path when I hear her tiny feet dance up behind me.

"What," I grunt, exhaling a breath so hard my nostrils flare.

"The themes of gender were really subtle." She smiles.

I stop. I wasn't expecting anyone to pick up on anything, or even give a damn.

"*Oppressive heft commands a woman's worth*," Ginny quietly remarks. "I think that was my favourite line."

I look down at Ginny, now walking next to me, her teeth worrying away at her bottom lip.

"*In the crooks of your body, I find my religion*," Ginny whispers, her arms hugging her textbooks as she bounces along. "Your sonnet had epic Sappho vibes. Have you read her stuff?"

You gotta be kidding me. She's talking about Sappho, like, legit. Ginny looks up at me with those blue eyes and I feel my legs wobble.

Who is this strawberry-haired goddess, full of the sun's beauty and brilliance?

I groan inward – now *I'm* quoting Sappho! I'm standing in the golden sun, staring at this golden girl who's apparently interested in me… quoting Sappho to me!

All I can do is nod.

"I'd love to read more of your writing one day."

I swallow hard. This isn't happening. Is this happening?

"And isn't bio this way?" the sweet-voiced maiden asks, her lips pouting after saying the letter 'o' in bi*o*… her slight overbite leaving an indent on her lower lip. Those cherry lips.

No, Fred. Bad Fred.

"Coming?" she asks.

I bite my lip, trying my utmost to not make a childish re-mark.

Again, I repeat: *No, Fred. Bad Fred!*

"Fine." *Shit.*

Walking back the way we came, the cicadas are bursting with sound – summer is definitely here. They're louder around this part of the school; the old gumtrees are full of them. But even still, all I can hear are Ginny's tiny feet tapping away on the concrete.

"So apparently, we have an assignment for biology –" Ginny says, breaking the awkward silence.

"First day back and you're already in the know," I smirk.

"How do you know it's my first day back?" I can hear the smile in her voice as her fingers twirl a strand of her strawberry hair.

Shit, Fred, think quick. "Cassie!" I splutter, feeling a flush of embarrassment creeping up my neck.

Ginny's laughter dances through the air, a light and melodic sound. "M'kay. Well, anyways, Mr Spriggs gave me a heads up. About the assignment."

I raise an eyebrow, playfully grinning. "Not bad having a

teacher in your pocket, hey?"

Ginny fidgets with her hair, a hint of pink colouring her cheeks. "I have Spriggs, you have Robinson. Clearly we should team up and take over the world! Or, the school, you know, kinda thing," she quips, her words stumbling a bit.

I notice Ginny's nervousness, her fumbling words giving her away. She's so shy, and it's kind of cute. "Yeah, I've been lucky with Robinson," I say with a smile. "She's been super helpful with my scholarship application process. I'm hoping to get into a creative writing course once I leave this hell-hole. My case worker, social worker, whatever, has all the paperwork sorted, and with Robbo as my reference here at school –"

I instantly stop talking.

Why am I sharing so much? This is the most I've said to anyone ever over the past twelve years. Who is this talkative Fred, and where did the tight-lipped recluse go?

"Well, I reckon you'll get it, easy. You have a way with words," Ginny offers, her voice warm and encouraging. I can feel the heat rising, all the way to the tips of my ears.

I cough. "Anyways. Bio assignment?" I ask, my voice now deliberately deeper and composed, a stark contrast to the gushing literary nerd that emerged seconds ago.

"Oh yeah. So, it's groups of two." Ginny natters on, words bubbling from her mouth with such passion and excitement.

Have I finally met someone that gives a shit at this school?

"I really need to make sure I get top marks," she continues. "And Cassie mentioned you do alright in class, and I was wondering…" Ginny pauses, the flurry of words stopping suddenly as she looks at me, all dimples.

Ginny's smile is dazzling. Yeah, dazzling. *Who am I?* Her little beaver-looking teeth jut out over her lips and I dig my hands deeper into my pockets.

"You were wondering why this school even bothers with assignments?" I tease, mustering a playful grin.

Ginny laughs, a melodic sound that lightens the air. "No. I was just wondering if you wanted to be partners on it?" she asks, fussing with another strand of loose hair. "Like, lab partners, assignment partners."

I keep staring at the ground as we walk, terrified if I look up I'll blurt out another candid, stupid thought.

The concrete path winds up behind a set of demountable buildings.

"We might need to book the science lab for it," I say, kicking at a stray rock.

"…or you could come to my place?"

Ginny's suggestion catches me off guard, and I can feel my eyes widen. *Chill, dude*, I scold myself, trying to hide the mess of feelings swirling inside me.

I've never been invited to someone's house before. Sure, for parties and stuff, but parties are different. That's a whole lot of people just doing dumb shit together. This would be just me and Ginny. Ginny… with her dimple cheeks and big blue eyes.

"Sure," I offer as casually as possible.

Ginny smiles. "Cool."

So, I guess I was right; today's turning out to be a good day. Maybe one friend is alright. Especially one that smells as good as Ginny. I smile at her, and she's smiling back at me. This feels right. Yeah, maybe I will make an exception to the no friends rule.

And just as that thought blooms, a thunderous laugh erupts behind us – Steven's voice, booming.

"Check out these two lezzos!" he whistles, his tone dripping with sarcasm. "Get a room!"

"I'd pay to see that." Tyson leers.

"Piss off – not that weird dyke one. What even is it?" Steven snarls.

The two boys burst into laughter and continue running down the path towards the football oval.

My feet feel like lead. All those dreams of friendship, or more, fall shattered, replaced with white-hot rage. I feel my stomach churn. I feel… hungry. My fists clench so tight my nails pierce the flesh of my palms. Blood gathers in the creases of my knuckles and trickles through the cracks of my fingers. I squeeze tighter.

"Oh, Fred, you're bleeding…"

I can hear the dull tones of Ginny's voice, like listening through water, but my focus is on Steven and Tyson. I can feel my eyes narrow. The hairs on my arms prickle with electricity. The whole world seems to fade away, and all I see are two little boys, like frolicking deer, prancing in the distance. A rumble, a howl, deep within my soul, awakens. I'm imagining the chase, and my heart quickens. I wonder what my teeth would feel like sinking into their flesh, how they'd taste…

The weight of a hand presses down on my shoulder.

"Fuck off!" I growl, pushing Ginny to the ground. Waking from my daze, I stare wide-eyed at what I'd done. Ginny looks up, confused, hurt, her hand slowly reaching towards her chest where four deep scratches begin to welt.

I stumble backwards, the anger, the hate, subsiding. But something else takes its place.

Shame.

"I'm sorry." My voice trembles, and so do my legs as I fall back, retreating, running. Back down the path, over a broken garden bed, and out into the car park, away from that moment, away from that primal urge.

Reaching the street, my heart thumps as I choke for air.

Peering down at my hands, at the deep gouges in my palms, I feel my stomach turn, the bile rising; the sour acrid taste filling my mouth and spilling onto the bitumen.

What the fuck just happened?

And I run.

Footsteps sound behind me and I turn abruptly, panting, the air hissing between my teeth as I struggle to breathe.

"Fred, it's ok, Fred…" Ginny's voice is a salve for my chaos.

I can't help but collapse to the ground. It's only then I realise I ran all the way back to Jocelyn's.

I can hear Ginny's tread fall soft against the footpath. She's approaching me as if I were a wounded animal. And I feel like one, scared and confused.

"I'm so sorry," is all I can offer through my wheezes.

Ginny gently sits next to me. She's quiet, but I can feel her eyes watching me.

"Did I hurt you?" I look up through wet lashes.

I can see her shoulders slump, her eyes darting to her chest, then me. She shakes her head and offers me a faint smile.

"I'm fine. Nothing a bit of iodine won't fix. I reckon you might need some, too." Her voice is careful, just like her movements as she gently reaches out, touching my hands, turning them palm up. She clicks her tongue, hissing inwards through clenched teeth. "Come on, come back to my place."

My hands draw back, retreating into my sleeves. "I'm fine." The words are abrupt, and I'm embarrassed all over again. I can feel the embarrassment turning to shame, to anger, the words bursting from my mouth. "Just, piss off, alright? I'm fine on my own."

Ginny's brow knits together. "And by *I'm fine on my own,* do you mean, *I like getting horrible gross infections in my hands and have them fall off?*"

I scoff. "Dramatic much?"

"Baby much?" Ginny sighs. "Let me help you."

I open my mouth to protest, but Ginny's finger slides over my lips.

"And I'm not taking no for an answer."

CHAPTER SIX

The front door of Ginny's house slams shut, sending thousands of tiny flecks of dust into the air. The midday sun streams through the stained-glass window, catching each speck in its rays.

The entryway looks like any other. Umbrellas in the corner, shoes on a shelf, a side table to the right with a dish, and something else…" What's with the little rake and the sand?" I ask, my finger tracing shapes in the soft powder spread out on a deep tray.

"It's for *fang shoey*, or something," Ginny says, locking the front door behind her.

"You mean feng shui?"

"Alright, oh worldly person. If you knew, why'd you ask?" I catch a smirk dancing at the corner of her mouth before she ushers me towards the bathroom.

Ginny's still here. She hasn't run away. The opposite, she's invited me *in*. I honestly thought I was going to be shoved into a room and locked up, have the cops here because I'm some angry freak. I peer down at my still-clenched fists, blood drying in the cracks of my fingers.

What the hell happened…

Padding down the hall, my shoes are silent on the carpet. To my left, I notice a heavy timber door, its deeply stained wood adorned with a multitude of locks and latches. I swallow hard, uncertainty rising from the depths of my stomach.

"Sheesh, what's that about?" I ask, my head tilting towards the heavily armoured door.

"Just my grandad's den."

Goosebumps prickle my skin as a strange smell tickles my nose, a sweet metallic tang that makes me feel queasy.

"Weird…"

"What's weird?" Ginny asks, standing at the entrance to the bathroom. She drops her head to one side, her strawberry blonde hair falling softly.

"Nothing," is all I can say. It's too hard to explain. My scalp tingles.

I've had this happen before, moments like this, where I can feel my body react in a way that's beyond my control. It's like my senses heighten, and I become hyper-aware of my surroundings. We learned about the body's natural fight-or-flight response in Biology class last year, and that's when I recognised this feeling, this evolutionary response to danger. A few months ago, when Cassie was cornered by Jocelyn's husband, Terrence, in the shed out back, my body reacted before my mind even had time to process what was happening. The rush of adrenaline, the increased heart rate, and heightened awareness. *The tingle.* I remember running out to slam the door open just as he was about to lay his hands on her. It's a feeling I've experienced before, but the first time was when my parents died.

Standing in the bathroom, my reflection in the mirror is a pale comparison to this morning's rosy hue, my raven hair stuck to my forehead with sweat. It feels like all my energy has been syphoned, sucked dry.

I watch as Ginny moves swiftly, all business. Her lips purse as she opens the cabinet door, taking out a brown bottle of iodine. Rummaging through the drawer, she pulls out a bag of cotton balls and sits on the edge of the bath.

"Sit," she says, tapping the closed toilet next to her.

"Yes, ma'am," I reply, awkwardly sitting, hands resting against my knees, palms up.

Ginny struggles with the child safety cap. "Damn, these things are a pain," she mutters, twisting the cap, the plastic spinning in place.

"Here, let me," I offer.

"With your cut-up hands?" Ginny scoffs. She twists one more time just as the lid pops off, the liquid splashing onto her chest. She winces, her hand reaching for the rip in her shirt.

"Hey…" I say, my hand touching hers. Our eyes meet, and

as I stare into those glistening blues, I cough, dragging my attention away, and back to her shirt, the scratches beneath. "Did I really do that?"

Ginny shrugs. "It was an accident."

My fingers gently shift her torn checker blouse, my eyes finding Ginny's – she's not saying no, she's not batting my hand away. Should I keep going? My mouth goes dry and sticky. I hesitate, my breath shallow.

"Is it alright if I take a closer look?" my voice shakes. "I – I just, I want to make sure you're okay."

Ginny smiles faintly, her fingers sliding up to mine, the pink buttons between our fingers.

How Eros shakes my soul.

I peel my eyes away from her intense gaze and peer down at the dry blood and swollen skin. Four distinct scratches tear down her chest, stopping just above the purple lace of her bra. Her chest is flourished in freckles like a starry sky. I blush when I realise I'm staring.

"They'll heal," Ginny says, buttoning her top again. "Accidents happen –"

"But I hurt you." Before I even realise what I'm doing, I gently place a hand on Ginny's cheek, cupping her face, my thumb grazing across her twinkling freckles. My eyes flicker, blinking rapidly as I swallow hard. "Sorry," I offer, my hand quickly retreating to my lap. But as I look away, Ginny's lips curl into a coy smile.

"So, what's the deal with needing top marks in bio?" I steer the conversation elsewhere, trying to divert attention away from whatever *that* was.

With an iodine-soaked cotton ball, Ginny dabs at the cuts on my hands. "I wanna study veterinary science."

I flinch as the cold liquid touches my wounds. Ginny smirks.

"It stings, alright?" I say, half smiling. "Guess patching me up gives you a chance to test out those veterinary skills, hey?"

"You're not *entirely* an animal." Ginny grins.

She's playing with me. A smile creeps at the corners of my lips. I let my mouth drop open, sarcasm oozing out. "How dare you suggest such a thing. Not *entirely*," I scoff. "I am 100% animal!"

Ginny laughs, the dimples in her round cheeks deepening.

My next words are low, and rasp past my lips. "Only in a fun way."

Ginny fumbles with the cotton balls, and it's my turn to see her flustered, her freckles coming to life on her crimson cheeks.

"So. What happened?" Ginny asks, nodding towards my hands, clearly changing the subject herself. The question startles me.

"Umm…"

"It's okay if you don't want to talk about it. We all have our *stuff*."

Stuff? Sure. Which stuff? My parents dying? My aunt dying? Nearly every foster family who's ever taken me in meeting their untimely demise? Or what about my gender dysphoria? The weird-ass dreams? The fact I just Hulked out? Where would I even start.

We sit in silence for a while before the clank of a handbrake sounds in the distance, then the buzz and whir of the automatic garage door. Ginny must hear it too. Her eyes widen.

"Shit, shit, shit!" Ginny spills half the iodine onto the floor, the mahogany liquid seeping into the bathmat.

"What? What's happening?"

Quickly screwing the lid back on the bottle, Ginny tosses it, along with the cotton buds, into the sink before grabbing the toilet paper off the roll and frantically wiping up the antiseptic. Its sharp, salty smell fills my nose.

Still confused, though catching on to Ginny's urgency, I follow suit and wipe down the iodine stains, then take the bundle of burgundy toilet paper from Ginny and flush it down the loo. Ginny rolls up the bathmat and dumps it into the laundry basket, underneath the towels.

"Now will you tell me what's going on?" I say, placing a hand on her shoulder. Her eyes find mine.

"My grandad's home. We had a bit of a fight last night, and I'm just... It's just..."

I see the panic fill her eyes as she pulls away, her head pressing against the bathroom door. She's listening. And she's terrified. I don't want to make this any worse for her than it must already be.

Searching the small, rectangular room, I notice an open window above the bathtub. It's narrow, but I've squeezed through tighter gaps.

"I was never here," I whisper, pulling myself up and out before Ginny even turns around.

As I land in the small garden below, the lavender now trampled beneath my feet, I see Ginny's head pop out from the window above.

"Thank you."

Her words are few, but her eyes say it all.

CHAPTER SEVEN

Sitting amongst the flowers, I hear the garage door closing at the front of the house.

"Possum, you home?" the gravelly voice sounds. "Gin, love, I know I'm back early, but I got us some chops for dinner."

Ginny's grandad's back. That's who she was worried about? I should leave; this is none of my business. Remember – head down, just get through the days, the weeks.

One more year, Fred. That's your mantra, now. Just one more year.

I close my eyes, but I can still see Ginny's face, the look she had. I feel as though I need to stay. Something is wrong. Why was she so nervous?

That's when I feel it. *The tingle.* Like icy fingers crawling up my spine, a subtle shiver that prickles my skin and quickens my heartbeat, leaving goosebumps in their wake. I have to make sure Ginny's okay.

"Since when does Fred care about people, huh?" I mutter to myself, my inner monologue screaming over the top, *Don't get involved. Walk away. People just let you down.*

But Ginny's something else. She's not just *people.*

I hear the bathroom door slowly creak open, followed by the soft patter of footsteps receding down the hallway. A second door sighs on its hinges, and soon the familiar beeps of a washing machine fill the silence.

"Hey Grandad, I'm just doing some laundry, got a bit messy in art today. Chops for dinner sound great!"

Her voice is muffled, but I can still hear the fear dangling like a noose on every word. I have to find a way to get closer. Gingerly moving through the garden bed, I follow the sound of the frantic beeps and find a tall, narrow window full of lint. This has to be the laundry. I can hear Ginny moving, and… is that her heartbeat? No, that's crazy, right?

"Oh, here you are," says the gruff voice again. I shouldn't, but I stand closer to the window, picking off pieces of lint, making a hole in the flyscreen to see what's happening.

Ginny's grandad is a big guy. His shoulders fill the entire width of the doorframe. He might be sixty or so, but he's fit. *Granddaddy Garamond*, I'd heard some of the girls at school call him. Gross. He's one of those old codgers who drinks protein shakes, eats loads of red meat, and bros it out at the gym. I remember Cassie telling me he always has his mates around, and they're all as bearded and burly as he is. *The secret society of buff, plaid dudes*, Cassie had joked… and if old mate here is anything to go by, she's not wrong.

"What exactly happened in class today, Gin?" The worry in Garamond's voice is evident, and I strain to listen from my hidden spot outside.

"Um…" Ginny's voice trembles, barely above a whisper. "It was, like, agriculture class, and I tripped over a rake…"

A creaking sound reverberates through the wooden floorboards, followed by a groan. Peering through the lint-free gap I've created in the flyscreen, I see Garamond brushing away Ginny's hand, his eyes squinting at the scratches on her shirt.

"Agriculture? I thought you said art class got messy."

Ginny stammers, "I meant art, yeah. Paint. My shirt got messy… and then, in the other class, the agriculture one… with the rake…"

The silence that follows is deafening.

"I worry about you at this school, Gin," Garamond sighs, and I can hear the creak of the wooden stool as he sits down.

Ginny exhales heavily, her frustration evident. "I'm not having this argument again. I told you last night –"

"You told me that those kids wouldn't bother you, but clearly…" his voice trails off, filled with unspoken concern. "Are you sure you don't want to switch schools? Enrol for your final year at Outwash College? They have a great science program."

"Grandad! No one hurt me. No one even knows, yet."

My curiosity piques. Knows what?

"I just worry, love. I know what this town's like. And it's your last year, I know how important it is for you. I'd hate to see it ruined because –"

"– because I'm bi?"

My hands instinctively cover my mouth, preventing any gasp from escaping. My stomach churns with anticipation. I read the signals right? Is this why Ginny was so anxious when she had me alone in her house? The realisation sends a jolt of excitement through me. My heart races, and I can't help but bite my lip. It's as if a door to a secret world has swung open, and the thought of Ginny being bi ignites a flicker of hope deep within me.

"Anyways, I'm not the only queer kid at school. There's Fred," Ginny finally speaks, her voice soft, and I can hear the smile in her words.

"Fred. Don't know a Fred. Is he new?"

"*Their* name's Fred. And yeah, kinda. They started around the time we left for Amsterdam."

Garamond grunts in response.

"Fred's actually acing every class," Ginny continues. "In fact…" She pauses, her feet shuffling on the tiled floor. "In fact, I've asked them to help me study. So. Expect them around."

I feel my insides warm at Ginny's words.

Garamond lets out a gruff laugh. "Is that who I saw jumping out the window?"

The silence that fills the laundry is explosive.

"I… they… it's just…"

Garamond's laughter subsides, replaced by a more understanding tone. "Did you think I wouldn't approve?"

"A little." Ginny's sounds so small.

"Gin…" Garamond's voice softens.

There's a deep vibrating sound.

"Bugger. I've gotta take this call, Gin. It's Sarge."

Then a creak of the stool shifting.

"What's that for?" Ginny asks.

I poke another lint-free hole. He's hugging her.

"I'm proud of you." He squeezes Ginny tighter. "I'm proud that you're proud." I can hear the smile in his voice. "And I trust you. You don't have to be worried about me, little love."

"You knew, didn't you? Before I came out…" Ginny gently steps out of his embrace. "How long?"

"A grandad can sense these things."

"It was me ogling Katy O'Brian on telly the other night, wasn't it –"

"– it was you ogling Katy O'Brian on television the other night, yes," Garamond laughs. "She's an attractive young woman. I can see the appeal," he adds with a whistle, opening the door.

"Grandad, ew!"

"What?" he laughs. "I'm just dropping truth bombs, or whatever you kids say."

"Yeah, no more trying to act young, ya old fart," Ginny laughs.

"I may be an old fart, but I love you, and I want you to be happy. If Fred's important to you, they're welcome here." Garamond's phone buzzes again, his face serious. "Just remember to put iodine on that," he says, his voice receding down the hallway.

The soft mumble of Garamond's voice echoes from the other end of the house as the back patio door opens with a slight creak, the flyscreen screeching as it slams shut. Despite my chunky boots, I tiptoe through the lavender, my destination clear: the small white picket-style fence that leads to Ginny's backyard. With ease, I throw a leg over and find myself standing in a native oasis. The yard is massive, full of banksias and wattles. The past few days have brought intermittent rain, leaving the air rich with the lingering scent of damp soil and pollen.

I take a step back, seeking refuge behind the water heater, as I hear Ginny's gentle tread against the concrete. From my concealed vantage point, I watch her step out onto the grass.

"Psst…"

Ginny jumps, throwing a basket of clothes pegs at me.

"Oi, it's me," I laugh as the plastic rains down. Ginny covers her face as her shoulders shake with laughter.

"What are you still doing here?" she asks, throwing one last peg at me. It bounces off my shoulder and onto the grass. Ginny moves closer and wraps her fingers around my wrist.

I hesitate, a maelstrom of emotions churning within me. I haven't let myself get involved with people in so long, to care so deeply. But here I am, staying against my instincts because I'm worried about her. I don't want to admit it, not even to myself.

Ginny's gaze is searching, her fingers warm against my skin, and I can't avoid the question forever.

Maybe I can avoid it.

"So. Katy O'Brian, huh?" I smirk, tussling my hair for emphasis. Clearly Ginny has a type.

Ginny's face scrunches bright red.

Shit, I berate myself inwardly, my own words tasting bitter in my mouth. The guilt of sidestepping Ginny's question and making her uncomfortable courses through my veins, like a cruel reminder of my self-imposed emotional barricades. Why do I always resort to deflecting, hiding behind sarcasm, when it's clear Ginny wants to open up to me? My silence now feels like an apology I can't bring myself to utter.

"You heard?" She lets out a small laugh, her eyes downcast. I watch as her toes curl in the lush green carpet of turf.

"Is that why you were freaking out?"

"Kinda." Ginny nods.

"I thought he was gonna wallop you, or something. You looked so scared."

"Grandad can get a bit… overprotective, is all."

"As long as he doesn't hurt you," I add, and I can't stop the rage tangled in every word.

Ginny laughs softly. "Grandad would never. I just, I was nervous because I thought he'd, like…" her voice trails off.

"Disown you?" I wince. "But he seems cool with who you are," I continue, genuinely happy for her.

Ginny looks up at me, smiling. "Yeah, he is."

Standing in front of her like this, as close as this, is when I notice her eyes. They're a deep shade of blue with flecks of silver, like the reflection of a tranquil sea under the soft, silvery moonlight, drawing me into their gentle depths. She's poetry in motion.

Ginny slides her phone from her back pocket, her fingers gracefully gliding over the screen as she searches for something. She taps a few times, and then, with a playful smile, hands me her phone. As I take it, I see my name, "Fred," displayed on the screen, but my contact details are conspicuously missing. I can't help but grin, and my fingers dance across the keyboard as I quickly enter my number. With a gentle chuckle, I return her phone, our connection now etched in digital ink.

Ginny bites her lip, her eyes darting back and forth between me and her phone. Confusion creases my brow.

"… what…" I snort, puzzled.

Before I can refuse or react, Ginny's phone flashes, my bewildered face filling her screen.

"Oh, no no no…" I try to snatch her phone, but she just giggles.

"Yes, yes, yes!"

"I look tragic!" I protest.

Ginny gazes down at her phone, then back up at me, a warm smile playing on her lips. "I think you look handsome."

Ginny's fingers find their way into my closed palm. I feel her soft, small hand in mine and our fingers intertwine. It's exhilarating, a rush of emotions I've never experienced before. Everything else seems to fade away and blur and it's just me and Ginny, standing here, in this moment. This rush of feelings is a tempest, a hurricane surging through me, as if the towering walls I've constructed around my heart are quaking.

"I'm starting dinner, Gin!"

Ugh, timing.

Oh, how I want to tell her to blow off dinner with her

grandad and come with me. I could show her the creek I found down near the campground – how it trickles into the river. Share with her the little oasis I've made in this shitty town.

"Guess that's my cue," I say, squeezing her hand.

Jumping the fence and running down the side of the house out onto the street, the late afternoon sun feels warm and inviting. My phone buzzes, and as I swipe to open, a message pops up from an unknown number:

```
Now you have my number, too.
- Ginny.
```

Maybe having a friend won't be so bad after all.

Or more than friend. The thought flutters into my mind, and I can feel my cheeks warm. Groaning, I push that temptation down. Just because she's bi doesn't mean I have a chance. And just because she slid her hand in mine… said I was handsome.

Here come those butterflies again.

No. Friend is enough.

Or maybe it's all just a ridiculous fantasy.

And just like that, the bubble bursts.

I think back on my past schools, past foster homes. Of the so-called *friends* I'd thought I'd had. Like the time I had gotten busted helping one of the other foster kids, Sarah, climb the latticework to go meet her boyfriend. She went off and had a good time, but me? No. I got in shit for it.

Or the time I let Michael study with me for our maths finals the year before. Bastard copied all my notes and aced the test. But who got accused of cheating and then suspended? Me!

And don't get me started on the number of girls who dated me purely to get back at an ex-boyfriend, or piss off their overly devout parents.

I look down at the glowing screen and see the words for what they really are. Trouble. This'll just end the same. *"Grandad can get a bit… overprotective."* Ginny's words hover amongst the angst. My jaw aches as I finally unclench my teeth.

"Not again…" I whisper. Swiping against the screen, the little red trashcan appears next to Ginny's text. "It's easier if I just delete it."

But yet, I can't. I look back over my shoulder to the golden-haired girl hanging out laundry. Such an ordinary, mundane thing… yet I wish I was still there with her.

I shove the phone back in my pocket and push every feeling down. Every side glance, every smile, those dimples and sapphire eyes… every touch, those small hands… I push it down and bury it. Just one more year, and I'm out. I don't want anything or anyone fucking things up.

I find myself reaching into my pocket, pulling out a rune-stone from its satchel as two very familiar sigils slip from my pocket – I catch them before they hit the ground.

"Wunjo and Laguz. Again?" I scoff. "There's no love here, you stupid rocks."

Cramming the stones back into their bag, I notice a stray stone loose in my pocket.

It's then my ears start to ring. A high-pitched whir of a noise. I dig my knuckle into my ear and cringe. Then comes a voice, familiar and gravelly.

"Say it was dingoes, or something. Look, just get it fixed!" it growls.

Garamond.

I stare back at Ginny's house. How could I hear that? I shake my head and the ringing stops. "Weird…"

Looking down at the runestone in my hand, I can't help but gasp at the trident carving staring back at me.

"Algiz? Protection? What do I need protection from?"

CHAPTER EIGHT

My body lies still on the bed, its heaviness sinking into the mattress. My fingers awaken, searching for my blanket. Through a cracked eye, I peer down onto the floor; the crotchet wool lies crumpled on the ground. Groaning, my head flops back onto the pillow until a strange, bright light catches my eye, then disappears. It's then I realise it's still dark. And I'm not in my bed at all, but at the campground on the outskirts of town. A numbing sense of confusion and fear washes over me. I jolt upright, my back stiff from sleeping between two fallen trees, a moss-covered rock as my pillow. A rush of adrenaline courses through me. All my senses are on high alert.

Exhaling a ragged breath, I rub my face, hoping to unscramble this confusion. My face feels different. My fingers trace over my jawline, cupping my chin. It's fuzzy. A soft, downy fluff spreads across my cheeks.

Lifting myself up and over the ancient fallen tree, I sit on the edge, my feet landing on the familiar shaggy rug on the bedroom floor, back at Jocelyn's. My mind eases. *I'm just waking up still.* I laugh nervously and rub my eyes. Attempting to stand, I stumble towards the mirror. Well, where my mirror should be.

In the shimmering glass, I stare on in horror at what looks back. Not me. *It*. A beast. Morphed and changed. Not quite animal, not quite human. A snarling monster with blood mad eyes. I can feel my throat tighten, my stomach heavy, filling with hot nails and bile. I tear at the fur, ripping until my chest is exposed, bare and raw.

Trembling, holding on to the mirror, staring at my reflection, I scream. A hollow sound of nothingness. When my eyes stare back into the silver glass, I buckle over in agony, my body contorting. Wrapping my arms around me as I fall to the ground, my fingers feel skin. I scurry back to the mirror in the woods. The beast is gone, and it's just me again. *Her*. I can feel my jaw clench as I stare at this soft, feminine form before me. My eyes sting, holding back the pain and anxiety dysphoria always brings. Collapsing to the ground, my tears break free. The salty anguish fills the room until I'm gagging, the briny liquid swamping my lungs.

Then. Silence. Stillness. Nothing.

In the acrid depths there's a hum, a thrum, of pounding hearts and surging water. With a *whoosh* I feel my being separate, and I watch my body from above. I watch as Winnifred succumbs. Her body floats, motionless, in the dark. Though not just her body. As I watch my naked form ebb and flow, I can feel a shift, a murmur deep within. Just as fast as the tears consumed me, I plummet to the forest below, my tears now raindrops falling over a valley.

With a splash, I plunge into a river, the force splitting me in two. Bobbing in the icy water, I stare wide-eyed at the animal in front of me: a wolf, its eyes glowing like amber. It gently nuzzles its nose into my shoulder and whispers, *Florentine*, before turning and running. Its soft paws skip across the top of the water. More wolves appear, leaping from the trees, running up into the clouds until I'm there with them, surrounded by a soft knowing.

Feeling the familiar stiffness of Jocelyn's cheap polyester sheets, and the itch from the laundry detergent she uses, I realise I'm awake. At least I think I am. I pull at the gold hoop hanging from my septum. *Ouch.* Yeah, I'm awake.

Sleep has always been a little problematic for me. I remember waking up many a night when I was small, creeping down the hallway to my parent's bedroom. They thought a nightlight might help, placing a glowing yellow star in the corner of my room so that the monsters would stay away. But the monsters still invade my dreams; they just wear different masks.

Dreams are weird. They can be windows into worlds beyond the ordinary, a peek into your most inner thoughts. Your fears, your joys. Dreams offer the dreamer a great insight into their consciousness. But what did this dream tell me? Lying in bed, I try so hard to remember it, but it's already drifting away. It felt so real. And they've been getting… more realistic. I've often been plagued with dysphoric dreams, as if dealing with my gender identity in my waking life wasn't enough, my dreams seem determined to mess with me, too. But the wolves…

"Yeah, that part was new," the words escape my mouth.

"What part was new?" Cassie's voice creeps from the crack in the door.

"Just dumb dreams," I say. I can tell Cassie's used to my noncommittal conversations as she happily continues.

"Yeah, right. Well, I'm getting a lift with Tyson this morning, if you want a ride to school?" Cassie steps into the room, her small frame yet again shrouded in another dickhead's jacket. I sigh.

"Tyson now?" I roll my eyes. Cassie just giggles. A horn beeps from the street. "That's me. See ya at school."

Sitting in bed, my hair a nest of knots, I groan at the thought of another day at Acacia High. My phone buzzes. Three new texts, all from Ginny. I'd forgotten about yesterday afternoon. About Ginny. I can feel my stomach churn, the memory of lashing out, of hurting her. I comb my fingers through my hair in contemplation as grass sprinkles down.

Hold on.

I pick up the long green strands. I don't remember going out last night. But the dream… It *was* just a dream, right?

CHAPTER NINE

Another Tuesday, another drama at school.

Walking up the concrete path towards the main building that holds the office, hall, and a sad excuse for a library, I see the blue flashing lights of a police car parked out front. I feel a tug at the back of my shirt and turn to see Ginny. The blue flashing lights make her eyes sparkle.

"What's going on?" She smiles.

"Dunno," I say, turning to look back at the police car. I hear Ginny let out a soft laugh behind me.

"I meant with you. What's going on with *you*. How are you?"

I scratch at my neck and grimace, remembering I never replied to any of her messages last night. Remembering how I had gone to delete her text, to delete her from my life. But I hadn't. I couldn't.

"Fine." I shrug.

"It's just…" Ginny continues. "I didn't hear anything, and I thought maybe you weren't –" her words cut off as Principal Jones stomps down the stairs, a police officer in full uniform idling behind. The waft of stale onions floats on the breeze.

Gross. Must be all these sweaty teens. We are truly a disgusting age. The police officer at the stairs adjusts his belt.

"Is that the sergeant?" the words crawl from the corner of my mouth, asking Ginny.

"Wow, the first full sentence of the day, and it's that?" Ginny scoffs.

I sigh. I'm a shit person, and this just proves it. She's already had enough of me. But then she knocks me with her shoulder and smiles. *She smiles.* Am I reading this all wrong?

"Good morning to you, too, Fred." She smirks. "And yes, that's Sarge. Or, yeah, Sergeant."

A group of kids and teachers gather at the steps and Principal Jones ushers us inside towards the Hall. My nose catches a whiff of something else, something familiar – sickly and metallic. It's then I see him, Garamond, standing in the Hall, just to the side of the podium with the sergeant.

My thoughts drift back to the conversations overheard yesterday. *So, you're 'Sarge,' huh?*

Despite the full police getup, he's a scruffy-looking guy. A sparse beard, mottled grey, covers his chin and cheeks. His eyes are heavy-set, and although he stands tall, he doesn't command the attention a police officer usually does. I've always been wary of cops. But he seems... weak.

Like you, I hear my inner thoughts hiss, making me question why I haven't mustered the strength to take the plunge with Ginny, even as friends. I think back to yesterday, her hand in mine, the way those golden strands smelt like golden honey…

"This is all new to me," I whisper to Ginny.

"Oh. You've never been in the Hall like this before?"

Now it's my time to give Ginny a cheeky nudge. "I meant *this*." I take her hand in mine. "Sorry I didn't text. Having a friend –"

"– just a friend?" Ginny raises a curious brow, a smirk twitching at the corner of her mouth.

My heart is in my throat, and I can feel my eyes widen, unable to blink. Before I can respond, the sharp screech of feedback from the microphone hisses through the room, the people inside moaning and swearing in retaliation to the sudden high-pitched squeal. Principal Jones holds the mic so close to his mouth, his words are muffled, but it's something along the lines of *shuddup*. He hands the microphone over to the sergeant.

Sarge barely opens his mouth to talk. His voice is husky and droll, like he's a pack-a-day smoker, lungs full of so much tar, the rasp of it hangs on every word. He introduces himself, but I'm distracted by a face in the crowd. A face I haven't seen before. I squeeze Ginny's hand and nod towards the kid.

"New guy?"

Ginny shrugs. "Probably?" she whispers. "I overheard

Grandad say the Rustmanes' cousins would be visiting soon. Manebarns, I think?"

I shake my head. "Rustmane… why's the name sound familiar?"

"They own the land south of the campground, you know the old horse farm on Carlisle Road?"

I nod, but that's not why it sounds familiar, I'm sure of it.

"That's them. Anyways, Grandad said I was to *stay away from that lot*." Ginny scrunches her face at the last part, her voice deepening to mimic Garamond's gravelly tone. I can't help but snort a laugh, covering the outburst with a fake cough.

Ginny smiles and playfully nudges my knee, her finger pressed to her lips, signalling me to be quiet. She points to the front, her grin never fading.

As my eyes drift back to the podium, I stop a moment on this new kid. *Manebarn*. His dark complexion pops against his tightly wound blonde curls. His head shifts and our eyes meet. Two glowing, amber eyes. I'm suddenly drawn back to my dream, to the wolves.

The trill of feedback makes me wince, a few students swear, and the sergeant apologises, stepping to the side of the podium, tugging at the chord of the microphone in his hands.

"As most of you know, I'm Sergeant Luis Pine of the Acacia Hills branch of Outwash Police Department. I have asked Mr

Jones to gather you here to inform you of some troubling news."

The crowd mutters.

"There's no easy way to say this," he coughs, his feet finding purchase, as if bracing himself for the onslaught to follow. "A Mr Randal Anderson – most of you knew him as Randy – was found dead yesterday afternoon, down at the campground off Carlisle."

"Holy shit…" I murmur, and I feel Ginny squeeze my hand, her eyes damp in the corners.

Gasps and murmurs wash over the crowd of students as Principal Jones steps towards the podium and directs us to be quiet. I search the crowd for Cassie. Nothing. *I hope she's okay.*

Sergeant Pine continues. He doesn't divulge much, though he warns us of feral dingoes in the area. My mind jumps back to that disembodied voice I heard near Ginny's place: *Say it was dingoes, or something… just get it fixed.*

What needed to be fixed? And why are these newcomers, the Manebarns, to be avoided?

The sergeant's voice cuts through my thoughts. "With the school term just starting –"

"– we don't want to have to instigate a curfew," Principal Jones interrupts.

"No, we don't." Sergeant Pine nods. "But we ask that students be diligent and smart about your comings and goings."

Sergeant Pine steps down from the mic, Principal Jones taking his place.

"And can Cassie Kelly please meet me in my office?" Principal Jones' voice echoes over the speakers, students and teachers slowly draining out of the hall when Cassie floats towards us.

"You alright?" I ask. I don't know what else to do or say. And I have no idea why she's being called to the principal's office. Ginny immediately rushes to her, her arms enveloping Cassie and her manic red curls. At least one of us knows how to be *normal*.

Cassie blinks slowly, adjusting the glittering butterfly nestled amongst her fiery hair. "The cop said it happened the night I was meant to meet him at the party. When he left without me…" her voice trails off. Ginny hugs her tighter.

"You, in my office, now." Principal Jones' voice is brisk as he pushes through the crowd, nudging Cassie in the direction of his office, just outside of the Hall and to the left.

"Hey," I growl, "no need to shove."

Sergeant Pine stands next to Principal Jones, giving me a look, all flaring nostrils. I shut my mouth.

"Gin." A gruff voice cuts through the crowd.

My eyes are still watching Sergeant Pine as Garamond walks out of the Hall. The Sergeant flinches, his hands falling to his sides as his shoulders slump. *Curious.*

"Grandad, what're you doing here?"

"I'll be assisting the sergeant –"

"– and your expertise is much appreciated, sir," Sergeant Pine adds. Garamond's head whips, his eyes on Sarge, the sergeant quickly averting his gaze like a cowering dog. I notice the corner of Garamond's mouth crawl into a faint smirk.

Ginny's hands are on her hips, her small frame puffing out as far as she can.

"Well, I'd like to help, too." Ginny's voice is absolute.

I can't help but smile at how fierce she is.

"That's not necessary, Miss Chase," Principal Jones interrupts. "The police just need Cassie."

Ginny folds her arms. "But doesn't Cassie need a guardian present in the case of being interviewed by police?"

Principal Jones sighs. "Jocelyn Carr's been notified –"

"– if she's even sober," I scoff.

"In any case, having Principal Jones here will suffice," Sergeant Pine says, his eyes darting back and forth to Garamond, as if for approval. Garamond squares his jaw, nodding ever so slightly. "This way, Miss Kelly. Your friends can wait out here."

I watch as Sergeant Pine and Principal Jones usher Cassie into the office, the door clicking shut behind them. The echo of laughter and teenage gossip bounces down the corridor as all the kids pile out of the school. Garamond sits across from me in the empty hallway and I can feel the runestones hum in my pocket.

"Gin, love, can you go to my car out front and get my notepad? It's in the glovebox."

I watch as Ginny's golden hair bounces out of sight.

"So. Winnifred. Now it's just you and I…"

It feels like his eyes are burning into me. I return Garamond's stare. "Fred's just fine."

"Ah. One of these alphabet kids, right?"

I can't tell if he's trying to be genuine or mocking me. I lift one shoulder in a very noncommittal shrug. My fingers slide into the canvas bag and gravitate towards a runestone.

"Fred." He smiles. "I hear you paid my house a visit yesterday." Garamond's voice is low and deep.

I swallow hard, my eyes blinking as my mind races. Am I busted? But what for?

"Ginny stacked it at school," I offer. "I wanted to make sure she got home okay."

Garamond sits back in the chair. "Ginny told me all about it."

All about what? How I mauled her?

"I just want to know what your intentions are with my

granddaughter."

Oh, wait, hold on. Is this *the talk*? Is this the boyfriend talk?

"We're friends, I guess?"

Fred, that's terrible, something else!

"I'm helping her catch up on schoolwork after being away."

Not a complete lie.

A sharp pain zaps between my eyes. The crunching sound of bare feet on loose gravel echoes through my memories. My dreams. They were just dreams, weren't they?

"You okay?" Garamond leans forward, eyebrows furrowed with concern.

I look over towards the closed door of Principal Jones' office. I can only imagine what questions they're asking Cassie. I can hear a faint sniffle.

I slump in the chair. "This is all, just, a lot to take in."

"It's never easy when someone so young is murdered," Garamond sighs.

Wait, what? "Murder? I thought the sergeant warned us about dingoes?"

Garamond pauses, clearing his throat. "You're right, sorry. Definitely a feral dog."

The latch of Principal Jones' door clicks, and Cassie bursts out, running down the corridor and out the double doors.

"Cassie was very helpful. Everything checks out in relation

to the party…" Sergeant Pine's voice trails off, eyes on Garamond. "Did you want to question her?"

Garamond stands abruptly, grunting in response.

"Here's your notepad, Grandad." Ginny, all smiles, skips up the steps.

Garamond is like Jekyll and Hyde – one minute he's giving death stares to the sergeant, the next, all smiles to Ginny.

"Thanks, Gin."

Ginny crosses her arms against her chest. "So, what are the plans from here? I can text some people, see if anyone at the party saw or heard anything, and maybe –"

"No, Gin. Leave this to us," Garamond says, scrawling something in his notebook.

Ginny rolls her eyes and stomps off. I turn to leave when Garamond's hand is on my shoulder.

"Do me a favour and help Gin get her mind off all this, yeah? Maybe head into Outwash, make a day of it." He slides a fifty-dollar bill into my hand.

All I can do is nod. This is turning out to be a super weird day.

Principal Jones nods in my direction, and I take that as a *get going.*

"Ginny, wait up." I easily close the gap and take her hand. Her eyes stare up into mine, then back to our entangled fingers.

"So, more than friends?" she says, nibbling on her bottom lip.

Gods help me, this is a very weird day.

I give the Fred Special, a one shoulder shrug, and Ginny laughs.

Walking through the front doors and down the steps of the school, I feel like I need to pinch myself. None of this is how I saw my last year of school going. But in true Fred form, it is absolute chaos. Love and death and creepy old dudes all rolled into one.

"Cassie's already gone." Ginny's voice breaks my train of thought. The sound of Cassie's boots walking down the laneway next to the school stomp against the concrete.

"Hey, if we run, maybe we can catch up, make sure she's okay…" I squeeze Ginny's hand and we follow, making it to the corner of the laneway only to watch Cassie's ginger curls bounce around the next bend, the sun shining off her diamante butterfly.

"She'll be okay…" I smile, weakly.

Yet why is my stomach churning?

Walking back to the main road towards the school, I look at the runestone I'd picked earlier from my pocket, and frown.

Algiz. Protection. I look behind me, up towards the stairs to the double doors of the school where Garamond's still standing.

I swallow hard. *Maybe I do need protection. Protection from the overly protective grandad.*

"What're those?" Ginny asks, her eyes on the moonstone rune in my hand.

I've never let anyone see them before, let alone talked about them.

"Just dumb rocks," I reply, when the new kid steps out in front of us, knocking the stone from my hand. With reflexes like nothing I've seen, he catches it and flashes me a toothy smile.

"Sorry. I wasn't paying attention," he says, the rune in the palm of his outstretched hand. "Talk about hectic first day of school. Is it always like this?"

"…s'pose," I offer, taking the stone and sliding it back in my pocket.

"Not really," Ginny laughs.

As Ginny and the new kid talk, I watch his face move. The way his full lips smile, making his high cheek bones squint his eyes shut. He laughs a lot. He seems nice – not sure what Garamond's issue with him is about.

"I just realised, I've been talking, and I haven't even introduced myself," he says, holding out his hand to me. "I'm Mathusi Manebarn."

Sliding my hand in his, I feel a jolt of electricity, like a memory being sparked to life deep within. My thoughts are immediately pulled back to my most recent dream. The wolves. And those amber eyes. The same amber eyes staring back at me right now – Mathusi's kind, warm, familiar eyes.

"I've gotta go," I say, pulling my hand away. "*We've* gotta go, actually," I correct with a smile, Garamond's request taking precedence in my thoughts.

Mathusi smiles politely and I watch him make his way towards the school.

"We?" Ginny raises a brow.

"Yeah, Good Time Garamond gave me a fifty and said we should go to Outwash for the day."

"You're kidding, right?"

It's not until we're in the laneway that I look back over my shoulder, but the new kid is gone. Not his eyes, though; they linger. *What was it the wolf whispered in my dream?*

Opening the internet search bar on my phone, I'm greeted with a blank, white screen.

"Shit. No internet connection. I've run out of data –"

The sound of a horn blaring thrusts me from my thoughts as the bus to Outwash slams on its brakes, tyres screeching, smoke pluming. My heart races, the bus driver yelling obscenities, opening the bifold door, while Ginny stands back on the curb, panting.

"Watch where you're going!" the driver curses.

Stuck on the glass of the folding door was a small poster for the newly renovated Outwash District Library – *free Wi-Fi and coffee* written in neon green.

"Are you even getting on?" the bus driver hisses.

"Yeah, yeah, two to Outwash. The library." Rummaging for coins in my pocket, I toss them into the till, Ginny stepping on after. She shakily sits next to me.

"Fred, you nearly got run over!"

I pat her leg. "I'm like a dog, or something. I have nine lives."

Ginny laughs so hard she starts coughing. "That's cats, you goose!"

"Ah, come on, which is it, cats or geese?" I tease. "And you wanna be a vet."

Ginny whacks me with her backpack, and I can't help but laugh. This feels so easy. Clearly I've been stressing about the *no friends zone*, or whatever this is, for no reason. This feels right.

The gears crunch loudly as the bus splutters down the main road towards the highway and Outwash.

CHAPTER TEN

I'm not entirely sure what's been refurbished at the library, as the flyer in the bus window proudly proclaimed.

"Wow, this is a flashback to a bygone era," I say, Ginny laughing beside me. I've never actually been here before, but it still looks like a throwback to the early nineties, the carpet full of neon colours and geometrical shapes.

"So, my grandad gives us fifty bucks and tells us to make a day of it, and you take me to the library?" Ginny smirks.

"I thought this'd be, like, prime date location for a nerd like you," I tease. Then pause. I had said *date*.

I look back over my shoulder to Ginny, standing by a rack of tattered lifestyle magazines, idly tracing the torn edges with her finger, her shoulders swaying.

"This is a date?"

She's trying so hard to hold back a giant smile. I can see it twitching at the corners of her mouth, the tips of her ears going red.

All I can do is blush back.

"Wanna help me look up something?" I cough, changing the subject.

Spying an old box-looking computer at the librarian's desk, I find the search function to locate books in the library.

"F-L-O-R-E-N…" I type.

What did it mean? Seeing that Mathusi kid had brought my dream rushing back to me. I remember falling, water… the wolf's whisper. Then there was this *knowing*. The knowing what this place was called. A valley, a river?

The search auto-fills for me and brings up a list of books.

"*Florentine Valley*. In Tasmania?" Ginny reads over my shoulder. "Have you been there?"

"Not sure…" Writing down the codes on a scrap of paper, I search for the aisle.

The musty, woody smell of books, old and new, fill my nose. It's as if I can pick the individual smells – the leather, the glue, the ink. I trace my fingers along the spines, landing on a book titled *Van Diemen's Land*. Flicking through the pages, pictures of giant billowing trees and rocky streams pass by. Opening the index, I find the page number indicating the Florentine Valley. The trill of fluttering pages stops when the book opens to a grand lake, surrounded by those same billowing trees. Huon trees. My eyes trace the page, my finger moving, then stops.

"Lake Gordon."

This is frustrating! What does some lake in Tassie have to do with anything? Am I reading too much into these dreams?

They just… they feel important. Ginny grabs the remaining books on the list, and we take them back to an empty desk.

"Hey, did you know Randy much?" Ginny's voice is so soft and quiet, I barely hear her.

Oh. Yeah. Randy. I've been so caught up in my own shit.

"Not really," I offer. "I only knew him in passing, kinda thing. You?"

"Yeah. Yeah, I do… did," Ginny sighs. "His nan and my grandad were both part of the Outwash police unit. So, when Grandad and I moved out here a few years back, Randy was the only person I knew." She shuffles in her seat. "I just…" Ginny sits forward, mouth opening and closing.

I've spent years perfecting the *not caring* attitude, but Ginny? I can just tell she wants to be making casseroles and handing out fliers.

"Screw old mate Garamond. Message everyone. Someone's gotta know something."

Ginny's face beams. "Exactly!"

Time seems to slip by. Between all the reading, Ginny's feverish texts, and an epic lunch break where we overindulged in Thai food, it's not until the afternoon sun's glaring through a window that I squint down at an old newspaper slide in front of me.

Tapping Ginny's shoulder, she moves onto the seat next to me.

"Check this out. An article about a murder in Huon, Tasmania." It's nothing that should have caught my attention, just another macabre incident documented in the news. "The, uh, the date…" I squint at the tiny slide. Only a few days after my parents' death.

Ginny purses her lips, then takes the slide from me, heading to the library's front desk.

"Excuse me?" Ginny's voice drips with sweetness as she approaches the librarian. "We were hoping to take a look at this slide?"

The old woman behind the counter shakes her head, her expression unyielding. "In the refurbishment, the council moved the old projectors to storage. I was supposed to collect and file all the slides, but I must've missed one." She carefully takes the square piece of film from Ginny's hand and places it in a tray on her desk. "I'm sorry, love. Maybe you could try the internet? It seems like everything's online these days."

"Surely we could take just this one slide?" Ginny asks, offering the librarian a charming smile, and I leave her to it. She'd have more luck than me in trying to convince the librarian.

I remember the sign on the bus – *free Wi-Fi* – and spy a row of computers in a far corner.

"Tch. Five bucks? So much for free."

"It's a bit steep, isn't it?" a somewhat familiar voice behind me sounds. A tall man leans against the cubicle divider, his blonde hair catching the light in a golden halo. But there's something off about his presence. Freckles sprinkle his chiselled cheeks, and a smile plays on his lips, but it feels too perfect, almost rehearsed, radiating warmth in a way that seems calculated. His eyes, a striking shade of blue, glisten as he watches me, but there's an intensity in his stare that sends a shiver down my spine, filling the room with an air of charm that feels anything but genuine.

Charm? More like wankery. A smirk tickles the corner of my mouth.

His smile drops slightly before signalling to the computer at the end of the row, the screen flickering. The glimmer of a green crystal catches my attention, the rock on his finger entwined in a gnarled band of gold. His choice of bling is gaudy, and I instinctively take a step away from him, feeling increasingly uneasy in his presence.

"Cool ring," I manage to say, trying to sound nonchalant despite the unease creeping up my spine. Where have I seen this guy before?

The man smiles, rubbing at the hunk of jewellery, a smile twitching at the corner of his mouth. "I'm done with the computer if you'd like to use it. Probably another twenty minutes left on the clock."

I turn to thank him, but when I do, he's gone, as if he was never there to begin with. The room feels colder.

"Pfft. Weirdo." I can't help but glance over my shoulder, and a strange feeling niggles, as if I'm being watched.

"Who's a weirdo now?" Ginny laughs, making her way back from the main desk.

"Just some Vampire Diaries-looking reject," I snort. "Any luck with the slide?"

"Unfortunately, no. But at least we can search it up here?" Ginny slides onto the swivelling desk chair, fingers tapping against the keyboard. Search engines flash on the screen, and it's not long until she finds a copy of the article mentioned in the slide.

"Alright, Veronica Mars," I tease.

Ginny stands, bowing deeply, sliding her chair across for me to sit down.

There it is, deep in the archives of the *Huon Post*, dated twelve years ago.

I'd always been told that the cause of my parents' death had been overdose. I had only been five when they'd died, so I had taken what people had said as truth. But despite having been told my parents had been dropkicks, told that they had been more interested in getting high than looking after me, deep down, it had just felt wrong. Deep down, I had known the truth. I had just been so frightened of finding out, on the off chance that, well… what if it was true? What if my parents had been useless junkies… so I'd never searched, I'd never investigated it, instead, I'd held on to the memories I'd felt were real.

"Blood Moon – murder on New Moon Island…"

No matter how hard I blink, trying to keep the tears at bay, I can't.

"Fred?" Ginny's hand is on mine.

I dab at the corners of my eyes. "I'm fine. It's fine."

"It's okay to show an emotion now and again."

A huff of a laugh tickles my throat, my fingers toying with the gold heart-shaped locket around my neck, opening the latch. The small features nestled between these golden hearts are now large upon the screen. I can feel the pinpricks, the sting of tears sitting behind my eyes. I swallow hard, pushing it down, but this is just all too much. I can't deal right now. This was meant to be a fun little excursion.

Using my phone, I click a photo of the screen and slide the device back in my pocket, wiping my nose on my sleeve.

"You know I'm here. Whenever you wanna talk." Ginny smiles softly.

I nod. Collecting all the photocopies, I tuck them into my

bag. Maybe one day. Maybe with Ginny I can open up.

Ginny takes my hand as we step out into the crisp evening air. The smell of rain still lingers on the breeze. Sliding my backpack over my shoulders, we make the Acacia Hills bus just in time. My mind is swirling in a thick stew of thoughts. Memories, dreams, all sloshing together with the new information gathered throughout the day.

We find a seat and settle in for the hour drive back to Acacia Hills. Ginny chatters away about the books she borrowed, how she found a stack perfect for our microbiology assignment this term. Glancing over, she's already excitedly organising the pages with coloured tabs, telling me what each colour references.

Swiping my phone with a pinch and zoom, I find the photo I took of the article. "Have you seen this man…" I read softly, a picture of a police sketch: a man, scruffy, wearing a tartan newsboy cap. "Person of interest…" I read on.

Maybe if I can figure out who you are, mystery man, I can find out what happened to my folks.

Ginny laughs over my shoulder. "That looks like Grandad."

I glance again at the pixelated photo, squinting. "Nah, this guy actually looks half decent," I tease.

Leaning my head against the glass window, the sun slowly setting, giving way to the starry night, I close my eyes and let the hum of the engine lull me into a dreamless sleep.

CHAPTER ELEVEN

My head is pulsing. Throbbing. It feels as though every single cell in my brain is alive, crashing into each other like Dodgem cars. Smashing. Bashing. The siren wailing in the distance doesn't help this ever-growing migraine howling in my head.

No! No, no, no! My alarm never went off. And even if it had, I doubt I would have heard it through the thrum in my head.

Rolling out of bed, a sprinkling of dirt falls from the cuffs of my jeans.

Why am I still dressed… and what's with the dirt?

Sitting on the edge of my bed, I hold my head still, trying to corral the bumper cars. I was on the bus with Ginny, coming back from Outwash. I walked her home, then went to my little lean-to to mull over what I'd discovered that day. Huon Valley, New Moon Island…

I stare out the window. I vaguely remember coming back to Jocelyn's. I think?

The alarm blasts.

"Bit late," I scoff, and cram my biology textbook into my bag, the photocopies from the library crumpling underneath. *Shit.* I pull the papers out, flattening them against my bed, then slip them under the mattress.

"Cassie, you home?" I yell through the open door of my bedroom, though Jocelyn's snoring is my only reply.

I can't believe it was only yesterday we found out about Randy. I'm sure Cassie's okay; she's probably already shrouded in a new guy's B.O.-stained jacket.

Walking down the hallway towards the bathroom, I hurriedly turn the shower on. That'll help clear the cobwebs. And the dirt. The memory of Ginny yesterday tangles in the webbing of my thoughts, all sticky and appetising.

I turn the hot tap off, blasting icy water onto the tiles below. "Maybe a cold shower is a better idea…"

Letting the freezing spray wash over me, I lean my head against the cold tiles, my thoughts racing, about everything and anything – the curve of Ginny's thighs in that skirt she wore yesterday charging ahead.

I've known since I was seven that I liked girls. I remember stumbling across *Xena: Warrior Princess* and getting all googly-eyed for Gabrielle. And now Ginny sashays into my life, like a real-life Gabby, all golden hair and sass.

My thoughts start to slip and wander, and before I know it, I'm back in my room, towelling off, staring at my wardrobe. Searching my drawers, I find a plain white tee and a crumpled plaid button-up.

No pants. Shit.

I feel my face scrunch, and I gingerly peek from one eye, spying the pair of jeans I had on yesterday… and the day before.

"You'll do," I sigh.

My alarm shoots off again. "Alright, alright! I'm going!"

Slinging my backpack over my shoulder, I'm out the door, power-walking down the street. With my legs pumping at full speed, I might make it in time for homeroom.

"*I might make it in time for homeroom*? Who *am* I?"

Ginny's smile fills my thoughts, and I can feel my headache subside.

~ 🐺 ~

"So, I was thinking." Ginny sidles up beside me, the bell signalling the end of the school day trilling down the hallway.

"Did it hurt?"

Ginny stops, her nose wrinkling, confused. "Did what hurt?"

"Thinking." I smirk.

"Hey!" she scoffs, slapping me with the back of her textbook.

"Ouch. Feisty today." I laugh, rubbing my arm. "Anyways, you were thinking…"

" – you should come over to my place this arvo. We can get a head start on this assignment. I've made notes…"

"Oh, so you're planning my days now, huh?" I say jokingly, though Ginny stops, stepping in front of me, her face staring up at mine.

"I'm sorry." Her voice is low. "I just. This is all new and exciting." She steps closer. "I've never done *this* before. And to be honest, I'm sometimes a bit…" She pauses, searching for the right word.

"Controlling?" I tease.

Ginny's head drops.

I slip my fingers under her chin, tipping her head upwards, my eyes finding hers. "I'm not complaining."

We stand like this for some time. Just. Staring. I can feel a warmth rush through me before the junior kids run past, bumping into us.

"Genevieve Chase," I say, taking her hand and walking towards the steps of the school exit. "I woke up late today." I pause, and Ginny's eyebrows wriggle upwards in question. "Normally, when I wake up late, I stay in bed. *Especially* when none of my classes are even remotely English-orientated." I squeeze her hand. "Until you." I smile. "So, control away!"

A giant smile spreads across Ginny's face, reaching her eyes. "I'm gonna hold you to that, McTire."

"Oh no, what have I done?" I reply, playfully cowering before bursting into laughter.

We walk down the steps and out onto the street.

"And anyways, am I even allowed over?" I ask, genuinely concerned. "I get such mixed vibes from Garamond."

Ginny smiles. "I already let him know."

Walking to Ginny's house from school takes a good fifteen minutes, the conversation jumping from how hot this summer is to whether Ms Robinson owns anything other than bold block colours. Then, to the inevitable…

"Do you wanna talk about the other day?" Ginny finally asks, rubbing at the scabbing welts across her chest. "And yesterday," she adds. "New Moon Island?"

We walk in silence a few steps. What *had* happened that day? "Steven and Tyson just really pissed me off," I finally blurt out, feeling the heat rise in me once more. "I didn't mean to hurt you…"

"They're dicks," Ginny says, matter of fact.

"But it's not an excuse," I say, stopping facing Ginny. I take her hand, leading her to the footpath. "There's never an excuse for what I did to you."

"I get it. And I kinda see why Grandad was worried."

"You're lucky you have him looking out for you," I say through a forced smile. Kicking at a stray rock, I add, "And as for the other… shit, that's a long story…"

I'm not sure if I want to go there yet. Maybe *I'm* Jekyll and Hyde. I want to open up to Ginny. But what if this all goes pear-shaped?

Ginny nods; the only sound accompanying us is our shoes scuffing in the gravel and dirt as we continue our trek to her place.

"Just know, I have two fully functioning ears, and I'm happy to use them."

With a grin, I flick her earlobe. "*What big ears you have…*"

"Hey!" Ginny covers them with her hands, elbowing me in the back. "You cheeky bugger!"

Full of giggles, we're up the driveway and in the house.

"I could hear the pair of you from downstairs," Garamond laughs, latching the door to his den behind him.

"Downstairs?" I whisper to Ginny, who just rolls her eyes.

"Grandad's den. *The forbidden zone*," Ginny mocks.

"And don't you forget it!" Garamond teases. "Gin, could I speak with you moment?" Garamond smiles at me. "I'm sure Fred will manage to find the kitchen? I've laid out some afternoon tea for you both."

"How very domestic of you, Grandad," Ginny laughs. Garamond scruffs her hair, then leads her into the lounge room while I walk the hallway to the kitchen.

Taking a ham sandwich, I stuff it crust-first into my mouth, pouring a glass of water, when I hear the mumbles of Ginny's conversation. Sitting at the kitchen table, my ears seem to home in on their words.

Garamond's voice is muffled, but clear enough. I shouldn't listen – this is private – but curiosity gets the better of me.

"Work wants me back in Amsterdam in two months."

"What? We just got home! I can't go, Grandad. It's my final year, I need good grades –"

"Gin, love…" he interrupts, then pauses. There's the sound of rustling papers. "I managed to get you into the veterinary hospital at Outwash on their entry program. It counts towards your final year of schooling. You get every Friday off to work at the hospital, and you get credit for your university degree."

Silence. I'm not surprised. This is huge news; even I'm sitting here in shock. I cram another quarter cut of sandwich into my mouth.

"Grandad…"

"Think about it." I can hear the smile in his voice. "You're nearly an adult, I reckon I can trust you on your own here for a month while I'm in Amsterdam for work?"

Laughter, followed by words I can't quite figure out. I sit back in the chair. Ginny has her life all planned out. I look down at my rancid jeans and sigh. What does she even see in me?

"Speaking of work, I'm heading over to Outwash now, but

I'll be back in time for dinner." Garamond's voice is closer now, and I turn around to watch Ginny skip through the kitchen door, papers in hand.

"Can you pick up –" Ginny smiles, the words barely making their way past that dumb grin.

"– pies from Nina's Bakery?" Garamond's beard twitches with a smile. "Yes, I can."

Ginny's shoulders wriggle with excitement, turning to me. "Nina has *the best* chicken curry pies. Her pastry is so deliciously crumbly."

"You're in for a treat, Fred." Garamond winks.

"Thanks, Grandad."

"Anything for you, Gin," he says, kissing her forehead before jogging down the hall.

Ginny sits across from me, peeling an orange.

"So. What's the latest, Chase?" I ask over the rim of my glass, knowing full well what the latest actually is.

Ginny spreads the paperwork and forms across the table. "The start of my future, McTire!" She beams.

Footsteps creak back up the hallway. "I forgot to ask." Garamond pauses, looking at me. "What type of filling do you prefer, *McTire*..." Garamond stands against the doorframe, his arms folded. "Did I get that right? McTire?"

Ginny looks at her grandad, scrunching her face. "What's

with the *McTire*?" she laughs.

"I just didn't realise that was Fred's surname." Garamond smiles, though I think I'm the only one who notices the smile never reaches his eyes, and the slight flare of his nostrils.

"Um, chicken curry sounds nice," I offer.

Ginny is so focused on all her paperwork, mumbling away, only I see Garamond's eye twitch as he speaks. "Chicken curry it is."

The sound of the front door closing finally lets my body sigh with relief. *What the hell was that?*

"I can't believe he did all this after I acted like an absolute bitch to him yesterday," Ginny says, flicking through the pamphlets.

"Yeah, right," is all I can manage, fixing my gaze down the hallway, the memory of those unsmiling eyes still staring back at me. I can hear Ginny at the cusp of my thoughts, and I'm drawn back to the here and now. "Well, hey…" I finally manage. "Something makes me think Garamond's been planning this for a while, and that he'd, in fact, do *anything for you, Gin.*"

Ginny laughs at my terrible Garamond impersonation, but I can feel my smile drop a little as I shuffle in my seat. Yeah, he might be a bit weird, but he really cares for her. "You're lucky you have someone who loves you so much."

Ginny reaches across the table, gently placing her hand on

mine. "Fred," she says softly, "I know it might feel like you're alone, but I want you to know you're not. You have people who care about you." Ginny pauses. "I care about you."

Ginny's hand remains on mine, her touch a lifeline in the sea of uncertainty. I struggle to find my voice, my mind racing with a whirlwind of emotions. The weight of Ginny's words settles deep within me, stirring a mixture of hope and fear.

Meeting her gaze, I see sincerity and compassion reflected in her eyes. In this moment, I want so desperately to believe her, to allow myself to be vulnerable and open up to the possibility of connection. But years of disappointments and broken promises have etched scars on my heart, leaving me hesitant to trust and afraid of being hurt. Again.

A fragile smile tugs at the corners of my lips, a small gesture to acknowledge the significance of Ginny's words. I take a deep breath, trying to gather my thoughts. "Thank you," I finally manage to whisper, my voice barely audible.

Ginny's smile widens, a glimmer of understanding in her eyes. She squeezes my hand gently, offering reassurance through that simple touch. "You don't have to thank me, Fred. I mean it," she says, her words carrying a warmth with them. "I want to be here for you."

I can feel her words battling against the walls I've built, the bricks crumbling. A part of me longs to believe her, to let go of the fear and allow myself to be seen and supported. But another part, scarred by life, whispers caution and reminds me of the pain that can come from trusting too easily.

"I want to believe you," I rasp, the sounds coming out all crackly and broken. "I want to trust that there can be someone who cares. But it's hard for me. It's really hard," I admit, vulnerability seeping into my words.

Ginny nods, her expression gentle and understanding. "I know. And that's okay. We'll take it one step at a time, at your pace. All of this. I'm here for you, whenever you're ready. Ears, remember?" She smiles.

In that moment, I realise that maybe, just maybe, I don't have to face the world alone anymore. And with that newfound hope, I take the first step towards trusting and letting someone in.

"Well then…" I pause, my mind swirling, trying to think where to start, what to say first. There's so much, too much…" Where are all these books with the colour coded tabs you got all horny for?"

Ginny laughs, slapping me on the shoulder as she walks by, retrieving her library haul.

Maybe I'll take that first step tomorrow.

CHAPTER TWELVE

Well, tonight got weird.

Pushing through the bracken, making my way to the river, I can't shake the ick from me. The way Garamond looked at me.

Ginny and I had been sitting at her kitchen table for a while, sorting through books on microbiology, working out the details of our science project, when she'd gotten a text from him – he had been held back, apparently, and wouldn't make it for dinner. She was seriously miffed about the pies, but we'd made do with some ramen noodles.

After the whole *New Moon Island* discovery, then the *McTire* thing with Garamond… maybe I'm just on edge. Maybe the Randy thing is affecting me more than I'm letting on.

But the memory of Garamond's face, how his whole attitude seemed to change when he found out my surname…

After dinner, I remember sitting on the couch with Ginny, her legs tangled underneath her skirt, her fingers tracing circles on my arm as we talked about books and movies, the headiness of it all colliding with the weirdness of the day, the weirdness of the last few days.

"Did you wanna see my room?" Ginny had asked, her cheeks

all blushed as she'd nibbled on her lip.

"I'm actually gonna get going," I'd replied, abruptly. "I think I just need to clear my head."

Ginny had smiled, but I'd seen the bob in her throat. I hadn't known why she'd been so nice, so patient. Caring. I'd squeezed her leg and shown myself out.

As I make my way along the rocky path, the rhythmic thud of my boots sends a couple of wallabies bounding away into the night, their silhouettes vanishing into the shadows. In the quiet stillness that follows, a pair of eyes, gleaming like distant stars, fixes its gaze on me from the thick undergrowth. I come to an abrupt halt, captivated by the entrancing luminescence in the darkness. Then, a snout emerges, and I recognise the familiar orange coat of the dog from Sunday night. It sniffs the air briefly before retreating into the bush. Just as I wonder if it's a mere figment of the night, my phone vibrates in my pocket. A text message, from my social worker:

```
Hey Fred. I know I messed up a bit, moving
you out to Acacia when that Harrison woman
wasn't even there (how's Jocelyn's?)

Anyways. Good news! I managed to get in
contact with another relative - cousin of
your mums. He's flying out from Norway, can
you believe it?

This is big news. I'll keep you posted.
```

Great. More weirdness. Why not? I don't reply and switch my phone off.

Breathing in deep, staring up through the leaves, the full moon peeks through the spindly branches. The damp smell of the river, all sweet and musty, fills me. Out here in the open – no walls, no assignments, no commitments, no weird grandfathers and distant relatives… everything feels right again.

Not a cloud betrays the night sky, the moon a dazzling radiant orb pinned to the backdrop that is the velvet night. A distant hum, drum, roll of thunder – a splash of light, a flash of white. I lean back against a billowing wilga and close my eyes, letting the poetry of the night engulf me.

I'll just chill here. Rest my eyes for a little bit. Just for a minute.

I try to open my eyes, but they feel sticky and heavy. They throb. My brain shrieks at me like a petulant toddler, devoid of any thought other than pain. Reaching for my pillow, I grab instead a strange rectangular shape, the contents raining down over my head. The smell of freshly baled hay, sweet and crisp, tickles my nose.

"Wwhaa?" is all I can muster, the sound croaking from my tacky, coppery mouth. My lips smack and it's then the taste hits me, and my stomach churns. The acrid bile bubbling until it bursts, sick spewing from my mouth onto the floor. My eyes peel open, finding the glob of muck that came from my stomach; streaks of red, and something that looks like chunks of wet fur, fill the mess.

Adjusting to the light, I squint and sit up. Suddenly, the cacophony of screaming toddlers within my mind falls silent, their relentless cries extinguished like fireworks fizzling into oblivion. The scorching embers of thoughts rain down, their fiery remnants dissipating into wisps of memories. Recollections, at least partially, of the night before. My body starts to shiver, a coldness from my core running up my spine. I raise my hands, and it's then I see it. Blood. Deep, burgundy red, all hard and crunchy against my skin. Imbedded under my nails, in the creases of my knuckles, running like dried-up rivers down my forearms.

The queasy, churning knots twist again in my stomach, my mind frantically leaping and jumping through memories. Whose blood is this? The last thing I remember was the wilga tree. The river.

I blink, squinting past the memories to the now. This isn't my bedroom. Bales of hay line the farthest wall. Troughs and buckets fill the stalls. The quiet bray of a horse sounds; the curious creature tips its head over the gate, flares its nostrils, and snorts at me.

"I think Norris is just a bit confused, you being in his house, and all." The voice is low and accented.

I find whatever strength I can and crawl towards a large metal barrel, wedging my body between it and the wall. It's only then I realise how much blood there is on me, and how very naked I am.

"I have a spare change of clothes. And the all-essential coffee," the voice beckons, the nutty smell of chicory floating on the morning air. "It's okay to come out."

I gingerly stand, peering over the barrel. It's the blonde ringlets I see first, all damp from a shower, I presume.

Mathusi?

His footsteps are soft against the dirt and straw.

"There's a shower in the stall behind you. My cousin uses it for the horses. It's even rigged for hot water."

I peek behind me, over my shoulder, and sure enough, the makeshift spout juts from the wall.

"I'll leave the clothes here." Mathusi gently places a pair of folded jeans and T-shirt on the hay. "And there's a towel, too," he adds, the plush fabric flicking over the stall gate. "I'll just be outside."

His footsteps recede, and I wait until I can hear the barn door slide shut.

Slipping behind the stall, I turn on the taps. The hot water streams out, steam filling the air, wrapping me in its ghostly warmth. The momentary comfort subsides as I look down at my hands. My legs. Even my torso. Red blood, muck, and dirt cakes my body like some gruesome Halloween suit. I take a rag hanging from a hook, a bristled bar of soap, and lather. Scrub. Scrub. My skin stings, it burns, but I keep rubbing and scrubbing, washing away the filth of who-knows-what. My fingers trace over my skin: no cuts, no scratches, no wounds. My eyes swell. I can feel the tears clamouring at the back of my throat, clawing at my eyes. I want to cry, I want to fall to the ground and sob like a child, but I can't. Not here, not now. I beat my fist against the wooden wall and keep scrubbing.

I'm soon dried and dressed. The shirt is extra-large, which I'm grateful for. Despite the horrible strangeness of all of this, I feel so naked without my binder. Where is it? And where are the rest of my things? I reach for my neck; the gold chain and locket still hang loosely. Where are the runestones?

I'm hyperaware of the way my breasts pendulously sway when I walk, so I cross my arms tightly over my chest before nudging the barn door open with my bare foot. The morning sun creeps through the distant gum trees.

Mathusi hands me an oversized mug of hot coffee, smiling as he nods towards the fresh brew. "It'll help," he says, and despite my trembling hand, I take it cautiously.

Staring at him over the rim of the mug, Mathusi continues to talk, but I'm not entirely listening. My mind drowns in a sea of thoughts. Is this shock? I remember a similar feeling washing over me the night I found my parents.

I pinch the bridge of my nose, then open my eyes wide, as if to take in as much of my surroundings as I can. As if opening my eyes as big as they can get will somehow help this all make sense, that I'll see everything for what it is, and life will miraculously go back to normal.

What even is *normal, Fred?*

Okay. This is a farm. Fields of horses graze on the long grass ahead, and I can see the homestead up on the crest.

This is the Rustmane house.

I sip at the coffee, but my stomach gurgles back angrily.

"Did… did I get attacked?" I interrupt. I have no idea how I got here, or what happened, and so far this kid is just talking about his family, or whatever. His cousin is missing? Their monthly run? I don't know. He doesn't seem too weirded out by my being here – by the gross, bloodied person hiding in his barn.

"Attacked?" Mathusi's smiling face drops slightly, his eyebrow ticking up.

"Yeah, dingoes. I think I saw one last night. Wasn't that

what the sergeant said at school the other day, about Randy and stuff?" I sip my coffee. "Speaking of, where's my stuff? My bag… I have some important family shit in there, and…"

Mathusi stutters but no words come out. He just stands, shifting his weight from foot to foot, tapping his toes.

"Yeah, I think my brother has your bag…" He flicks a pointed finger to the house on the hill, a look of confusion on his face. He pauses, rummaging in his pockets. "Actually… here."

The familiar scratchy canvas bag with Mum's runestones sits in Mathusi's hands.

"These looked important, so…" his voice trails off.

I feel at least one knot in my shoulder release as I take the bag and slide it into the pocket of the baggy jeans.

"Thanks." I nod.

"Yeah, no worries. And hey, it's not every day you find a bag of rocks and a naked chick in your backyard." The boy snorts awkwardly. His eyes soon dart away from mine to watch the sunrise. I can see him glancing at me from the corner of his eye, and I sigh.

"I'm not a *chick*."

Mathusi heaves a sigh of relief, throwing his hand on his hip. "Oh, good, so you know?" His shoulders slump and a big dumb grin spreads across his face. "That makes this, just, so much easier –"

"Makes what easier?"

"– to be honest, I wasn't sure how to even *tell* you, you know?"

"No, I don't know."

"– it's like, how do you have *that* conversation: *oh, by the way, you're a werewolf.*" Mathusi laughs.

I can feel the blood rush from my head and sink to the depths of my intestines.

What did he just say?

"I'm a what now?" I feel as though my jaw is hanging on the ground.

"A were-what?" I ask again, my chest tightening. That knot I just loosened in my back wrinkles up again right under my shoulder blade.

Mathusi quickly wraps his arms across his chest, his shoulders stiffening; the whites of his eyes are whiter than white, growing bigger, taking over his face.

I don't feel so good…

"Yeah, so, *you* said, *I'm not a chick*?" he mimics, swaying from side to side, trying to make light of whatever this is. His hands reach for his temples, moving to his hips, then settle back in a knot in front of his chest.

I can feel the bile rising in my throat.

"I meant I'm non-binary," I finally manage to say, each word laced with the potential to puke.

"Ooh…" Mathusi's jittering stops as he stares, his face blank.

Silence falls over the barn. Well, more like silence came crashing down and smothered us. Even the distant croaking of frogs at the pond has stopped.

"…well, so, um. Another thing…" Mathusi weakly continues, scratching his head.

Flashes from the night before jolt to the forefront of my mind like bolts of lightning. Memories of the moon full in the sky, waking up with an itch deep under my skin. Flashes of trees zooming past. The crunch of gravel. And the metallic tang of blood.

It's then I start to feel dizzy. My head feels like freshly-spun cotton. That same, soft, fuzzy feeling trickles down my body as I unravel and slump against a bale of hay, succumbing to the warmth of darkness.

My eyelids flutter to life, my fingers tingle. The hay bale seems to be bouncing, jostling me slightly from side to side.

Why is it moving?

Through heavy lashes I see the flash of a car and a set of traffic lights. The last thing I remember was the barn. *Why are there traffic lights at the Rustmane farm? At the Manebarn barn?*

"The Manegal barn farm," I mumble, a snorting giggle bubbling from my nose. The cotton wool wraps me again and draws me down into its cosy embrace, and I plunge into nothingness.

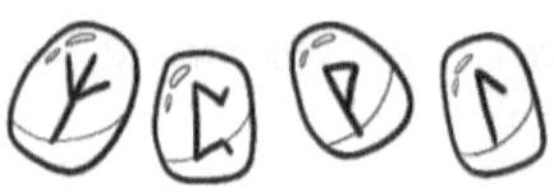

CHAPTER THIRTEEN

A snarling howl, guttural, echoes in my mind as my eyes fling open. The stark light of the room is blinding; I can feel my pupils retract, adjusting from a groggy sleep. Ugh, the ache. My whole body is so stiff, as if I've spent the day at the river and been burnt to a crisp. I wince, peeling my body from the sheets.

I think I dreamt of the lake again, a moon as bright as the sun. My knuckles squelch against my closed eyes, and the images fade away to bleary stars.

I feel the start of a yawn deep in my chest, and stretch. Waves of exhaustion course through me. The distant toll of the school bell rings out – the lunch bell? Midday?

"Fuuuuuu…" I groan. *What happened?* It's unsettling having so much time unaccounted for, the skin-crawling anxiety of trying to think back on a past that doesn't exist. It's as if someone else took the wheel while I fell asleep in the backseat.

Backseat.

The memory leaves as fast as it came.

What day is it? Everything is starting to just blur together – dreams, life.

"You're awake," a voice from outside the room sounds, soft

and sweet.

I open my eyes wide and feel my body tense instantly. I look around. Like, *really* look around, seeing where I am for the first time. Shit.

Again, I'm confronted by the terrifying reality of *what the hell is happening!* How can I not know how I got here? Wherever *here* is. And what have I said during that time? What have I done? If I can't remember it, could it really be me who's been doing it? I feel my chest tighten. My throat… it's closing; I can't breathe. My cheeks prickle as I hold back the tears that want to break free.

The door creaks open, Ginny's concerned face peering through. I offer a weak smile, and the door clicks shut behind her.

"Imagine my surprise when I found you passed out on the back porch this morning. I had to MacGyver a little pully system with sheets just to get you inside." Her brow furrows, and she bites her lip, a flicker of worry passing over her features before she quickly masks it with a small, forced smile.

She's playing it cool. But why? I can feel my chest tighten.

"W-where was I?" Panic starts to set in as I struggle to recall the events leading to this bewildering moment. I remember Ginny, our assignment… walking back to the campground… a barn? I bury my face in my hands.

Ginny joins me on the bed, and I peek out at her through the gaps in my fingers. She starts to say something but hesitates, words hovering on the tip of her tongue.

"– How did I get here? –"

"– Are you hurt? –"

Our words come out tangled. Ginny's eyes dart to my head, her fingers tracing over my temple.

"Hurt? Apparently…" I wince.

Ginny tuts, pulling random pieces of straw from my hair. "I don't know how you got here. I think I heard a car, but…" her voice trails off, her eyes wide and round, taking all of me in. I must look like shit. "Did you get attacked?"

I think back to the dingo I saw Sunday night, and I reckon I saw it again last night. The warning from the sergeant about wild dogs. Randy.

"I don't know…" The words are barely a whisper.

Silence blankets us.

"Does this have to do with Randy?" Ginny asks softly. "Grandad has been going back and forth to Outwash with Sarge. They keep talking about dingoes, but I think it's got something to do with drugs. Are you mixed up in that? What Randy was mixed up in? Some drug thing with gangs and –"

"No." The word comes out abruptly, cutting her off. I sigh, falling back on the bed. How do I explain any of this to her when

I have no idea what's happening to me?

Ginny shuffles next to me, peeling my hands from my face. "Talk to me."

I sit up next to her, my back against the wall. "I keep having these… dreams. Maybe blackouts, I dunno. But it's not drugs. I don't touch the stuff, not since my parents…" I sigh, reaching for the cup of chamomile tea Ginny had placed on the bedside table; the floral smell wafts up my nose, and I blink back the memories. The runestones quietly click in my pocket as I sit forwards on the bed. I open my mouth to speak, to open up, but the words that I hear aren't mine.

"My parents died when I was young, too." Ginny's admission is sudden and soft. Unexpected. "I don't really remember Dad. I know he smoked, Grandad still bangs on about it," she laughs. The sound is so small and sad. "I was only two. A hunting accident or something." She pauses, swallowing. I can see the edge of a tear in the corner of her eye. "My mum died when I was five. I don't really know what happened. I don't have much to remember her by, besides her name – my middle name."

"What is it?"

"Malena." Ginny smiles, though her eyes are still wet. Rubbing her hands against her knees, she stands. "I'm going to make something to eat. Are you hungry? I'm hungry."

Watching her leave, I sit for a few seconds, trying to corral my thoughts. I've never spoken a word about my past to anyone. But with Ginny, maybe I can. Maybe it's okay to open up. Maybe she can help me make sense of it all.

As the honey sweet smell of her leaves the room, I take in the space around me that is Genevieve Malena Chase.

Her bedroom is like a dusty sunset, all powdered pinks and warm greys. It's just how I imagined it to be. Soft peach throw cushions sprawl across her double bed. A cream writing desk stands underneath the window where fairy lights fall from the curtain rod above – each tiny light a bright peg clasping a photo; the pictures light up like twinkling golden memories. Glancing over the photos, I catch a glimpse of my own shaggy black hair in a few of the shots and blush. Standing, I edge closer to the pictures, pinching one of the little Polaroids between my fingers. It was from months ago, maybe even my first day at Acacia High. I can't help but smile at the thought Ginny might have had her eye on me for a while now.

The far wall of Ginny's bedroom is covered with shelves, each filled with a rainbow of books. Literally. Rainbow. She's arranged the books by colour, because, of course *Rainbow Brite* over here arranges her books by colour. I roll my eyes but can't help smiling. Just a little. I read some of the titles and notice most of them are fantasy or queer fiction. I pluck a well-loved book off the shelf, *Carmilla*, its pages bearing the marks of countless readings and thoughtful highlights.

The touch of the book brings back memories of holding Ginny's hand earlier. I slide the book back into its very designated spot.

Down the hall, the springing release of the toaster sounds. I can hear Ginny busying herself in the kitchen, the clink of cutlery falling into the sink. Sitting on the edge of Ginny's lilac bed, I bury my face in my hands once more, pushing my palms deep into my eyes, trying to squeeze out some image of what happened last night.

How did I end up here?

Staring down at my hands, mud and filth thick beneath each nail, I frantically pick at the muck. Ugh, I need a shower. What even is this gunk? I feel so out of place, sitting here all grotty in this plush pink palace.

"Shit, I gotta go. This is stupid," I say, shaking my head.

"You're not going anywhere." Ginny's voice is gentle, though the plates of toast in her hands tremble. The smell of strawberry jam fills the silence. "If you don't like jam, I think there's peanut butter. I have vegemite, too."

Ginny walks across the shaggy purple rug, the plates softly scraping on the desk.

I can't help but scratch the nape of my neck, my fingers

rubbing the base of my skull as if the action will shake free the lost memories of the night. Ginny's staring at me, expectantly.

"Nah, jam's fine. I just, like… I don't know why I came here." *Or how I got here.* She doesn't need to be caught up in my bullshit. Standing, I brush past her. "I should go."

"Please stay." Ginny's voice trembles.

My mind feels like a bag of popcorn, thoughts jumping and exploding, until Ginny's hand slides into mine.

"Please."

I can feel my rushing thoughts slow, my inner demons gobbling the popcorn, nestling down for the show. *Kiss her!* one goblin screams. *Nah, leg it, fuck off outta here!* another goblin laughs, all the while chowing down on my popcorn thoughts. The competition to see which goblin wins halts when Ginny squeezes my fingers, grounding me. Her eyes search mine. For the first time in so long, I feel as if maybe I can lower my guard. Is this what *safe* feels like?

And just when I feel as though my feet have found themselves firmly on solid earth, the memories of the day before force their way to the forefront of my thoughts…

"Your grandad was super weird yesterday."

Ginny rolls her eyes, letting out a long exhale. "Yeah, he was. He didn't get home until heaps late, so I'm glad you didn't stick around –"

"– but maybe if I had, none of this…" I pause, looking down at the dirt under my nails, the clothes that aren't mine. "Maybe none of this would have happened. Whatever *this* is."

"We'll figure it out. Together," Ginny says, her hand running gentle circles on my back.

"Wait…" I frantically search my pockets. "Have you seen my phone?"

"No, you didn't have anything on you. Just… you."

Ginny's voice is a beacon; the whirl of worries subsides. The feeling of dread, however, lingers. I swallow hard.

"I don't know what's happening to me, Ginny. And I don't even know where to start…" I whimper, on the verge of tears. I stare into Ginny's deep blue eyes.

"Maybe let's start with New Moon Island, hm?" Ginny sits next to me, her presence a gentle nudge.

I nod, wiping my eyes with the back of my hand. "I was five when my parents died, too. I remember it was late winter – it was still cold; I had my pink mittens on. Mum crocheted them for me." I think back to the details of those gloves and how the yarn sparkled in the sunlight, the wool flecked with pieces of gold thread. "Pink like the cotton candy trees –" I pause, letting out a small laugh. "– cherry plum trees."

Ginny smiles, placing the warm teacup in my hands. "I used to call them cotton candy trees, too."

I sip at the tea; the sweet chamomile and honey is soothing. My thoughts jump between dreams and memories. "The backyard was an explosion of pink, like my gloves. I went into my parent's bedroom to tell them the cotton candy trees were awake, and that my gloves were like the blossoming flowers…" I can feel the smile on my face, like the memory, fade.

"It was the smell I noticed first." My voice is low and monotone, drawing the past into the present.

Suddenly I'm back there. Tiny Fred with their crochet gloves, reaching for the brass handle to their parents' bedroom. I speak as if in a trance.

"I tiptoed across the carpet; the morning sun hadn't reached that side of the house. The room was black. There was a familiar smell, like wet dog." I inhale deeply, the memories coursing through me. "Stretching out, I found the switch for the bedside lamp…" My hand reaches out, reliving the horrid moment, before Ginny takes it in hers, beckoning me to continue.

"Vinegar."

Ginny blinks. "Vinegar?"

"Yeah. Wet dog and vinegar, that's what it smelt like. I found out way later the vinegar smell was drugs. Apparently shit heroin has a vinegary smell."

I venture further into the past.

"There was a chunky squelch under my foot. When the light

came on, I stumbled backwards. And there they were. My parents sprawled out on top of the bed." I swallow hard against the tears stinging my throat and eyes. "Mum's bloodshot eyes hung open, staring at me; her vomit stuck between my toes."

"Fred…" Ginny squeezes my hand.

"But it wasn't just the musty smell of dog, or the sharp vinegar. There was another smell…" I feel my voice trail off, my mind searching the memory, recalling the article we'd found in the *Huon Post*. "But I don't think they OD'ed. It just never felt right, you know?" I pause, wondering if I'm ready to admit what I'm certain really happened. "I think they were murdered. That it was, like, a coverup."

Ginny's mouth drops. "Hold on, what?"

"*New Moon*, that article we found, those faces? They were my parents' faces. And that article said they were murdered."

Ginny opens her mouth to speak again, when the creak of a floorboard squeaks in the kitchen down the hallway, snapping me from my thoughts.

My fingers slide to Ginny's lips. "What was that?" I ask, standing, tilting my head towards the sound.

Ginny arches a brow. "What was *what*? I didn't hear anything."

I focus on the kitchen, blocking out Ginny's voice, her breathing, even my own ragged breath. I can sense my heart slowing, and then I hear it. A deep, shallow hum coming from the kitchen. My nostrils flare, inhaling; a nauseatingly sweet copper scent invades my senses. My stomach groans.

"We gotta go." My voice is a low growl.

"Go where?" Ginny whispers. "What is it?"

I don't know why I feel this urge to run. Something unsettling ripples through me.

"Oh, I didn't know Fred was visiting, Gin," Garamond's voice sounds in the distance as he swings the kitchen door open, his footsteps heavy down the hallway.

How long has he been listening?

CHAPTER FOURTEEN

Ginny's bedroom door flings open.

"Ah. Fred *McTire*." Garamond emphasises each syllable of my surname. His eyes dart from me to Ginny. "Has *McTire* over here told you where they were last night?" He moves swiftly, standing between us, his face inches from my own. "A little birdy saw *McTire*, here, at yet another crime scene –"

"– since when was there even a first? Didn't know you could charge dingoes." My voice is low, the jigsaw of my memories slowly sliding into place.

Garamond's eyes are grey swirling pools of anger.

"Wait. Another?" Ginny swallows. "A murder?"

The raging clouds in Garamond's eyes subside, turning to his granddaughter. "Yes, Gin. You might want to take a seat," he says softly, all the malice and anger ebbing away.

I step forwards to take a seat next to Ginny.

"Not you…" he growls.

I guess not *all* the anger.

Crossing my arms against my chest, I hold his gaze. A twinge of a smirk prods at the corner of Garamond's mouth as he stares me down, his back to Ginny.

"There was something about you I couldn't quite put my finger on, you know? I first noticed it Tuesday, when we spoke at the school."

"Grandad, what's happening?" Ginny's voice trails off, confusion wrinkling her face.

Garamond turns to Ginny. "You need to know what lurks in plain sight!"

Ginny groans. "If you try and lecture me about *monsters* one more time…"

Garamond and Ginny keep talking, but everything they're saying is muffled, my thoughts elsewhere – everywhere. Everything that's happened over the past week comes crashing through the memory banks like a carousel of horror.

How I attacked Ginny.

Those scratches.

The rage.

My lost time.

The memories of blood… so much blood.

Garamond is all seriousness, kneeling before his granddaughter. "Gin, have you heard from Cassie lately?"

Ginny's eyes widen and she shakes her head.

The last memory I have of Cass is her diamante butterfly as she turned the corner.

"I'm sorry, love," Garamond continues, standing. "Sergeant

Pine found young Cassie Kelly's bag amongst, well…" He turns to face me, that smirk from before itching at the corner of his mouth. "Amongst parts of her."

My pulse hammers against my temples. Wait, what? Cassie? Dead? It doesn't make sense. It can't be true.

My eyes find Ginny's; her face pales.

I try to focus on my breathing, but it feels like I'm suffocating. It's as if a heavy weight has settled on my chest. I can't think straight. I scuttle through my memories, searching for an explanation, a way to make sense of what's happening.

Garamond pins me to the spot with those rage-filled eyes, outlining the gruesome details. An arm at the campground… entrails by the river…

I was at the campground. I was at the river.

I feel like I'm drowning. Grief, confusion, anger, and fear, all swirling around me, threatening to pull me under. I want to scream, to cry, to lash out at Garamond, tell him to stop.

I look to Ginny, but I can't tell what she's thinking. Her freckled face looks as still and cold as marble.

"Those wounds on your chest, Gin." Garamond kneels before his granddaughter again, trying to get her to focus on him. "I've seen them before. When we found Randy…"

Ginny's eyes break, the shock overflowing, bursting with tears. Her trembling hand reaches for the now healing score marks along her chest.

"What're you trying to say?" I cough, my voice wavering slightly despite my efforts to stay steady. I don't want to give Garamond the satisfaction of seeing me crumble. I'm stronger than that. Stronger than his lies. Because they are lies… right?

Garamond's monstrous stare locks onto mine once more as he rises swiftly from the ground, charging towards me. I instinctively retreat, my back pressing against the far wall of Ginny's bedroom. With a swift and threatening gesture, Garamond's knuckled fist slams into the drywall just inches from my head, sending dust and particles scattering into my face.

"Grandad, that's enough!" Ginny shrieks, standing, her face damp with tears, her breath ragged. "And why do you think Fred's even involved?"

Garamond's lips are a thin white line, his remaining hand sliding into his pocket. I follow his movement and watch. Encased within his meaty fist is… a phone.

"The fellas found this with the, uh, filth." He steps back, shaking the plaster of his knuckles and tosses me the device; I can still see the blood and bits stuck in the grooves.

My mouth is dry. I try to speak, yet nothing comes out. I feel like I've been left in the middle of a desert with no water or shelter, exposed and vulnerable to the harsh elements that are Garamond and his lies. Cassie can't be… no… I didn't…

Staring at the lock screen – a photo of the sunrise I took a few weeks ago at the river – a shiver crawls over me. *My phone.* But how? The dreams, lost time. The blood. So much… I was covered in it! Fuck, what is going on? I remember Cassie's ginger curls swishing as she walked down the laneway. The library. Ginny's house. The river. The full moon. Crunching of bones, screams, *changing*. Running. Soft fur. A barn… The Rustmane barn. Mathusi!

A knock rattles the front door. Then again. A pounding. Garamond glares at me, his eyes like daggers pinning me to the chair.

"Stay, dog," he spits, feet stomping down the hallway.

The front door explodes open under Garamond's rage, the wood slamming into the wall with a thunderous crash.

"What!" Garamond snarls.

Peeking past through the bedroom door, a tall man, taller than Garamond, strides in, all pinstripe suit and combed back hair. His eyes shine as they meet mine.

"Come on," the man says, the words thrown at me. "We're leaving."

"Get out of my house, Vargus. Your kind aren't welcome here!" Garamond's voice is like a landslide of rocks.

Mathusi walks from behind Mr Pinstripe, followed by another person. A woman. Dark like Mathusi, with long curls of silver.

"You…" The word barely makes it out of my mouth.

Mathusi reaches his hand to me, beckoning me to follow.

"The barn…" *It was real.*

Mathusi puts a finger to his lips. Garamond and Mr Pinstripe continue arguing in the background.

In the haze, I feel Ginny's hand grab mine as she stands, following to leave.

"Let the bitch go, Gin." Garamond's square hand envelopes Ginny's arm.

"Grandad…" Ginny squirms, panic in her eyes.

My feet root to the ground. Those feelings from before, at school on Monday, that same screaming rage. Garamond is just another bully, like the douchebags at school. My fists clench, squeezing so tight the blood trickles and pools, warm and thick, in the cracks of my skin. I feel the blistering rage swell within me, roiling and bubbling. And as if in slow motion I watch Ginny writhe and scream, her ghastly grandfather gripping her tight, and all I see… is red.

Raising my arm, a surge of adrenaline coursing through my veins, I feel my nails tear from my skin like hidden needles. With a primal howl, thick with anger, I slash out at Garamond. The man stumbles, his body crashing into the side of the room. The impact sends Ginny sprawling backwards onto the couch.

Garamond's chest heaves; a fresh score of torn flesh mottles with blood on the back of his ripped shirt.

"Get that mutt out of here!" Garamond's command echoes through the room, and Ginny sinks into the couch, her wide eyes locked onto her grandad's back.

A crushing weight of guilt settles over me. What have I done…? But I can't suppress the surging rage. I lunge at Garamond, my voice trembling. "If you hurt her…"

"That's your job, dog," Garamond snarls, his remark stinging like venom.

Mathusi holds me back, and I wrench myself free from his grip. My hands tremble, sending flecks of blood splattering across the room. "Fine," I growl, relenting. I turn to leave, the seething anger gradually subsiding.

Ginny isn't safe with me here. And as long as Garamond's around, I can't be. She had a happy life before I came into it.

The burning heat within me dwindles, replaced by an ice-cold sorrow that gnaws at my insides. I watch helplessly as Ginny quivers beneath a cushion on the couch, her eyes filled with fear. She's terrified. Of me. Am I a monster?

I can't be here. I can't be with Ginny. I don't deserve her, and she doesn't deserve this chaos. I know what I have to do. Even though I don't want to.

"You know what?" I feel my shoulders square, my back

rigid. My jaw clenches and I grimace, sizing up the hulking old man in front of me. My gaze then falls to Ginny, and I push it all down, flood those warm feelings with ice and lead. "You can keep her. Apples and trees and shit. She's probably just as fucked up as you…"

And I leave.

I force my feet to walk, pulling out the roots that feel as though they'd found their home in Ginny. And I leave. Stomping, trampling out of that house, away from her. Tears burn in my eyes and my frozen heart shatters.

The silver-haired woman wraps her shawl around me; a musky, earthy smell drips over my body and I feel a calmness with her by my side.

Mathusi opens the car door and I slip in. I'm in a daze; I don't even remember walking outside. The muffled sounds of an argument come from the house, then the slam of a door. Lurching footsteps on gravel, then the car shakes as Mr Pinstripe sits in the driver's seat. His knowing eyes meet mine in the rearview mirror.

"Let's go home."

I look back over my shoulder, Ginny's face a smudge in the window of the house, my reflection in the glass staring back at me, contorted and full of shame. I always considered myself my only home. And then I met her.

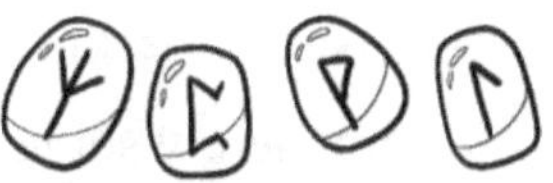

CHAPTER FIFTEEN

Days and nights roll into one giant depressive blur.

This couch is my home now. A lush pillow of security within a tumultuous world. It's been a week, and here I sit, beneath a window that looks out over the farmland of the Rustmane residence. I can feel the sun on my back, feel it move across me until the night creeps in and darkness surrounds my darkened heart. But this couch, with its velvety softness, has cocooned me. It's my safe place. Sure, it's old and scuffed on the armrests, and smells strangely of stale toast and vegemite, but I sink into it, my body heavy with the weight that only loss can bring.

Funny, huh? How losing something can make the vastness of everything consume you.

The world rushes by, a blur of motion and energy, of reassurance and honeyed teas, but I remain frozen in this stillness.

Do I exist purely to provoke this haunting curse that clings to my every step? Why does everyone around me, everyone I dare care for… leave…

Die.

I feel a hand on my shoulder, what has now become a familiar touch. The woman from the car, with her silver curls and warm, brown eyes. I know she's speaking to me, I can see her lips move, but her words are merely sounds. Mumbles laced in honey. She places another cup of warm tea in my hands and adjusts the blanket around my shoulders. This has been our ritual for some days now.

Red curls wrap around my thoughts, strangling me until I sweat. The same knowing hand brushes my brow. I hear her this time. And I hear the name she mentions…

Cassie.

Another abrupt and sorrowful end thanks to yours truly, as if I were a vessel of their tragic farewells, an omen of their impending goodbyes. There's an eerie presence, like a ghostly spectre of loss, that follows me wherever I go. Its sinister dance leaves behind a trail of shattered dreams and anguished cries. In this never-ending tale of heartbreak, my spirit throbs with agony as I find myself questioning why love around me dies.

I wanted to love Cassie. Like a sister. She was the first who made my heart crack a little.

The autumn curls fade, bursting into golden summer, laced in freckles.

Then there was *Ginny*.

"Fred, *cheri*," Bett's voice is a soothing whisper, breaking through the storm of my thoughts. I feel the couch dip beside me as she sits. "We have some news to share –"

"Cassie?" The name bursts from my lips. I refuse to believe she's gone. I refuse to believe that I… that I…

"No, my dear, no…" Bett sighs, her warm hand enveloping mine. "We've been speaking with your social worker."

I try to focus on her words, to pull myself out of the turmoil inside my head. My social worker? Why would they be talking to her? A vague memory of a text message bubbles to the surface before popping.

Bett's silver hair shimmers in the dim light, her dark eyes softening. She continues, her words measured and gentle. "Your social worker, she's been in touch with us. She found us last month."

"Last month?"

Bett nods. "You see, Varg, well…" She pauses, looking past me out into the fields before continuing. "I was hoping he would be here."

I uncurl my legs from beneath me and sit forwards on the couch, squeezing Bett's hand for her to continue.

"Varg is a Manebarn," the woman says, as if that means something to me.

I shake my head. "Okay?"

"Your mother was also a Manebarn."

The dawning of what Bett is saying slowly blossoms.

"Varg, he's your mother's cousin, Fred. We're your family."

My heart skitters in my chest. "From Norway…" I manage, not so much a question as the memory coming back.

"We didn't know you were here, that you survived, that…" Bett shakes her head. "Your mother…" Bett's voice trembles with unspoken emotions. "She was part of something, something that goes back generations." Bett's grip on my hand tightens, and her eyes bore into mine with a fierceness that demands my attention. "Your parents, they wanted to shield you from this world. They knew the dangers, the darkness that lurked. But sometimes, the past catches up with us, no matter how hard we try to escape it."

A ripple of unease trickles through me. "Shield me from *what* world?" I finally ask, my voice trembling.

Bett leans in closer, her gaze unwavering. "We are werewolves, Fred," Bett says with pride. "Your mother was one, and your father, too. And so are you. And it's time to face the truth of what that means. There's a shadowy presence, an enemy from your family's past, a wicked adversary who seeks to extinguish your bloodline. We thought you had escaped it, but it's here, closer than ever. They know about you, Fred. And they'll stop at nothing to destroy you and anyone you love."

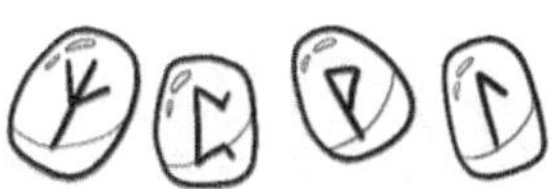

CHAPTER SIXTEEN

Loss is a void, a chasm that devours,

A wound that never fully heals,

An ache that lingers and haunts,

A weight that bears down and steals.

It takes many forms, loss does –

Of people, of things, of time,

Of dreams that never come to pass,

Of love that couldn't survive.

It leaves us feeling hollow,

Numb. Angry. Depressed.

And though we try to fill the space,

The emptiness persists.

CHAPTER SEVENTEEN

Nearly one month has passed. Well, maybe not an entire month. The moon is edging closer to full, so more like three weeks.

Three weeks since Garamond accused me of murdering Cassie.

"They didn't do it. No matter what bullshit Garamond spews, it's lies." Mathusi's voice had been full of anger and frustration when he'd spoken those words last week. "Where's the body, where's the proof?"

Another memory flits to the surface of my thoughts – Cassie in that oversized, sweat-stained jacket – and I wince, squeezing my eyes shut. Everyone here keeps reassuring me I had no part in it. But, what if Garamond's right?

"Garamond…" The name is so bitter on my tongue. It's been three weeks since I clawed into his flesh. Felt the tear of it. I can sense my anger rising, but I push it down, sighing as all the memories seem to come rushing back, to the smudged face in the window of that hellhole.

"And three weeks since I last set eyes on her," I say, my words soft and sweet. Like her. Like Ginny. The last time I stared into those limitless blues.

Oh, yeah. And three weeks since I turned for the first time.

"Were-wolf. *Were*wolf. W-O-L-F." I roll the sounds around my mouth.

I still haven't quite wrapped my head around it, what it all means. I feel like my life shattered and I'm here, picking up the pieces, trying to fit this shitty jigsaw back together again.

A lot has happened.

That's the biggest understatement ever made.

Bett's words are still rattling around in my brain, too: *And they'll stop at nothing to destroy you and anyone you love.* Just add that to the list of 'W-T-F.'

For real though, werewolves exist. Like, seriously. And I happen to be one.

What. The. Actual.

I feel as if I'm constantly teetering between being a regular human, person, *thing*, and having this beastly creature inside me.

I can't help but snort a laugh at the thought of *regular*. There's never been anything *regular* about me, so why should this be any different? Like the moon's changing phases, my sense of self is constantly shifting, never fitting into those typical male or female boxes. And now I've added lycanthrope to this crazy mix. Sure. Why not? Talk about a complicated recipe, right? Being a teenager is hard enough. Dealing with gender and sexuality was already a challenge. But now werewolf? Yeah, that's like the cherry on top of this fucked-up cake called *adolescence*. Thanks a lot, life.

I rest my cheek on my knuckled fist, staring down at the words I've been scribbling on the page in front of me, all coffee stained and smudged.

The past few weeks have been a blur of screaming, of crying, of sailing down that river in Egypt. You know. *Denial.* But somehow, amidst the chaos, I've found the space to confront it all – confront the emotions, the fears. To sit with it all and let it consume me. That's healthy, yeah?

But here's the thing that keeps baffling me: how the hell am I so okay with all of this? I mean, seriously, I look at my hands, and I swear I can see traces of blood staining my skin. Whose blood is it? Is it mine? Does it belong to Cassie?

No... I didn't, I couldn't...

The pen in my hand snaps, the ink flicking over the lined page of my journal.

"Shit..."

I dab at the paper and breathe.

Why does everyone around me die? As if I were the harbinger of their goodbyes.

"Oh, that's actually really good."

The remnants of the shattered pen scratch against the paper.

"Sad, but good."

I think my writing has made a difference. Putting my thoughts into words has always helped me to make sense of the world, and my world is a bit fucking bizarre at the moment. But pen to paper enables me to express the words I'm unable to speak. Last year we studied sonnets and terza rimas, but I think my favourite was when we looked at experimental writing. The flowing, free form lets you push the boundaries, daring a writer to bend language to their will. Yeah, a bit wanky, but I like it. And it's helped me since coming here. *Here* being the Rustmane farm, with the Manebarns. My family.

Red fills my vision. Viscous and coppery.

Breathe.

I listen to the sounds of the house, the distant whinnies of horses, and the croaking of frogs in the pond.

Breathe.

Writing isn't the only thing that's been helping me lately. I've discovered this awesome technique thanks to Mathusi. Whenever I feel the overwhelming panic attacks and anxiety creeping in, he's taught me how to control it by concentrating on my breath.

Closing my eyes, I take a deep breath, feeling the cool morning air enter my nose, filling up my lungs like a balloon. Slowly letting it out, I imagine all the stress and fear leaving my body with each exhale. It's like releasing a bunch of balloons into the sky, watching them float away with all those negative emotions. By controlling my breath, I can take control of my thoughts and emotions. So, whenever I feel that familiar rush of *holy shit, what the frick is happening* creeping up, I take a deep breath, focusing on the sensation of air filling my lungs, and slowly release it, allowing all those worries to drift away.

Well. Some of them. They don't always like to leave, clinging on for dear life.

I can hear Mathusi's music softly thudding from the room next to mine.

Mathusi's got his own take on why I've managed to hold it together in the midst of all this bullshit. According to him, it's because of my past, the constant shuffling from one foster home to another. He thinks that all those transitions have shaped me into someone who can adapt to change with ease. I guess there's some truth to his words. That's one benefit of trauma.

Oops. The 'T' word. I'm sure some therapist out there is tingling.

Maybe that's why, in the face of this supernatural madness, I've managed to keep my cool. All that past… pain. My mind has become conditioned to embrace change, to adapt and adjust like a chameleon in a kaleidoscope of shifting circumstances. It's as if I've become an expert at compartmentalising, finding a way to detach myself from the chaos and simply go with the flow.

But there's something about this particular *flow* that feels different, more natural. It's like a gentle current that carries me along, bringing me closer to a sense of belonging. This house, these people around me, they feel more than just temporary. They're family, a concept I haven't fully grasped in a long time. It's an incredible thought, and one that warms my heart.

Amid uncertainty, a glimmer of hope flickers within me. It's like a small flame, delicate yet resilient, that refuses to be extinguished. Hope becomes a word that dances in my mind, painting colours of possibilities. And what's even more amazing is that it's accompanied by a genuine smile, one that springs up effortlessly.

Could this be the moment I've been waiting for? Is it possible that amidst the struggles and hardships, there's a silver lining shining through? The thought fills me with a mixture of excitement and wonder. Maybe, just maybe, this is my chance to build a stable and loving home, to find the acceptance and warmth I've yearned for.

I can't help but let my imagination soar, picturing the days ahead filled with laughter, shared meals, and heartfelt conversations. It's a vision that brings comfort and a renewed sense of purpose. I'm ready to embrace this opportunity with open arms, to nurture the connections forming around me, and to weave my own story of resilience and love.

There's still a part of me that holds caution, aware of the fragility of life's blessings. But for now, in this moment, I choose to let optimism guide me. I'll savour the joy that has found its way into my heart and cherish the hope that lights my path. This chapter feels like the start of something beautiful, and I'm ready to embrace it with all my might.

But aren't you the harbinger of goodbyes?

"Thanks, inner demons," I sigh, rolling onto my back, spreading out on the carpeted floor.

I feel that all too familiar churn in my gut… But you're right. *I'm* right. There's no *moment*. No silver lining. I know this will all end soon, whenever Mathusi and his family go back home to Norway, or wherever. But I can't help but savour this giddy feeling as I lie in this borrowed room.

In this borrowed house.

With this borrowed family.

On borrowed time.

I think back to Garamond's accusations. I've half expected the police to rock up and arrest me. Every day I anticipate seeing those flashing red and blue lights, feel the latch of cuffs.

A flash of a memory… maybe a dream?… rushes to the forefront of my thoughts. Blood

Breathe.

The coppery tang heavy in the air.

Breathe!

Cassie's ginger braid.

Fucking breathe!

Instead of big balloons and deep breaths, my lungs tighten, the air wheezing in and out at a ridiculous pace.

Screw this. *Squash those thoughts back into the cracks of your mind, Fred, and slam the door shut.* Fuck balloons. I gotta lock this shit down. Garamond was wrong, okay? I didn't do it. I couldn't have done it.

…but why can I see it?

Reaching for my headphones, I push them over my frazzled hair; the worn pleather of the headset surrounds my ears, filling them with distraction. Drum and bass, to be precise. The pounding beat grounding me in the now.

The last three weeks may have been a bubbling cauldron of confusion, anger, fear… but there's been something else, something more. Potential.

And learning, too. I think back on the many conversations with Mathusi. He's been my tether between worlds, teaching me, showing me what this life is. What it can be. The history, the lore. For example, werewolves can't be *made*, by, like, biting someone. It's not like the movies or television or books…

if a wolf bites you, they just bite you. Someone might get rabies if they're unlucky enough, but that's it. Mathusi reckons that's where the horrible stories about werewolves came from – some poor bloke got bitten by a normal wolf, got rabies, and the townsfolk thought he was a rabid monster. Anyways, there's no transference of werewolf genes; that only happens *the old-fashioned way*.

"When a mummy werewolf and a daddy werewolf love each other very much," Mathusi had joked. Being his usual humorous self, he hadn't been able to resist giving me a playful demonstration of how werewolves come into existence, his hands and fingers making crude gestures while he'd tried to keep a straight face, but we'd both burst into laughter. I'd jokingly remarked that it was too 'hetero' for my liking, and we'd laughed even harder. According to Mathusi, the queer folks outnumber the cisgendered ones in the wolf world, and from what I've observed so far, that statistic seems accurate.

He shared stories about his own queer wolf family: his gay sister, his trans cousin, and his queer uncle. It made me wonder about my own parents and their connection to all of this. I had asked Mathusi about them the first day I'd woken up here, my mind flooded with questions. He hadn't had the answers, but he'd said who would: Vargus Manebarn, his dad. The guy I'd coined initially as *Mr Pinstripe*, who'd barged into Garamond's to rescue me. And my cousin. No, wait, *first* cousin. Once re-moved? Either way, he's been away for the past few weeks, dealing with some family business. Whatever *that* means. Ma-thusi said he'll be back today; just in time for a little Q&A with Fred McTire.

I idly scratch my scalp and adjust my headphones, scrolling the volume to max, so grateful I got my stuff back from Joce-lyn's place.

I haven't been back to Jocelyn's. I couldn't face going there. Apparently, Jocelyn's papers have been revoked and the re-maining kids in her care shipped out elsewhere. Varg and Bett have signed all the paperwork to be my foster carers. Mathusi said Jocelyn signed the papers when he and Varg collected the rest of my stuff from her dump of a house.

Stretching out on the floor of my borrowed bedroom, Nir-vana's melancholic droll throbs in my ears. Discarded chocolate wrappers litter the space around me – *can I even eat chocolate? Isn't it, like, bad for dogs?* I shrug, stuffing another gooey car-amel in my mouth and doom-scroll social media, eyes glued to my phone, and sigh. Nothing. No updates, no texts. Nothing at all from, well, you know. From *her*.

I pinch at the skin on the nape of my neck, itching.

No trace of Ginny. It's as if she's disappeared. I even snuck over to her place last week, crawled through that tiny bathroom window. The house was quiet. Empty. Her room was cold. I found that book on her shelf, *Carmilla*, and slid a letter inside, hoping she'd be back, would find it, and maybe understand what had happened.

You can keep her. Apples and trees… I wince at the memory. I hope Ginny knows I didn't mean it. That I was just trying to keep her safe. But how could she know? I *am* Fred the Fuckup, after all. I shake the thought from my mind – she's better off without my chaos in her life. Especially now.

I reach for the small tote bag next to me, the moonstones clinking as the canvas bounces softly along the carpet. Before I even try to set an intention, a runestone falls out, right side up.

"Ugh, come on, something other than *Algiz*. I get it, I need protection. That's pretty obvi now, you stupid stones."

The bag topples over, another stone rolling out. *Wunjo.*

I roll the stone in the palm of my hand. "Oh, and you're going to protect me, hm? Love? Love's my protection?"

The sound of voices and laughter echo from the kitchen, and the golden glow of possibility, of family – is this the *love* it means? – ebbs deep in my stomach. Will this family's love protect me? I feel a smile crease the corner of my mouth again. However, as soon as it comes, the glimmer of hope leaches from my gut, my lips sour. The heaviness of solitude, like lead, winds through me. They'll leave, like everyone does.

A knock, soft, taps at the door. "Breakfast is ready, *cheri*." Bett's voice is just as silky as her silver tresses.

"Be out in a bit," I say, popping the stones back in the bag, my nails once again grating against my scalp. Why am I so itchy? "Hey Bett, we can't get fleas, can we?"

A laugh booms from the room next to me. "No, ya goof!" The voice is muffled through the drywall.

Mathusi's door opens. Footsteps sound, then more chuckles; his head pops around the corner, ogling me.

"Fleas? Really?" Mathusi laughs again, his eyes squinting shut. His whole face lights up when he laughs. I've never seen laughter take someone over as it does with him. It's infectious, and I feel a giggle bubbling up inside me.

"Yeah, well, I dunno," I say, sitting up. "One place I lived had a pet dog, and they had to give it a special collar for fleas."

"I'll add it to Mamma's shopping list, hey?" Mathusi teases, his laugh echoing as he makes his way down the hallway to the kitchen.

I crawl towards the open door, my head poking out. "What about chocolate?"

The sound of a shoe hurtling down the hallway and hitting the doorframe makes me recoil, a giggle bubbling from my mouth.

A giggle. From me.

I freeze, startled by the foreign sound that fills the room. It's a moment of sheer astonishment, and I catch a glimpse of this person in the mirror across the room. They're smiling, despite the absolute shitshow around them. Around me.

The laughter echoing from the other room, the banter about fleas and chocolate – it all feels oddly comforting. Sitting back against the bedframe, I slide my feet into my boots, a tentative smile tugging at the corners of my lips. *Perhaps this family life isn't so bad after all*, I think to myself, eager to see what other surprises the day may bring.

CHAPTER EIGHTEEN

A metal wind chime sways musically outside on the patio; the clear notes dance on the morning breeze through the open window, bringing with it the smoky smell of a distant bushfire.

Sitting at the kitchen table, the linoleum tacky on my bare feet, I bask in this family life, even if it will be short-lived.

Mathusi and his little brother, Koba, bicker about which fighter is better in *Mortal Kombat*. Their sister, Alma, and her girlfriend, Tosh, share giggles over the morning newspaper. And Bett, mother of this raucous pack, stands at the stove, stirring a pot of pungent herbs, important for her magic against *je wouj*. I've heard the name whispered over the past few weeks, but I'm still unclear who or what *je wouj* even is. To be honest, there's been so much going on, I don't think I have the mental headspace to take all of it in.

As for Bett's herbal remedies, I've experienced some of her potions and teas and have been thankful for their calming and healing aromas. The shawl she'd used to whisk me away all those weeks ago now hangs over her shoulders.

The back flyscreen door creaks open and in walks Varg, the leader of the pack.

I smile at the thought. *Pack.* As if this is all the norm. This mixed bag of wolves. *Wolves.* This all feels like one of my lucid dreams. Which have stopped, come to think of it. Since that night, since that *change.* Thanks to Bett's special tea, I sleep deep and long, the dreamless sleep of healing.

Varg sits across from me, plate in hand. The suit is gone, replaced by a singlet and cargo shorts. And what I mistook for wiry is actually lean muscle, like a greyhound. His hair falls loosely over his face, long and white. He ties it into a low ponytail before reaching towards the stack of pancakes.

"So, Fred. You're settling in okay, *ja?*"

"*Ja.*" I pause, my cheeks instantly burning. "Sorry. Yes." I cringe.

Varg laughs heartily.

I'm still getting used to the way he melds Norwegian and English. For the most part it's easy to follow, and he only ever slips into it occasionally.

"This actually feels… familiar," I say, flinging my fork around the room. "Like I've been here before? Or maybe it's just, like, a vibe."

Varg smiles widely through a mouth of pancake, and I feel myself smiling back.

Don't get attached. They'll leave, just like everyone else. Enjoy the moment, but remember it'll be over soon, and you'll be on your own. Again.

The chill of loneliness creeps back into my bones, and I can feel my posture shift as it enters my body. The pancake is dry in my mouth.

"Your blood knows," Bett says, interrupting my thoughts. She sits next to Varg, kissing him gently on his brow.

"*Ja*. That and, well…" He puts his fork down on his plate. "We are family. I remember your *bestefar*," Varg says, loading his fork again and stuffing the pancake into his mouth.

I shuffle in my seat. "My what, sorry?"

Bett laughs, waving a hand at Varg to keep eating. "Your paternal grandfather. You come from a long line of wolves. Celtic wolves, that often mingled with Varg's Norwegian line."

This is some serious info dumping happening here, and they're all so casual about it. The chill in my spine shifts. Warms. *Family.*

"How did you know my family?" I sit forwards in the chair. "My parents…" I open the locket hanging around my neck. "My mum was your cousin?"

Varg stops chewing and swallows hard, his eyes finding Bett's.

"Up pups, breakfast is finished, off you go," Bett says, ushering everyone out from the kitchen, all except Varg and I.

Varg pushes his plate to the side. "Yes. Aasta was my

cousin," he finally says, sitting back in his chair; the grunts of video game violence and bickering already hum from the loungeroom.

"What happened on New Moon Island?" I lean closer, my fingers still wrapped around the locket. "Were they murdered?"

Varg sighs, his face serious, and he stands. "Come."

Following Varg from the kitchen, my mind swims. It feels as though I'm jumping from raft to raft, my brain drowning in all this new information.

Is this why I feel so safe here, because these people, these… wolves… are blood? Are family? Is this why I'm so okay with being a werewolf? I think back to being young, to the house I grew up in…

"There were always dogs." The words escape my lips. "When I was young, in our house. I remember big grey, fluffy-looking dogs."

Varg nods. "I'm sure there were. *Wolves* more like. But, dogs, yes. We come in many shapes, many forms." Varg opens the door to the basement. "Aksel, my cousin who owns this property, his *Norsk* mother moved here and fell in love with a local man. So instead of the Manebarn White Wolf, he took the form of his father."

Descending the stairs, Varg crosses the stone floor and leans up against a tall bookshelf.

"Help me with this," he grunts, and we slide the bookcase away from the wall.

Finding the light switch hanging from the roof, I tug at the string. The room lights up, showcasing a wall covered in maps, charts, and a giant tree etched into concrete, each branch spindling off with names. It's then I spot it.

"*MacTíre*?" My fingers trace the carved lines.

"Your ancestors simplified your name over time. *Mac tíre* is the traditional Irish for *wolf*."

"That's my dad…" My voice trails off. "*Connor MacTíre*." I follow the lineage and find my mother – "*Aasta*." It feels so surreal reading their names, saying them out loud.

Varg slides a stack of books onto a large square table in the middle of the room, flicking one open. "Here," he says, pointing.

"A photo album?" I ask, excitedly turning the pages.

"This is the Rustmane pack. Aksel's family."

"What was Aksel, then? Like, what did he change into? You said he took his father's form?"

Varg turns the page and taps the sticky film covering the photographs. The photo has that old seventies' blur, where it yellows and browns, but front and centre, outside this house's very own front door, sits a dog.

"He's a dingo?" My fingers trace over the photograph.

"Hold on, wait." I slam the album shut. "The cops are saying dingoes attacked Randy. Was it him? His pack? Is this why you're here? Garamond said –"

Varg growls and spits. "*Han er en drittsekk!*"

"Yes, he is a shitbag." Mathusi walks down the stairs. "And if I'd have known what Garamond was, I would never have left you there that night, Fred."

"Is he another type of monster?" *How many types of mythological creatures are real?*

"*Ja.* The worst kind of monster."

"He's a Hunter." Mathusi's voice is cold.

"Hunter?" I stare back at the wall of names.

"His dream is to irradicate our species," Mathusi continues, opening another book on the table. He points to a page. "There was a truce made by our families with the Hunter clans, many years ago. Most Hunters still abide by this agreement –"

"Except him." Varg says, his voice is more mellow now and level-headed. "We don't harm anyone. We don't hunt people."

"But, in movies, and stuff, don't we eat human hearts?" I ask, turning the pages.

Varg laughs. "Propaganda. Put out there by Hunters."

"Like the rabies," Mathusi adds.

I nod, lost in thought. Mathusi takes more books off the shelf, Varg speaking to him in Norwegian. They laugh and joke as if this is all normal. I find Aksel's photo again. A dingo.

"What am I?"

Varg and Mathusi look at each other, then to me.

"We don't know yet," Mathusi says. "We didn't see you out in the Moon."

The full moon. The night I changed. The night Cassie died. I breathe deep, and I feel my throat tighten thinking of her: her smile, her stupid flouncing around in that big, gross blue jacket.

The jacket. Randy's jacket. The blue jacket…

"I thought it was a dream," my voice whispers. Varg and Mathusi stop, and I can feel their eyes on me. "I dreamt about a monster, snarling. A boy yelling…" *Randy.*

"When was this dream?" Varg places his hand on my shoulder.

"Sunday night, three weeks ago, maybe?" My eyes search the room, though really I'm racing through my memories. "I was there. I must have been. How could I know?" I shrug Varg's hand away, the tightness squeezing the air from my lungs. "And the night Cassie was killed, that's when you found me, in the barn." My eyes are on Mathusi. I gasp, finding no air. "I was covered in blood."

Varg's voice is gentle and soft. I know he's talking, saying words, though I'm not hearing any of them, only the frantic whooshing of my blood pumping in my ears. He nods to

Mathusi, who runs up the stairs. His footsteps recede towards the kitchen.

"That night was your first turn, Fred." Varg's voice sounds distant, even though he's in the room with me. "Cassie's death was just a coincidence. It wasn't you."

"Yeah, but Mathusi just said no one saw me. You were all out, but where was I?" I'm walking backwards now; I can feel the cold concrete wall pressing against my back. Cold like death. "What if it was me? Garamond found my phone with Cass…" I can feel the hairs on the back of my prickle. "What if I wolfed out?" My teeth ache. "Did I kill them both?" My eyes burn. "Did I kill my friends?"

Footsteps thud down the stairs, and Bett sashays towards me, pushing Varg to the side with a tut. "*Cheri.*" Her voice is calming. "My love, it's okay." She hands me a mug of tea. "Drink."

I nod, and sip. The warmth fills me; I can feel it cascade down to my toes.

"This is all too much for the young thing." I can hear Bett's voice. "It's too much, too soon."

"They can handle it. They're a Manebarn!" Varg says with pride.

I smile. "Woof."

"Fred's cooked," Mathusi laughs. "How much of that California poppy did you put in their tea?"

"They're also only seventeen," Bett adds, her arms around me.

I boop Bett on the nose. "Good puppy."

Bett snarls. "Don't just stand there laughing, Mathusi. Help me, would you?"

The scrape of metal on stone sounds in the corner, then a creak and click. I can make out the vague shape of a trundle bed and clap my hands. "Naptime!"

My eyes are so heavy now. My whole body is mellow, and exhaustion seems to creep into every bone. Falling onto the bed feels like sinking into a marshmallow.

"Have a rest, *cheri*. Things will make a little more sense to-morrow."

Closing my eyes, I let the marshmallow consume me.

"Wait…" I mumble. "Will the marshmallow mat my fur?"

CHAPTER NINETEEN

I'm starting to get a little tired of waking up groggy and confused. Surely this isn't my new *normal*, is it? The trundle bed creaks as I swing my legs over the side, burying my face in my hands.

"Good morning, sunshine."

"Rack off, Mathusi," I groan.

I can hear him snort a laugh, his footsteps on the stone tiles.

"Here," he says, putting a mug of steaming coffee between my feet. He sits down on the bed next to me.

"Thanks."

"And no, waking up feeling like shit is not the norm. At least, not as you get used to it. The first month is always rough," Mathusi says, sipping his own frothy brew.

My head swings, eyes wide, staring at him. "Did you… can you…" I pick up the mug of coffee and take a huge gulp. "Can you read minds?" I whisper.

Mathusi stares at me, eyes slowly crinkling until a roar of laughter makes its way from deep within his stomach. He has tears in his eyes and everything.

"Piss off," I laugh. "How am I supposed to know what we

can and can't do?"

Mathusi coughs as if trying to stop himself from laughing any further. "No, you're right," he finally says. "Not about the mind reading, ya goof, but about the whole *you don't know* business." His smile fades. "It wasn't you, alright? I reckon you were just there, like, you saw it happen. We don't attack people."

I offer him a faint smile. I want to believe him. I should. They know – they've been wolves far longer than me.

"This is so not how I expected my last year of school panning out," I sigh, the realisation hitting me that I haven't been to school in three weeks.

Mathusi huffs a laugh. "Don't worry. You haven't missed out on much. Principal Jones said you can make up for it over the first break for holidays."

I stare at him, wide-eyed. "Are you sure you can't read minds…?" I ask, eyebrow twitching.

Mathusi rolls his eyes. "Just drink your coffee." He smiles.

We sit in silence for a while. Well, the silence of no one speaking. My thoughts, on the other hand, are a cacophony of voices vying for my attention, Cassie's red braid wrapping around them all. My heart hurts every time I think of her. I should have followed her that day after school.

Maybe I already did.

"No…" Mathusi's fingers intertwine into my own.

I gaze at him, his eyes curving into delicate crescent moons, as if the weight of his knowing stretches them upward.

"And I don't need to read minds when your whole body goes rigid." He squeezes my hand.

It's almost unnerving how he effortlessly decodes the nuances of 'Fred,' as if he has a hidden lexicon of my micro-expressions.

I clear my throat, changing the subject. "Varg told me he turns into a white wolf, and that's, like, rare." I unwrap my fingers from his. "Aksel's a dingo because of his dad…" I continue, then pause. A question I've been wanting to ask finally untangles itself. "What are you? Is that something I can ask. Is it polite? Or not…"

Another laugh.

"Your nickname is officially Chuckles, now, Mathusi."

Mathusi laughs even more. "Valid."

Silence.

"Well?" I ask.

"Well!" A cheeky smile spreads across his face. "You'll just have to wait!" He grins. "Not long until the next full moon."

"Shit, don't remind me." I stick my nose into my mug of coffee.

Mathusi taps the bottom of the mug, coffee splashing my

nose.

"Oi!" I say, wiping my face.

"We'll be with you this time. It'll be easier, I promise."

I raise a sceptical brow.

I hate intimacy. I hate sharing, and feelings. I've built walls so tall I can barely see over them, stopping others from getting in. Ginny made me want to peek over it, but being here? With family, with Mathusi? I can feel those walls crumbling big time.

Mathusi leans in closer, his voice soothing and reassuring. "I know it's scary, especially not remembering your first transformation." He takes a deep breath, a hint of nostalgia in his eyes. "You know, I don't remember mine either. It happened last year. I woke up in the woods, surrounded by a bunch of very confused sheep." A small chuckle escapes him, and he continues. "There's a sheep farmer back in our hometown." He clicks his tongue. "Now he sure has some vivid memories of that night."

Mathusi's smile grows wide, his tone lightening. "But the point is, you're not alone in this. We all go through that same bewildering experience. It's like a rite of passage. And I promise you, we'll help you navigate it smoothly."

He pats my back gently, the camaraderie between us growing stronger. "So, don't worry too much. Chuckles' got your back." He winks.

"I feel better already." I smirk.

"So you should." He grins. "We'll make sure it's a howling success."

I snort a laugh.

"Prepare for a 'fur-tastic' outcome."

"Please stop," I laugh.

"We're 'pawsitive' you'll have a 'grrr-eat time'!"

I sit back, digesting Mathusi's words. Not the nonsense. He's still prattling on, pun after pun. But the idea of not being alone in this strange journey, of having a support system. The thoughts begin to chip away at the anxiety that's been festering within me.

As I stare at the remnants of my coffee, swirling the last dregs in my mug, I can't help but reflect on my life so far. Being non-binary, embracing my identity, and facing the challenges that come with it has been a lonely journey. There were nights when I wished for someone to guide me, to tell me that everything would be alright, just as Mathusi is doing now about being a werewolf.

"I wish I'd had a talk like this when I came out," I admit softly, my voice carrying the weight of my past struggles. "Would have made life so much easier."

The puns cease.

Mathusi's gaze is understanding, and he nods. "I get it. But know you're still the same person, just with a few extra layers."

I meet Mathusi's eyes, gratitude welling up within me. "Thanks, Mathusi. Seriously, I appreciate you being so open about, well, everything."

He smiles warmly, patting my shoulder. "Anytime. We're in this together, remember?"

I can't help but smile back, feeling a sense of belonging and acceptance. It's something I've been craving for a long time, and now, maybe I can find the support and understanding I've always needed.

Mathusi squeezes my hand. "You know, I was really starting to think you were absolutely devoid of emotion." He smirks.

I can't help but laugh at that one. "I've even surprised my-self."

The smell of pancakes and bacon wafts down into the base-ment, my stomach growling in response.

"Am I allowed to come upstairs?" I ask gingerly.

Mathusi holds back his laugh. "Of course. Mamma has breakfast ready."

"Breakfast?" I gasp. "How long was I out?"

Mathusi downs the last of his coffee. "About a day."

I just stare at him. A day? Is he serious?

"It happens when you first turn. It takes a toll on your body. You're prone to small changes throughout the month of your turning. Your body's adjusting and needs plenty of rest."

Small changes. That explains me lashing out at Ginny all those weeks ago. And Garamond. "Yesterday morning, I was starting to wolf out. I could *feel* it. I thought my teeth were going to shatter. That's why Bett gave me that tea?"

"California poppy? Yup."

It's then I remember why I was getting so emotional. I exhale heavily.

"What if it was all my fault? If I'd just have gone after Cassie… and Randy…"

Mathusi puts his cup on the ground, then takes my cup and does the same. He turns on the bed so he's facing me, my hands in his, his eyes locked to mine.

"You didn't kill Randy. And you most definitely didn't kill Cassie."

"But I was covered in blood, that morning you found me in the barn."

Mathusi sighs. "Look, the first turn is always ugly. When you shed, it can get messy. And most likely, you probably killed a rabbit, or two." He winces.

I cringe, remembering all the fur when I'd vomited.

"Trust me when I say it. You didn't kill them."

I search his eyes. They're so round and open, inviting me in, wanting me to see the truth.

"I trust you."

Mathusi smiles. "Good," he says, and pats my hands. Standing, he picks up the mugs and makes his way towards the stairs. "Come on. All this talk of rabbit – I'm hungry. Let's eat!"

Walking into the kitchen, a shyness fills me. If I had a tail right now, it'd be between my legs. I feel so ridiculous for losing control. Mathusi keeps reminding me it's to be expected, but I can't help that old familiar feeling of not fitting in.

"Look, Freddy, look what I found for you!" Koba grins from ear to ear. He has the same tightly wound curls as his brother, Mathusi. And an equally mischievous grin.

"Hey, that's my bag!" I smile; the tie-dyed canvas is heavier than I remember. "Where'd you find it?"

Mathusi raises a brow at his little brother. "Yes, little brother. Where?"

"Some big old ugly guy. With a beard." He giggles. "I'm fast like a cheetah!" Koba says, zooming around the kitchen table, pretending to punch and kick invisible enemies. "Them Hunters got nothing on me!"

"Excuse me, Koba Manebarn?" Bett steps into the kitchen. "You got it from whom?"

Koba's face turns ashen before he bolts out the backdoor, Bett in hot pursuit hurling a flurry of curses. The flyscreen bangs shut.

"Did he really pinch it from Garamond?" I whisper to Mathusi.

"Dumb kid seriously thinks when he turns, he's gonna be a cheetah." Mathusi tuts, then looks at me. "Yeah, but by the smell of things, I think he may have had some inside help." He winks, grabbing an apple before walking back down the hallway to his bedroom.

Inside help? I close my eyes and inhale deeply. The sweet earthy scent of honey drifts from the bag. *Ginny.*

Moving aside the stack of pancakes and jug of orange juice, I plonk my bag onto the kitchen table. It really is heavier.

Rummaging through the pockets, I find all the research and books from the library, other bits and pieces, but nothing to indicate why it's so heavy.

I take out each book, a library sticker plastered on every spine. Except one. A dense book, leatherbound. A piece of torn paper pokes out from the top, writing frantically scrawling across the page:

Fred,

I got your letter. I'm nowhere near as poetic as you, and your words were beautiful, but... Grandad has lost it! He took my phone... but even still, no one was answering my texts before that, other than Tyson, and he seemed really confused when I'd asked if he was okay about Cassie. There's been no obituary. I even rang the morgue pretending to be from the local paper, but they had no clue, only mentioned Randy.

Grandad's taken me to Outwash. I snuck back home, into his den, and found this book. I also found... something else. Files. He's been telling me horrible lies, Fred. About monsters. But monsters aren't real! Are they?

If you can, meet me in Outwash. At the library. I'm gonna go every day at 1pm and hope I see you. Just be careful; Grandad's lugged me with two of his goons.

Ginny x

My stomach knots up, and I read Ginny's words again and again. The worry clenches my insides as I sink onto the wooden chair behind me. Okay, at least Ginny's safe. Kind of. And she doesn't hate me. Right? And the news about Cassie? Maybe she's not...

The leatherbound book slips from my hand, landing on the kitchen table with a heavy thud, the cutlery rattling.

Focus, Fred. Breathe.

What even is this book? I run my fingers along the paper,

yellowed and crackling with age. It feels almost like cloth beneath my touch.

At the beginning, it's as if the book is written in a language from another world, maybe Latin? As I delve deeper, the pages trilling, the ink transforms, mingling with French phrases, creating a mesmerising blend of tongues that speak of, well… I don't know. What am I meant to do with this?

I reach the book's final chapter, and there, on the last pages, I discover a cryptic ledger, letters and numbers interwoven like an intricate tapestry of codes.

AW	O	100ml	negative
RUW	B	100ml	neutral
EW	A	150ml	positive
REW	A	150ml	positive

There are more lists going back a year. Longer, even. Maybe these other languages are the same kind of lists. Maybe Varg might know.

I look at the letter from Ginny, her words etched in my mind.

Later. I'll ask Varg later about the book, about these lists. I pack everything into my bag and hang it over the chair.

"Hey, Mathusi, wanna go to Outwash?" I yell down the hallway.

Mathusi sticks his head out of his room, a pearly grin on his face. "Let me find my shoes."

CHAPTER TWENTY

The sun is high in the burnt sky, the radio announcing a total fire ban as firefighters rage against a current blaze further north. Fragments of charred scrub rain down on the car as the wind picks up, leaving behind crumbling, ashen remains.

Mathusi has borrowed his sister's Volkswagen, a relic from the late sixties. The little car splutters along the highway, its tyres tacky against the bubbling bitumen.

"Hey, so, Varg and Bett. How old are they?" I ask, opening a bag of chips.

Mathusi gives me a sideways glance. "How old do you think they are?"

"I dunno. They don't look much over forty. I'd even say in their thirties, but that can't be right?"

"You're kind of right."

"How can I be *kind of* right?"

The gears shift with a crunch as the bright yellow Beetle careens towards the intersection for Outwash.

"When wolves turn, we age to a certain point. Roughly to your thirties. Then the aging process kind of… slows down."

I consider this. "So, like dog years?"

Mathusi laughs. "You and dogs."

"It's my only point of reference, alright?"

Turning off the highway, we're greeted by modern-looking houses and apartment blocks.

Mathusi laughs and continues. "But, yeah, I guess you're on the right track. *Like* dogs." He snorts again. "We just slow down. Dad looks mid to late forties, sure. But you wanna know how old he really is?" Mathusi glances at me as he checks the side mirrors before indicating.

I groan. "Obviously, out with it!"

"One hundred and thirty."

The car's brakes squeak as we come to a stop at the traffic lights, and all I can do is sit here, dumbstruck. I've never been great at math, but I think my dog years thing works.

"And your mum, Bett?" I ask.

"She's about the same."

I turn my body in the bucket seat and face Mathusi as he drives. My eyes search him, every slight crease of his face, every blemish and mark. "What about you? This isn't some *Twilight* bullshit, is it?"

"Tch. Fred! I'm offended! In so many ways…" he scoffs. "Do I look *that* old?"

I sit back in my seat, laughing. "Guess not." I stare out the window. "Wait, what about Alma?"

"She's about fifty. And before you ask, Tosh is thirty."

I lean in my seat as we make a right at a roundabout.

"Hold on, hold on… so when you say Varg is one hundred and thirty, is that how long he has been, like, *here*, alive on earth?"

Mathusi laughs. "Look at you, doing math."

I throw a chip at Mathusi's face, which he amazingly catches and proceeds to eat.

"Sheesh… this town's a bloody maze!" Mathusi grunts, his voice thick with a very forced, very fake, Australian accent. He elbows me. "Hey mate?"

"Please don't."

"What, it's my best Aussie accent, isn't it spot on?" he continues. Mathusi's accent is already a muddle of French and Norwegian – Norway being where he and his family spend most of their time – but he has a knack for accents, and I must admit, he does the stereotypical Australian accent well.

We continue driving past houses and flats, along with an old set of terraces adorned with pink flamingos; the sun-scorched plastic birds sprawl out drunkenly on the lawn.

"Big night!" Mathusi points to the flamingos, nudging me again. "Hey mate!"

I give him a sideways glance, brow raised.

Mathusi chuckles. "Yeah, you get me."

I can see the tower of the library up ahead, behind a row of single-storey shops. A newsagent, a butcher, and a bakery.

I point. "It's right here, I think."

"So, you're telling me we came all this way to go to the library?" Mathusi pulls up to the curb. "Who're we meeting?" he sighs, turning the ignition off.

I bite my thumbnail and stare out the front window. I look at the time on my phone. "Ginny. She left me a note, and some weird book."

"What book?"

"I dunno, I'll show you later. But she found other stuff in Garamond's den."

"Oh, I bet that was a treasure trove of horrors."

"Yeah, from the smell of it, I'd reckon so." I check the time again. "I'm not meeting her until one o'clock. You hungry?"

Digging into the crumbliest meat pie I've ever eaten – Ginny wasn't wrong – I notice Mathusi watching me. He hasn't even touched his food.

"You not hungry?" I ask through a mouthful of lamb.

Mathusi picks a piece of the crust. "Yeah, I just" – he pops the pastry in his mouth – "so, you really like this Ginny chick, right?"

I can feel my cheeks warm. "Yeah, I guess I do."

"How'd you know?"

I think back to the party, Ginny all pink and pretty and sweet. Her little bucktooth pout.

"I usually don't pay much attention to people, but with her, it was different. Something about her just drew me in."

Mathusi's eating now. He swallows. "Ever think it's because she's the granddaughter of the Big Bad? Very Romeo and Juliet of you." He smirks.

"Except I'm not some Romeo fuckboi, having a thing for Juliet's cousin," I laugh. But it does make me wonder. What if it is because of some weird *star-crossed* thing…" Nah," I continue. "I just have a thing for cute blondes." I grin. "And anyways, why are you so curious? Did you have your eyes on her?"

"Maybe…" he says, sipping his soda, a smirk teasing the corner of his mouth.

I choke on the last piece of pie. "I didn't think your boat floated that way?"

"It doesn't," Mathusi laughs, his eyes following the cute guy from the bakery clearing the table next to us before sighing. "And anyways, I think I'm broken."

"Aren't we all?"

"Yeah, but, when you think of Ginny. You want to… *do* stuff with her, yeah?" He pushes the last piece of pastry around on the napkin, his eyes slowly meeting mine.

I snort a laugh. "Heck yes." I think back to us in her bathroom, how close she was. The dusting of freckles across her chest.

"Yeah, I'm broken," he sighs, stuffing remnants of butter chicken pie in his mouth, the sadness of his words creeping past the flecks of pastry.

"Oi…" I stretch out to take his free hand. "You're not broken, alright?" I wipe my fingers of pastry flakes and sit back in my chair, watching him. "I thought I was broken. For a long time."

This is it; I'm talking. This is how talking goes. You got this.

"To be honest, I fight it every day – this *broken* feeling." I tug at the binder under my shirt. "It's why I keep to myself." I pause. "*Kept* to myself." I smile at Mathusi. "You just have to find where your puzzle piece fits."

Mathusi nods.

"Who cares if you're gay –"

"– a gay guy who doesn't like dick." He snorts, rolling his eyes and throwing his napkin on the table.

The flaky pastry finds its way to the back of my throat as I gasp a laugh. *Well, that took me by surprise.*

"Sorry, I'm being obnoxious," Mathusi sighs.

"No, no…" I offer, I hope, reassuringly, through the pastry-induced coughs. "Pastry. Stuck," is all I can manage before having a drink. I've never spoken about this kind of stuff with anyone before. I'm not gonna lie, that despite wanting to be on my own, to not rely on someone else, that there's a part of me that wants *this*. This comradery, this friendship. Being able to talk openly, to confide in someone. And I think Mathusi feels the same.

"So, I know why I don't like that particular part of the human anatomy." I shudder, and to that Mathusi snorts a laugh. *Thank you, humour.* I watch as Mathusi squints, and I can just tell his mind is running through all the possible answers, trying to find a palatable response.

My shoulders stiffen. *I'm taking this conversation by the horns. This is it. Serious talk.*

"So, you like guys…" I venture.

Mathusi sighs and nods.

"But you don't like the idea of being intimate with them?"

Mathusi squirms in his seat, his eyes cast down. "It's not that I don't want to be *intimate*. I like kissing. Cuddling. I want all that nice relationship closeness… just not the *other* stuff. It's just all too much… mental effort," he sighs.

I lean back in my chair, studying Mathusi's expression. "You know, there's a whole rainbow of sexual orientations out there."

Mathusi folds his arms across his chest, nodding. "I've been thinking that, maybe, like, I might be ace?"

"Like, asexual?"

Mathusi's arms unwind, and he smiles, taking out his phone, tapping vigorously. "Yeah, exactly!" he says, showing me his screen.

"Wow, you even have an infographic at the ready." I smile.

Mathusi laughs. "Yeah, well, it's kinda been a big thing figuring it out. Finding out what all this" – he gestures with his hands, arms waving around his body – "is about."

I watch as Mathusi's smile fades and his shoulder slump.

"You know, there's nothing wrong with" – and I make the same gesture at the vague area of his body – "any of this."

"Yeah, there is." Mathusi's voice becomes stern now, almost harsh.

"What makes you say that?"

"Psh," Mathusi spits, "you're really gonna make me come out and say it, aren't you?"

"Only if you want." I wait patiently, until finally Mathusi works up the courage and blurts out what he's been holding back for so long.

"If I'm ace, then that means no sex. And if there's no sex, then that means I can't have any of the other stuff." He nods towards the guy behind the counter at the bakery. "And as if a guy that hot wouldn't wanna fuck."

"Hey." I take Mathusi's hand once more, and he rolls his eyes. "Some Chucklehead once told me that we all have our moments of figuring ourselves out. It's like a rite of passage, discovering who you are."

Mathusi scoffs and looks away.

"And that's just it, it'll keep changing and you'll find out more about who you are, and what being ace means to you. You're not broken because you don't wanna have sex. And you know what? Relationships can work without it."

Mathusi purses his lips, eyeing me up and down. "This is three for three, Fred. I'm worried. Your feelings are showing." The corner of his mouth curls into a smirk and I kick him under the table.

As Mathusi finishes speaking, the cute attendant from the bakery approaches us with a friendly smile. "Hey there," he greets us, placing a couple of straws on our table. "Need some straws for your drinks?"

Mathusi's eyes widen, and he stammers awkwardly, "Uh, yeah, thanks. Straws. Right."

The boy smiles, a deep dimple pressing into his cheek. "No problem. I'm Dan, by the way. My, um" – he clears his throat, his pitch lowering – "my aunt owns the bakery." He extends his hand towards Mathusi.

Mathusi nervously takes Dan's hand and stammers,

"Mathusi. I mean, *I'm* Mathusi."

Dan grins. "Nice to meet you, Mathusi. Enjoy your meal!"

Mathusi nods, still blushing, "You too."

Dan leaves our table, and I can't help but chuckle. "Smooth, mate."

Mathusi's cheeks turn ruddy. "Shut up," he mumbles, avoiding eye contact.

The phone in my pocket buzzes, distracting me. I swipe the alarm off.

"It's nearly one o'clock."

Mathusi slides the straw into his soda, sipping deeply, then stands, sliding his phone in his pocket. He stops. "Hey, thanks for talking with me about all this."

"And we're gonna keep talking about this later, okay?" I poke him in the chest.

"And here I was thinking you were the lone wolf type. Look at you, feeling emotions and talking like a real person," Mathusi teases.

"I guess feelings are contagious." I link my arm in his.

This does feel good, having someone to talk to. Is this what family feels like? Maybe I'll let myself enjoy the moment. Even for a little while. If even it is short-lived.

"Okay. So, Ginny's note said Garamond has left two goons watching her."

"That's just wonderful." Mathusi tuts. "Guess we're on the lookout for the plaid army, then, hey?"

Passing the newsagency, Mathusi stops to read a magazine, and I can see the library ahead when I notice a familiar-looking bloke. The same blonde hair and air of confident arrogance from before. The library guy? He smiles at me, his hands sliding into his pockets. I blink, but he's gone.

I squeeze my eyes shut. "Great, now I'm seeing things."

"Seeing what?" Mathusi asks, not really listening, his attention glued to the open pages of some men's fitness magazine.

"Nothing. You just enjoy your eye candy," I laugh, my attention drawn back to the library steps. Mathusi mutters something, though I'm transfixed on the man sitting on a fold-out chair at the bottom of the steps, his red trucker cap shading his bearded face. I'm certain that blonde goth guy was there before.

Trucker-cap man shifts in his chair, adjusting the sign he's holding, but the crowd milling around him doesn't seem to notice it.

Tell me your best joke. Cash prize $50.

"Well, am I gonna make you belly laugh today." I smile. Easiest fifty bucks I've ever made.

Casually meandering in and out of the crowd towards the guy in the deck chair, Mathusi rushes up behind me.

"What're you doing?" he asks, his voice sing-song, a fake

smile stretching across his face.

"Dude, relax." I smile. "I'm just making some easy money."

"It's bait, you idiot," Mathusi snarls, his eyes darting over my shoulder to the bearded man and back to mine.

"What do you mean?" I stare at him.

"He's a *Hunter*," Mathusi whispers, barely moving his lips.

I freeze. "W-what?" I turn my head to catch a glimpse of the defenceless-looking man in the yellow deck chair.

"Stop looking at him!" Mathusi smiles again and laughs as if I told the funniest joke ever.

"How can you tell?" I ask, sniffing the air. "I can't smell anything."

"You've been a wolf for three weeks, and suddenly you know all, huh?" Mathusi rubs the back of his neck. "It's written in special ink. Humans can't see it. Only *we* can." He pretends to show me something on his phone. "Have another smell, notice something bitter?"

I turn my head, sniffing.

"That's wolfsbane," Mathusi continues. "They hex it and mix it with ink." Mathusi smiles as if the conversation is sweet and not as harrowing as what it truly is. "Has anyone else approached him?" he whispers under his breath.

I twist at my knuckles. "No…"

"And why might that be?"

I sigh. Shit, I'm an idiot. "Because no one else can see the sign." Looking behind me, I realise the chair is empty. "Oh, crap, he's coming over. We need to run!"

Mathusi's hand clenches my shoulder, and his eyes flash golden. "Bad idea. They'd be ready for that." He loosens his grip, blinking as his eyes fade to their usual earthy brown. He smiles, his canines showing. "Just relax and act normal."

"Hi there, friends," comes the man's voice, sweet and rosy. "Saw you eyeballing my sign. Got a joke for me?"

"Don't know what you mean." Mathusi shrugs a shoulder.

"I was asking your friend. I saw them checking it out."

"Oh... I, um..." *Think quick, Fred.* "I was just wondering why you were holding a blank sign, is all. Bit weird," I say, forcing a laugh.

The bearded man stares at us, then suddenly chuckles. "I suppose that is a bit weird, huh."

More fake laughter, fake nods. Surely this guy knows. He knows. Oh, shit, I'm panicking...

Mathusi can sense my nervousness, I'm sure. "Come on, *babe*," he emphasises, taking my hand as if we were your average teenage couple. "Let's go."

"You know what else is *weird*?" the man continues.

Mathusi rolls his eyes and turns to face him. "I'm sure you're about to tell us..."

The man points to the sign. "It ain't blank," he says, a wicked smile spreading under his thick beard. He takes out his phone, snapping a photo of the sign on the steps. "Some of it's written with a regular old marker. That way, even sly dogs like you might slip up."

Staring at the photo, I notice the start of the sentence is completely missing.

The crowd of people edge closer. More Hunters. Pinned on each of their shirts sits a small silver dagger.

The old man slowly removes a blade from an inside jacket pocket, the silver glistening in the midday sun.

"Now we can do this the easy way," the old man says, nodding to a white utility van parked on the side of the road. "Or the hard way." The Hunters move in closer.

"Oh dear, oh dear, what do we have here?" Varg steps out of a sleek black sedan. "Whatever happened to our truce?"

Bett, Alma, and Tosh step out of the car, walking towards us.

"Where's my car?" Alma growls in Mathusi's ear. I watch him wince. Guess he never asked if he could take it.

"It's parked outside the bakery." Mathusi hands Alma the keys, though she pushes them back in his hand.

"Take Fred and get back to Aksel's," Alma says, and turns to the closest Hunter. "My little brother was just leaving."

The Hunter looks to the bearded man, who reluctantly nods.

"We don't want any grief," the Hunter says; a smile like a snake winds its way across his face.

Mathusi takes my hand and pulls me from the crowd, back towards the car. Nearing the corner, I can see the Volkswagen up ahead.

"But, what about Ginny?"

Mathusi scoffs. "She's a big girl. These are *her* people," he snarls.

"They're not *my* people." Ginny's voice is shaking. Scared. She steps out from the alley where the car is parked.

I can see out of the corner of my eye Mathusi recoil, just slightly. I, however, am fighting every urge to not launch myself at her, wrap my arms around her, and never let go. I can feel my heart racing as Ginny steps forward. It's been three weeks since I've seen her, and I can hardly contain myself. My breath catches in my throat as I nervously wave, my hand trembling by my side. I'm aware of every movement my body makes as I shuffle towards her, my feet heavy and clumsy.

A clamour sounds behind us and Ginny pulls me into the alleyway, my hand instinctively grabbing for Mathusi's as we tumble into a stack of plastic milk crates, my body pressing up against Ginny's, a surge of electricity shooting through me.

"I thought I'd never see you again," I whisper into her

golden hair, my hands trembling as I reach up to cup her face.

Ginny flinches, stepping to the side. "I have something for you."

My face flushes with embarrassment. *She hates me.*

"Take these," Ginny says, dragging a stack of document folders from her bag and into my hands. Her ocean eyes peer around the corner, then settle back on mine. Her long brown lashes sway up and down, beckoning me to tumble into those limitless blues. I'd happily drown.

Mathusi sighs heavily through his nose, the toe of his shoe kicking my heel.

"Wait, what? What are they?" I finally find my way back to the now.

"Answers." Ginny's face is stern and unyielding.

Echoes of voices sound from around the corner, calling Ginny's name.

"You guys gotta go –"

"– not without you!" I cut her off, grabbing her hand. Her small, soft hand. My thumb runs circles around the inside of her palm. "Not again."

Ginny smiles softly, her face turning a bright scarlet, though she shakes her head. "You were right," she says, her eyes wet. "Apples and trees." She drops her hand from mine.

"No, Ginny, I was just saying that to keep you safe." I reach for her hand again, dropping the folders. Mathusi scurries to collect them.

"I know," she whispers. "And now I'm returning the favour."

Ginny's hands are on my chest, grabbing my shirt, and I smile, licking my lips in anticipation. This is it. This is the moment. For real. Ginny's mouth on mine. *This is it.* But instead of pulling me into her, she shoves me backwards, towards the open door of Alma's yellow Vee Dub. I tumble into the back seat, Mathusi jumping into the front. The ignition is on, the door not even closed as the Beetle splutters off down the street. The papers flutter gently in the backseat as my heart flutters and breaks, watching as I drive away from Ginny. Again.

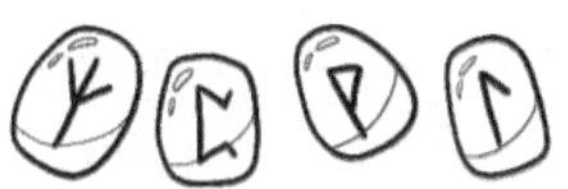

CHAPTER TWENTY-ONE

The drive back to Acacia Hills is quiet. The wind has cleared most of the smoke from the sky. It's been at least half an hour since we bolted. What would have happened if Varg and the family hadn't shown up? And how had they found us?

"Mathusi, I'm sorry."

He sighs. "There's nothing to be sorry for. These Hunters can be tricksters. I'm just glad the pack showed up when they did."

"Yeah, how did they know where we were?"

Mathusi shifts gears and the car cruises along the highway. "You said you found a note from Ginny?"

"Yeah, in a book."

"And where are they now?"

"Where's what now…?"

Mathusi rolls his eyes. "The book, the note."

"Oh! They're in my bag."

"Honestly, this is like pulling teeth!" he scoffs. "And the bag is where?"

"Back at home. At your cousin's place, I mean."

Mathusi grins. "You called it home."

Wow. I did. I don't know if I've ever thought of any one place as home. "Yeah, well, it is." I smile.

The car bounces over a pothole.

"So. Your bag, which has this book, and the note, is back *home*," he says again, smiling. "Put two and two together, Fred." He tuts.

The letter from Ginny.

"Yeah, right,." The words barely make it past my lips. I'm too busy thinking about Ginny – her smile, her blushing cheeks. Maybe she doesn't hate me. Maybe not all hope is lost.

We travel in silence for the last twenty minutes, only the sound of the tyres on the road and the droll of talkback radio.

Ginny keeps dancing through my mind, how close we were, the way she smelt. The fantasy of her mouth dancing across my lips. I sigh, imagining the taste of her, and cross my legs, squeezing my thighs tight. I imagine my tongue flicking across those adorable buckteeth and my skin tickles with goosebumps.

I wind the window down fully and stick my head out. I need some fresh air.

"Oh great, you're truly embracing your inner dog, now, hey?" Mathusi laughs.

I laugh too, and howl into the afternoon sky as the car turns into the long dusty driveway of the Rustmane Farm.

The black sedan from before lurks under the trees.

"How did they make it home before us?" There, I'd said it again. *Home.*

"Well, if you weren't making googly eyes at your girl-friend…"

Girlfriend. I like the sound of that, too. I blush. I don't know if that will ever be the case. But then again, she saved *me* this time. That's gotta mean something.

"Then maybe we would have made it back sooner," Mathusi continues, stepping out of the car and making his way to the front porch.

"Nah, Grandpa, it was definitely your driving," I tease.

"Look, I'm a safe driver, okay? Just because the sign says 110 kms, doesn't mean I have to drive that speed."

"Or maybe it was when you stopped to check the pressure of the tyres."

Mathusi knocks me with elbow and smirks, taking the steps two at a time, his voice sounding over his shoulder. "I wanted to make sure they weren't flat. The car was veering to the left."

I jog up after him. "Hey, wait." I reach for Mathusi's elbow, juggling the folders in my other hand.

"Look, before you start at me, I'm just a cautious driver, al-right? And that Bug is a breakdown waiting to happen."

I look back at the yellow Beetle and laugh; the side mirror seemed to teeter and fall as if right on cue. He's not wrong.

"No, no. Not that, I'll tease you more later, old man. But about before, when you were talking about being broken. About… sex, and junk." I cringe. I suck at this *real talk* business.

He shushes me and pulls me away from the door to the veranda. "Yeah, what about it?"

"Labels can be helpful, but they're not everything," I say. "You're you, Mathusi, and that's what matters most. You're not broken; you're just finding your own place in this insane world."

He gives me a smile, gratitude shimmering in his eyes. "That's four, Fred. Watch out." He smiles.

The front door creaks open.

"Where're my keys, Mat?" Alma leans against the wooden frame, her hands on her hips. She blows at a stray strand of hair, a white streak that falls from her widow's peak. The rest of Alma's hair is obsidian. Where the white steak meets her scalp, the skin is mottled and pale compared to her ochre tone. Mathusi said it's called *vitiligo*. I can see the patches down her neck and shoulders.

Mathusi tosses her the keys. "Sorry, sis."

"Not me you have to be worried about," Alma says, raising a brow before walking back inside, the door squeaking shut.

I look up at the house. "It's pretty quiet. You think we're in shit?" I ask, reaching for the door-handle.

Mathusi crosses his arms, exhaling a long breath. "Yup."

"What were you thinking?" Varg barks as we enter the kitchen.

I go to speak, but Mathusi tugs at the hem of my shirt.

"There are Hunters hellbent on your demise, Fred," Varg continues, "And you walk right up to them?"

What the fuck? "Yeah, nah," I reply, shrugging Mathusi's hand away. "How was I supposed to know? I've been a stupid bloody werewolf for three stupid bloody weeks, and you expect me to just *know* shit?"

Varg sighs, his body slumping onto a chair at the kitchen table. He looks tired.

"You're right. It's not your fault. I'm sorry… I just." His eyes find mine, and shift to Mathusi's. He takes the piece of paper wedged between the pages of the giant leatherbound book. "I was worried. And if it weren't for this note" – he waves Ginny's letter in the air – "and Koba's *telling* story –"

"–sorry!" Koba yells from the loungeroom.

Bett brings over a pot of tea, placing it on a heatproof pad on the table.

"I haven't been here, and, well. I haven't exactly been help-ful, or told you anything, given you a reason to be truly wary." He taps his fingers on the table. "Sit down. Both of you."

I eye the pot of tea. "No California poppy in this, yeah?" I ask, genuinely concerned.

Bett laughs. "Not today. Today we have a kind of…" She pauses. "Let's call it macha."

I look down at the frothy green tea and shrug. *Looks alright.* I take a small cup and go to pour myself some when Bett taps my fingers, taking the cup from my hand.

"But not for you," she whispers, her mouth twisting into a smirk.

I can feel my nose scrunch. *Why not?*

"Mathusi knows why we've come back," Varg continues. "Why we're here –"

"– my social worker contacted you, right?" I ask, trying to remember all the details. I watch Bett as she moves around the room towards the hallway.

Varg nods. "Yes. That's one reason."

"Wait, wait…" I can feel the dawning wash over me. How had I not put this together already? "Your cousin's missing… Aksel?" I think back to the conversations with my social worker, the texts exchanged. "Mum's cousin, Aksel. That's why I was shipped out here, that's who I was meant to meet. But there was a mix-up, and I ended up at Jocelyn's." I pause. "But wait, who's Harrison? I was meant to meet a woman with the name Harrison."

"Rueth Harrison. Aksel's wife." Bett nods.

My stomach twists in knots. "But where are they?"

"They're missing," Mathusi says, his eyes downcast. "They all are."

"All?" my eyes move from Mathusi to Varg.

Varg sighs. "Yes. But we may have a lead."

Mathusi sits forwards in his seat, twisting his knuckles. "What is it? Have you found him? Any of them?"

The distant crunching of tyres on gravel sounds outside.

I swallow. "I didn't realise they were all actually missing."

"His entire pack." Varg takes a breath. "They've all gone missing. Well, except one."

There's a knock at the door, and it's then I smell it. I've noticed that certain emotions have a particular smell attached to them. When someone is exceptionally excited, it smells like treacle, or syrup. Sadness smells like rain, earthy and damp. And this guy smells of onions. Fear. I'd smelt it before but hadn't known my snout from my tail then. I had smelt it at school when the cops had rocked up.

Footsteps creak on the floorboards and the stench wafts into the kitchen, and so does he.

"Hello Varg. Bett." Sergeant Luis Pine nods. He looks at me, and subtly takes a step back, clearing his throat before he speaks again. "Winnifred –"

"– it's Fred, actually," Mathusi interrupts before I can say anything. I knock my knee against his under the table, giving him a *thank you* smile.

Sarge nods, his lips a thin line. He then looks to Varg. "Wondering if we might have a word, mate?" He nods his head towards the backdoor.

"I think here is fine," Varg replies, and kicks a chair out from the table. "Sit."

"Please, Luis. Sit." Bett's voice is welcoming, unlike Varg's; she taps Mathusi and me on the shoulder.

"Hey, Fred, I think Koba wanted to show us that new level on his game," Mathusi says, standing.

I look to Bett, who raises her brows slightly.

"Right, yeah. I think he wanted help, hey." I follow Mathusi into the loungeroom.

"Don't forget your *homework*," Bett adds. She hands Mathusi and me the stack of folders and the book Ginny sent me, then closes the door behind us.

"What the hell's that about?" I whisper to Mathusi as the door shuts.

"Dunno. But I think we should stick around and find out," he says with a wink, sitting on the floor to the side of the door.

I swallow hard, a worry creeping its way through the small of my stomach.

It's okay. It'll be okay, I breathe, trying to reassure the knots forming in my chest.

As Mathusi and I huddle outside the closed door, the air thick with tension, I can't shake the feeling of unease settling in the pit of my stomach.

Even as the seconds tick by, I realise that whatever is happening behind that door is far from okay. And suddenly, the re-assurances I whispered to myself feel hollow, drowned out by the ominous weight of the unknown.

With a sinking heart, I know one thing for certain: whatever secrets lie beyond that closed door, they're about to change everything.

CHAPTER TWENTY-TWO

"You've got the wrong idea about Garamond," Sarge says. His voice is muffled, but we can still hear him. Mathusi and I sit on the floor, our backs against the wall.

"Sarge is one of us?" I whisper to Mathusi, absolutely gobsmacked.

"Apparently…"

"And why is he working with Garamond?" I can feel the anger in me start to twist. "And not to mention the fact he's out for my blood. And what about…" My voice trails off. I have so many questions, but my mind is going faster than my mouth. Mathusi squeezes my thigh, his finger to his lips.

"Just listen," he whispers back, and tilts his head towards the closed door.

"And what do we have wrong, hm? Your *boss* rolls back into town and then your pack mysteriously goes missing. Wolves are missing. All except you," Varg growls. "Seems a little suspicious."

I can hear Sarge make a noise, as if he's going to speak, but Varg cuts him off again.

"Working with Garamond," Varg spits. "A renowned

Hunter bastard, known for dismissing treaties, trouncing truces, and gutting anything he deems a monster."

"What is he doing back here?" Bett's now talking, the sound of tea pouring. "Last we heard, Garamond had been called back to Amsterdam to meet with the Guild about his… project."

Sarge scoffs. "What do you know about the project?"

"Only that the cure is a lie." I can hear the knowing lilt in Bett's voice.

Cure?

A slurping sound and the scraping of porcelain on wood fill the silence that follows. But only one person is drinking.

"What's in the tea this time?" I whisper to Mathusi. "Macha?"

"Looks like macha, sure, but Mum calls it *verite posyon* – truth potion."

No wonder I couldn't drink it. That could have been awkward.

"What do they think Sarge is hiding?" I ask, straining to hear the voices from the other side of the wall.

Mathusi turns to face me, mouth open to speak, when he cranes his neck, looking behind me to the pile of folders scattered on the floor. He reaches over. "What are these?"

"It's the stuff Ginny gave me. *Answers* was all she said."

Mathusi flicks through one of the folders. "These are police files."

"What?" My breath catches in my throat. Crossing my legs, I place the folders on my lap. I take one and open it, the contents spilling out. A photo. It's a crime scene photo. Of a house. I slide my phone from my pocket. Unlock, tap, swipe. I find the photo of the article about my parents' murder. It's the same house from the article.

"This…" My eyes jump from photo to report, to a photocopied document. Blood results, toxicity… silver nitrate? I spread the photos out across the wooden floor in front of me. "This is…" The words are stuck in my mouth; my eyes sting, my throat tightens. Reaching for a photo poking out from the pile, my fingers trace over its yellowed edges.

"Use your words, Fred." Mathusi half laughs, not looking at me, his ear pressed up to the wall again.

I pick up the crime scene photo. It seems so innocent amongst the blood and grime of the other photographs spread out on the ground, but this means I was right. That my dreams meant something.

Mathusi shuffles next to me. "What's that… a mitten?"

One lone pink crotchet mitten with a yellow-and-black number token next to it. My mitten.

"This is the police report from, um…" I cough, trying to make the words come out. "From my parents," I wheeze, gathering the hem of my shirt, pressing it to my face, wet with tears. "From their murder."

I can feel Mathusi's eyes on me. "Oh, shit. Yeah, no…" he says, scooping up the photos and reports. "We don't need to be looking at this right now."

"Why would Garamond have these?"

The chairs scratch heavily along the kitchen floor, the wall behind us thuds loudly, the picture frame above Mathusi wobbles and falls, glass shattering on the floor.

"I've had enough of these games!" Varg barks.

Koba pauses his game. "What was that?"

Mathusi stands. "Nothing. Hey, why don't you try out that new game on my console?" He turns, smiling at his little brother.

"For real?" Koba beams and is off like a cheetah, skittering down the hallway into his brother's room.

Mathusi's smile drops, his focus now on me. "Take those files, the book, put it somewhere safe in your room."

The voices in the kitchen are getting louder.

"He's trying to make a difference!" Sarge, Luis, whoever – his voice is raspy, like someone has him by the throat.

Another heavy thud.

"Why are you covering for him?" Varg's fist bursts through the wall, dust and particle board sprinkling the floor in front of us. Varg peers through the gap, his eyes a bright yellow.

There's a scurry of feet, then a metal *click.*

"Luis, there's no need for that…" Bett's voice is low.

Mathusi takes my hand, dragging me up. "We gotta go."

"Is that a gun?" My eyes are wide.

Heavy breathing, followed by another click, the chafe of leather.

"Good, no need for weapons." Bett's reassuring tone is cut off by Sarge.

"What did you put in my tea, witch!" Sarge groans.

The kitchen door bursts open, Sarge staggering through. Mathusi and I back away, falling onto the couch, Sarge stumbling through the loungeroom, Varg prowling behind.

"All we want is the truth, cousin," Varg pants.

Sarge turns, his hand on his weapon. "I'm not your *cousin.* And Aksel and his mutts were never my pack," he scoffs, pacing the rug. "They felt guilty for me. A lone wolf with no home. Pathetic."

"What did he promise you, Luis?" Bett edges around the corner, her voice soft and sweet, but her eyes are glowing amber.

Sarge's eyes dart upwards, meeting Bett's. "Hope," he says, resolute. Standing tall, he straightens his police blues. "I'll do anything for a cure. To be *normal,*" he spits.

His stare finds mine; a dry laugh escapes his lips. "I hope

Vargus is a better lawyer than he is a wolf," he scoffs. "You'll need it."

I hold on even tighter to the folders in my arms, watching Sarge slam the front door as he leaves.

Why do I need a lawyer?

Varg snarls, then sighs, his fingers running through his hair, tugging at the roots. The sound of a car speeding off down the driveway recedes into the night. Varg looks from Bett to me. "What's this *homework* Bett mentioned?"

"I think the main question is – what is he on about a cure?" Mathusi makes his way back into the kitchen and sits at the table.

I follow him, sitting next to him, making sure I *really* don't drink that tea. "And why do I need a lawyer?"

Varg waves his hand dismissively. "I don't know, I don't…" he sighs again, falling onto the bench. "Later. What's with the files Fred brought in?"

"Oh shit, that's a whole other kettle of fish…" Mathusi exhales sharply.

The files! Does Sarge think I stole them? Is that why I need a lawyer?

Mathusi shuffles in his seat, facing Varg. "What was Sarge on about…"

Varg rubs his temples. "There's been talk of the Guild

attempting to create a cure for wolfism."

Bett sighs. "Some in the Guild are of the opinion that since we can't be *put down*, thanks to the truce –"

"– and by *some*, you mean Garamond," Mathusi scoffs.

"Not naming names, but…" Varg rolls his eyes. "They decided to come up with another plan to eradicate us."

This is well, fascinating and all, but I'm not interested in this cure they're all talking about.

"Seriously, though. Why do I need a lawyer…?"

Mathusi sits back, folding his arms, oblivious to anything I've been saying. "Okay, but a cure's old news. They've tried before. Even Van Helsing gave it a crack."

Van Helsing? What is this conversation? And why is no one listening to me! Maybe I need a lawyer because Garamond is saying I assaulted him…

Varg continues. "Sarge came to Aksel a lost lamb. Aksel took him in."

Bett shakes her head, her eyes staring into the cup of green sludge Sarge left behind before placing a hand on Varg's shoulder. "He's still a lost lamb."

"Lamb. Delicious. Come on, guys. I'm really getting nervous, now. Why did he say I need a lawyer?"

"So, what, Garamond is working on a cure out of the goodness of his heart?" Mathusi ignores me. "And Sarge is helping him?"

Varg shrugs.

"It's beginning to look like it," Bett sighs.

My upper jaw starts to throb.

These fuckwolves aren't listening. Why do I need a lawyer? Are they charging me? Are they going to arrest me? Are the Manebarns covering for me? Did I do it? Did I kill Cassie?

The taste of copper fills my mouth.

"Lawyer!" I bark, smashing my fist on the table. The silence after is broken by the *tink* of enamel on the wooden tabletop. I look down. Teeth. My fingers rush to my mouth; two large canines hang from my aching gums.

I cover my mouth and make a run for it, down the hall to my room, slamming the door.

Standing in front of the mirror, I peel back my lip. Two large canines have broken through my gums. I push on one, in a hope it retracts, or something.

Muffled voices sound from the kitchen.

"The lawyer jab, from Sarge, was just a threat," Varg says, but I can sense doubt in his voice. Uncertainty.

"I think there's more to it," Mathusi speaks next, and I can hear the rustle of paper.

I look back at my reflection; the large canines are slowly receding. I sigh. *Thank fuck.* Mathusi did say there's an adjustment period, but this is ridiculous. My left canine is back to normal, replaced with a gummy gap. Awesome.

Bett curses. "That's him, without a doubt."

Wait, who *is him?*

"He's younger, but that's Garamond. I've stared at that face far too many times." Bett tuts.

"Isn't that the hat you ripped off his head last time we were here?" Varg laughs.

The newspaper article. The person of interest – that must be what they're looking at, that's gotta be what they're talking about!

Opening my bedroom door, I'm back down the hallway, standing at the kitchen entrance, everyone's eyes on me. "He knows who I am. He's come back to finish the job, hasn't he?"

CHAPTER TWENTY-THREE

We started off, Varg, Bett, Mathusi and me, in the kitchen. The conversation soon spilled out to the loungeroom. There was a lot of pacing – by me, mainly. They told me about my parents, who they were, what they were like. We went through what I already knew – that my mum, Aasta, was a Manebarn. She, Varg and Aksel were cousins, and the last of their kind. They told me how Mum and Dad had left Europe to settle in Australia, how they'd found a home in Tasmania. They'd even found another pack. Life had been good. Until it hadn't.

"Aasta befriended a human…" Varg's voice was low.

"Mal." Bett nodded. "Lovely thing."

"Yes. *Mal.* They became friends with the pack. Ended up dating one of the young men," Varg said.

"We don't know all the details. But what we did find out was that this person came from Hunters," Bett added.

"But this *Mal* wasn't a hunter?" I asked.

"No. Their family were Hunters," Bett corrected. "Not them. They'd left that life behind. They'd hated it."

I thought on this for a while. I had so many questions swirling through my mind, colliding into realisation, until one final question pieced together.

"Were my parents killed because they were friends with the wrong person?"

I looked down at the news article, at the sketch of the *person of interest*.

"And that's Garamond?"

Now, curled up like a little bagel on my bed, my mind is going a hundred miles an hour, my emotions teetering. What am I missing, what's the connection? Who the hell was this *Mal* person, and why had knowing them put my parents in so much danger?

Mathusi's behind me, hugging me. He was cracking jokes for a while, mainly around how wolves make a killing with the tooth fairy, but now he's content to just lie here with me and wallow in this information overload. I can smell the sweet chamomile tea Bett's left on my nightstand.

My phone chimes.

"Can you reach it? I think it fell down the crack of the bed behind you."

The bed bounces softly, and Mathusi grunts, squeezing his arm into the gap.

"Huh."

"*Huh*, what?" I ask, rolling over.

He hands me the phone and crawls over me. "I'll leave you two alone," he says, winking. "Oh, and your fangs are back to normal now, too," he adds, pointing to his own incisors, and shuts the door behind him.

"Weirdo," I mutter, rolling my tongue across my teeth, then look at my phone. Unknown number. Well, not a number I have saved in my phone. And a text.

```
Hi Fred, got a new phone. It's Ginny.
Can we talk?
I'm back in Acacia. Come over? :-)
```

I smile. She's forgiven me. She must have.

What about your grandad? I type back. He's gotta be back in Outwash; Ginny wouldn't invite me over if he was hanging around. I excitedly slip my feet into my boots. My phone buzzes.

```
He's away still. Come over.
```

I bite my lip, thumbs tapping over the screen. *And maybe we can pick up where we left off? We have so much to talk about.*

I sit on the edge of my bed, the familiar '…' flashing on the screen. Then, nothing. Oh, no… no no no, maybe I've made her nervous. Oh, shit, maybe I shouldn't have been so forward.

It was all such a rush, and…

My phone buzzes again.

```
Totes.
```

I laugh. Who says *totes*?

Goosebumps rush down my arms. I crack the door open and sneak down the hallway, out the front door. Koba's BMX bike is leaning against the porch.

"That'll work," I say, throwing my leg over the frame and kicking back the crank. Dust and dirt flick up as I ride down the driveway and out to the main road. The night is fresh; a southerly breeze has washed away all the smoke that sank over the valley earlier in the day, and the air smells like distant rain. The sky is open, and the stars are blinking, like a little cheer squad in the sky. It's been a crazy day – ups and downs – I need this. After everything I've learnt today, after everything I've learnt these past few weeks, I just want Ginny. She'll help me make sense of it all. Everything will be better. *She'll* make everything better. Sheesh, who am I? I can't help but laugh, thinking of Mathusi, Varg, Bett, *the pack*. And Ginny, too? I could get used to this *family* gig.

The tyres skid as I make the bend onto the long stretch of street where Garamond's house stands. It's a pretty big property, and backs right onto the western edge of the campground. I back-pedal into a brake and let the bike fall against a myrtle, making a beeline for the front door.

All the stress of the day is gone, standing here, knowing Ginny is waiting for me. My stomach bubbles with an explosion of twinkling stars. I knock, straightening my pant legs, when the door flies open. Gasping, I step back.

"I knew the bitch would come." Garamond's husky voice crawls from the doorway. Before I can turn and run, Sarge is behind me, pushing me inside. The door to Garamond's den is open.

"Make sure she wasn't followed," Garamond grunts.

"Yes, boss," Sarge replies, then pauses, turning. "Shouldn't we take her down to the station?"

"I just want to have a little chat, first." Garamond grins.

Sarge nods, then leaves.

"This is a bad move, even for you, *murderer*," I spit.

Garamond smiles, stepping closer. Close enough that I can smell the rage on his breath, like noxious fumes. And something else… something, metallic.

"Murderer?" he quips. "Well, I'm not sure who I murdered, exactly."

"How about Randy, for a start."

Garamond scoffs, rolling his eyes.

"I saw you," I growl. "You and your red eyes."

Garamond's smile falters, and he steps back slightly. His eyes widen, and I catch a flicker of something like surprise dancing across his face before he quickly regains his composure, his lips twisting into a sly grin. Is he surprised that I know? Did I catch him off guard? *Just say it, and let me sink my teeth into you…*

Garamond shakes his head. "Oh, *Winnifred*, that was you." A grin spreads wickedly across his face, his beard twitching. "You killed Randy. And Cassie, for that matter."

I swallow hard against the sick edging up my throat. "And we can't forget Tasmania," I continue, ignoring his false words. "New Moon Island, to be exact."

Garamond folds his arms, his eyes narrowing as he leans against the wall. His lips curl into a faint, knowing smile. "Well. I was right? You are the Mac Tíre kid. Look at you, all grown up."

"So, you admit it." I can barely keep my voice level. *Is* he admitting it? Is it true?

"I always hated that police artist's sketch. Didn't quite get the nose right." He smirks.

"Who'd you have to bribe, hm?" I think back to the scattered police files. "Funny how the cops glossed over the blood report. Silver nitrate."

Garamond's smug grin wavers once more before he slides a silver blade from his belt. The same kind of blade the old guy had at Outwash.

"Maybe I'll prove to you just how much of a murderer I can be." Reaching for his pocket, he retrieves a small glass vial, popping the lid before chugging the contents. The smell is over-powering, the pungent scent of iron and decay.

That's the smell from the den. *What is it?*

Garamond keeps talking, but I'm not paying attention. I stare at his mouth and sniff, deeply. Is it some kind of plant? A drug?

Garamond's pupils flash and contort; he squeezes his eyes shut for a moment, then grins again, staring back at me, his irises almost iridescent. He points to the opened door of his den.

"In. Now," his voice booms.

"Screw that…"

"Now!" Garamond barks.

I take a step back, remembering Ginny's *fang shoey* tray on the side table, then peer behind me. Sarge never closed the front door when he left; the streetlamps blink in the distance.

"Fine!" I say, throwing my hands in the air.

Stepping forward, I see Garamond's grin widen, his eyes flickering. Bringing my arms down, my right hand grabs a fist-ful of the white sand. With a flick of the wrist, I fling the grit straight into Garamond's face, his meaty fists reaching for his eyes as he screams and howls, lunging forward, lashing out. But he's too slow, and I'm already out on the curb, running. Running as though my life depends on it, because, well, it does.

I don't know if Garamond is following. I can't hear anything. All I can hear is my blood pumping through my body, thrusting my legs forward. My thighs burn, my calves are cramping, but I keep running, lunging over fences, up over the hill and past the barn, straight to the farm. I can see Varg already on the porch, running down the steps towards me.

Sirens wail in the distance, the flashing blue and red lighting up the darkness like bad news twinkle lights.

I fall into Varg's arms, panting, gasping for breath, my ears thumping, my legs jelly.

"Get them inside. Now!" Varg barks, Mathusi rushing to my side, helping me up the steps.

Alma and Tosh walk down the hallway.

"What's happening?" Alma asks, concern laced around every syllable.

"Take Tosh and Koba," Bett says, handing Alma her keys and her phone. "Drive." She hands her daughter a bag. Alma looks inside.

"Why are our passports in here?"

"Because you're going back home. It's too dangerous –"

"– We're not going anywhere." Alma throws the bag on the

ground. "We stay together."

Bett growls. "Just find somewhere safe."

I watch as the three leave out the back door.

The sirens scream louder; the flashing is right outside the door.

"How can I help you, fine officers?" Varg's voice is silken.

Mathusi pulls me into the loungeroom behind the sofa in front of the large bay window. Pulling the curtain aside, I see two officers dressed in their matching blues.

"We're just here for the girl –"

"Person," Varg scoffs. "Teenager, even. *Faen*, can't anyone in this backwards town get it right?"

Bett slides onto the porch, pulling her shawl over her shoulders, and steps down onto the gravel driveway.

"Why are you here, officers?" Bett asks.

"We have an arrest warrant for Winnifred McTire," the younger of the two says, matter of fact.

Mathusi squeezes my hand. "We can make a run for it, out back. Alma might still be there."

I exhale a stunted breath, squeezing Mathusi's hand back. "No," I mouth, shaking my head. *This is all my fault.*

"Arrest warrant for what?" Varg scoffs, snatching the paper from the officer's hands. "Murder? This is a joke, right?"

"Afraid not. We have proof that puts Winnifred at the scene

of the crime," the young officer adds.

Bett reaches for the paper, both Varg and she searching the paperwork.

"Cloth?" Bett asks.

"Yes. Torn from the jacket of a Randal Anderson. Found after we conducted a search of the accused's previous lodgings."

"This is circumstantial, at best. Fred moved out of that house weeks ago. It could have been planted," Varg spits, tossing the warrant back into the policeman's face.

The young man fumbles with the paper.

The second officer steps forward, a smirk twitching his lips. He stretches his hand out. "Constable Dale, sir."

Varg folds his arms across his chest.

Dale drops his hand. "Well, I'm sure if *Miss* McTire comes down, willingly, to the police station for DNA testing, we can disprove this, and everyone can go home."

"I'm going with them," Varg adds, straightening his shirt, turning to walk back inside.

"That won't be necessary," Dale adds. "It'll be over quick smart."

"That's not how the law works," Varg growls, turning to face the constable.

Constable Dale eyes him up and down. "Fine. But you come on your own. Ensure you get your paperwork in order – all her documentation – before you come. We'll take her now."

"*Them*," Bett grunts, rolling her eyes, then walking back up the steps with Varg.

"You can't go," Mathusi whispers.

"I have to. I've caused so much shit already," I sigh. "Look, if I go, do this DNA thing, they can see I have nothing to do with it, and it'll be over."

"But what if they're part of Garamond's posse?"

"Varg will be there," I offer.

I stand, walking towards the front door, to Varg and Bett.

"I'm sorry. I've been nothing but trouble." My voice is low. "I get it if you guys just wanna go back to Norway," I say, wiping my nose with the back of my wrist. "I'm cursed."

Varg laughs dryly, his hand on my shoulder. "You, Fred, are far from trouble. And we're not going anywhere without you. *Vi er familie.*"

I don't need to know Norwegian to know what he's saying, and I feel a lump form in my throat.

Varg glares out at the flashing lights. "Where's your birth certificate? And the foster papers?" he asks.

"I know where everything is," Mathusi interrupts. I stare at him, my eyebrows raised. "What…?" he says, coyly. "You hide things in the same place I do." He smiles.

I bury my face in my hands, then comb my fingers through

my very tangled hair. "Alright. Let's do this."

Walking out the door and down the steps towards the flashing police lights feels surreal. Constable Dale steps in front of me, and I notice a small silver dagger pinned to the collar of his police blues. He's one of them. A Hunter. He snaps the cuffs around my wrists.

"What the…" I hiss through clenched teeth.

"Silver," Dale whispers in my ear. The younger officer opens the car door, ushering me into the back seat.

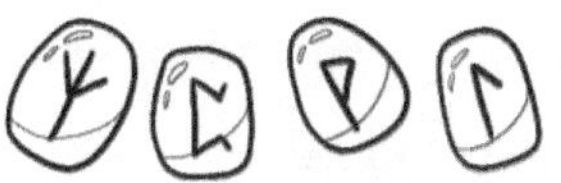

CHAPTER TWENTY-FOUR

I'm certain Constable Dale is deliberately hitting every pothole in the road. My head thuds against the window once more and I let out a soft groan, Dale smirking at me in the rearview mirror. I grimace, adjusting myself in the pleather seat, gritting my teeth against the aching itch in my wrists. Glancing at my hands in my lap, I see the small blisters forming a pustulant bracelet on my skin.

"Comfy back there?" Dale laughs. The other officer laughs along, but it's hollow. I didn't notice a bladed pin on his collar.

I pull the sleeve of my hoodie under the cuffs, like a cottony barrier between me and the silver. It works a little.

The handbrakes crunch, and I watch Dale jump out of the driver's seat, eagerly slamming his door and hurrying past the younger officer before yanking me out of the car. He pulls on my jacket, my cotton barrier leaving me, the silver hissing against my bare skin once more.

Dale escorts me through the double glass doors of the Acacia Hills Police Department. The fluorescent lights are harsh; I'd gotten used to the dark of the night, the dark of the car.

"Taking this one to the back," Dale says to the front desk

clerk, a burly-looking woman with bulging biceps. She's wearing a similar silver pin, and I deflate. How many are there?

"If you need any help, just let me know." The woman grins, buzzing us through a metal gate.

"Oh, Chris, mate," Dale says to the younger officer. "How about you get that paperwork sorted on that drunk and disorderly, hey?" He smiles, viciously. "I got this one."

The young officer nods, his eyes glancing towards me, uncertain, then walks in the opposite direction.

Leading me down a clinical-looking hall, Dale shoves me around a corner and into a windowless room. Sergeant Luis Pine stands at the opposite side of the aluminium table.

"Sit," Sarge grunts.

I fall onto the chair. "I know my rights," I blurt out. "I'm a minor. I don't have to talk until I have my guardian present." I slide my balled-up fists onto the table in front of me. "Where's Varg?"

"Oh, come now, we won't be needing him." A husky voice creeps around the corner. Garamond steps over the threshold and into the room. His eyes are bloodshot, probably from the sand I threw into them.

I shuffle in my seat. "Not sure why you're here, *Grandpa*." I smirk, trying so hard to hide the fact I am absolutely shitting my pants. What have I done? I've walked right into a trap.

Again.

Garamond sneers.

"That other officer, Chris?" I swallow hard, sitting up straight in my chair, trying to appear more confident than I feel. "He's not one of your little followers. He'll know something is suss if I go missing from here." *Please* let me call Garamond's bluff.

"Little runts like you often end up breaking free, doin' a runner. Always drugs," Garamond says, holding a baggy of white powder. "Tsk, tsk, Winnifred McTire. Just like your parents."

"You prick," I spit. "…that's not mine."

"Oh, but I believe Constable Dale, here, found it on your person upon arrest." Garamond grins.

I look over to Sarge, hoping that somewhere, deep inside, he remembers who he is. That he'll break from whatever hold Garamond has on him and get us out of here.

Sarge looks away, scuffing his feet against the edge of the table. "Yup. Dale radioed it in. I took the call," Sarge adds, his eyes still downcast.

Garamond laughs. "See? Now. Back to work," he grunts at Sarge. "Those bloodbags aren't going to move themselves."

I'm certain if Sarge had his tail right now, it'd be between his legs. He sulks from the room, the door slamming heavily behind him.

Wait, bloodbags?

"I'm not talking," I insist.

"Well, that works out well." Garamond lets out a wry laugh and nods to Constable Dale. "We don't want to talk."

I catch the glint of silver as Dale slides a shining piece of metal over his fingers.

A wicked grin smears its way across Garamond's face before he steps forward, forcing a hessian bag over my head. I try to lunge backwards, kicking my legs.

"It burns!" I howl.

"Silver thread," Garamond chuckles, as if he's the smartest piece of shit on earth. "Gotta get creative with you mutts."

Garamond's voice is close. I try again, thrusting my body upwards, the crown of my head connecting with Garamond's chin.

"Fucking bitch!"

I can smell his blood. I lash out again towards the stench.

Sticky steps on the linoleum rush forward. I kick, hoping to connect, but instead I'm met with the full force of Constable Dale's meaty fist of silver, straight to my nose.

The snap and crunch of cartilage makes my stomach churn. The pain fills my head and gushes out of my nose. I can feel the throb in my mouth, the points of my canines piercing through the silver infused hessian bag, and I scream, lunging forwards and grabbing onto Dale's arm, biting down with all my force. He hits me again, square in the temple, as he swears and stumbles backwards. I can hear him falling into the wall opposite.

"Get it out of here!" Garamond yells. "Dump it with the rest. And find Ginny! She needs to see what these animals really are."

Two more people enter the room and I hear the buzz of electricity. *Tasers.*

Then. Nothing.

CHAPTER TWENTY-FIVE

Ugh, my head…

The ground is cold. Hard. Grimy. My body feels as if it's stuck to it, as if I'm a cinderblock, part of the concrete floor. Wait, concrete floor?

My head is pounding, the ache rushing and throbbing in my ears. Bile rises in my throat as I wake further into the pain. I can feel the blood pumping through my face, hear it pulsating with each beat of my heart.

My neck burns. Why? I roll over onto my back and the world spins. The lone halogen light above me flickers and cracks into darkness, and I squint my eyes shut against the roiling room, pressing my hands against my forehead. It's then I realise my wrists aren't cuffed anymore. Trailing my hands down towards the stinging feeling around my neck, a cold burn prickles my fingers.

"Oh, sh…" I recoil, but the fast motion sets me off again, the room spinning. There's no holding it back now, and I manage to move onto my side, the bitterness spewing from my mouth, yellow and sticky.

I reach for my neck again. *A silver collar.*

Haunching over, I'm able to prop myself up on my knees and elbows, rocking back and forth, willing this sickness and pain to go away. The pressure of leaning forwards makes my face throb. Reaching for my nose, I flinch, the dusty air sharp against my teeth as I inhale. My finger traces over the bridge. Don't remember it being *that* crooked. A glob of blood falls from my nose onto the ground with a heavy *splat*.

"Lovely…" my voice croaks.

Sitting back, body slumps against the wall. It's only then I start to take in my surroundings, a new wave of unease washing over me.

"This isn't the cop shop…"

My throat is so dry. I spy a bucket and dish across from me. Crawling forward, I notice the ceramic bowl has a name, like a pet bowl.

Winnifred.

"Oh, fuck right off." I kick the dish away. I don't care how thirsty I am, I'd die of dehydration rather than be that old prick's pet.

I can feel the tears sting behind my eyes. I shut them. Tight. Pushing them back. Pushing down the vomit. Pushing away everything.

Opening my eyes, I breathe. A deep, musty inhale, filling my lungs. I hold it there, as if the air will squeeze out all my fears.

Then scream. I scream out every last molecule of air from my lungs until I feel as though I am a withered husk. The sound doesn't echo, though. The room I'm in isn't empty.

Adjusting to the dim light, I take in the space around me. The entire room's long and rectangular, the walls some kind of stone. It may as well be a tomb. I can just make out in the darkness the shapes on the walls, the heads of boars and kangaroos, mounted like trophies of death. There's a hatch further ahead on the ceiling, stairs cascading down from the trapdoor to this concrete crypt. I'm certain I can hear footsteps pacing the room above.

From where the staircase drops, a rickety bookcase lines the wall. Glass jars, stacked haphazardly, books with tattered spines, and dusty boxes occupy every available inch of the shelves. The jars, covered in a fine layer of dust, catch my attention, glistening with an amber liquid.

I pull myself up and hobble towards the shelves. The stuff in the jars is all wrinkled and pale; a pungent, pickled smell lingers around them. A yellowing plastic container of sharp, jagged incisors labelled *homo sapiens homovorus* sits nestled between wooden chests, each box carved with intricate shapes and letters.

I have seriously stepped into a horror film. I pinch myself. Hard.

"Shit. Wishful thinking. Okay, so, *not* a dream. This is real. What the actual…"

On the opposite wall, in the far corner, stands a wooden bench, its shelves filled with small cardboard boxes and…

"Fuck, yes!" They're covered in dust, but they're vacuum sealed, by the looks of things. "Water."

My legs are feeling a little more awake now, so I'm able to gingerly walk across the room. The familiar sound of rune-stones clinking in my pocket settles me somewhat.

"Guess the douchebag Hunters didn't search me." Small miracles.

Rummaging through the boxes along the workbench, I tear at the plastic, eagerly unscrewing the cap of a water bottle, and guzzle it down. It dribbles and stings, and I cough, but I keep drinking. Wiping my chin, my eyes graze over the remaining boxes. Maybe there's some food or something.

"Bullet casings… can't eat them."

Stepping back to inspect another box below, I nearly trip over a big plastic bucket. Stumbling, I grab onto a pile of hessian bags, the contents spilling across the floor. I bend down.

"Salt? What kind of screwed up Sam and Dean Winchester shit is this?"

The glint of something golden catches my eye, hidden beneath the fallen bag of salt. Bending, I pick up the shining trinket, turning it over in my hand. A hairclip. A chipped gold hairclip with a diamante butterfly at the end.

My breath catches in my throat as I stare at this simple thing. At Cassie's simple thing. I swallow hard, the lump in my throat bobbing, ready to burst from my mouth, my tears soon to follow.

"She was here!" My breath hitches. "It wasn't me. Maybe Ginny was on to something. Maybe Cassie's alive." I run my thumb over the sparkling gems, trying to make sense of what this means. What any of this means.

Teeth grinding together, my jaw clenches, suppressing the explosive wave of sorrow that threatens to claw its way up my throat.

Breathe.

Opening my eyes, I'm back where I started, in the middle of this claustrophobic basement. Is it a basement? Or a dungeon? Either way, besides the sliver of light coming from that little hatch, it's dark. There has to be a light somewhere.

My fingers scrape across the wall, following the shelves and dips. Cold concrete, cold concrete, gritty concrete… plastic. A light switch. I flick the switch and just as the light fills the void, the receding darkness takes my breath away. My stomach sinks into my bowels, groaning and churning.

I fall heavy onto a stack of boxes behind me, my eyes fixed, staring at the horror show in front of me. Monstrously presented in the centre of the painted concrete wall, with two hunting rifles on either side, hangs a large, taxidermy head of a wonderous white wolf, *canis lupus* engraved below it. But there's another word, something else. I manage to get up and step forward, hand shaking, wiping the grime from the plaque.

"MacTíre…"

No. No, it can't be. My insides churn, and those tears I've been pushing down for so much of life, those tears eating their way through my soul, making me hard as ice… melt. Their salty heat dissolves the grief, the sorrow, the denial.

My throat is thick, tight. The silver burns even more as the tears trickle down my cheeks and under the collar, burning against the already blistering wounds.

I sob. The sound bubbles from me until it's an all-consuming wail, gasping for breath, for life, in this rancid room. All that effort to hold them back, in vain. I look up at the wonderous beast before me, my broken nose to its. Or should I say… *hers*.

"Aasta MacTíre."

CHAPTER TWENTY-SIX

I don't know how long I've been down here now. One day. Three. A week. I find myself passing in and out of sleep, if you can even call it sleep. It's tortured and sweaty. I keep having nightmares about that day – the day I went into my parents' bedroom to tell them the cotton candy trees were awake, instead finding them in bed. Dead.

The dreams are twisted now. I dreamt I was hiding in my parents' wardrobe, or maybe it was some secret room. I remember them laughing and felt so overwhelmed with love and joy, I could feel their happiness tickling my skin like butterfly feet dancing all over me. But then those butterflies turned into pinching scorpions, the feeling ripped from me as a shadow blanketed the room – my parent's screams soon followed.

Waking, dreaming. But as my mind explores these nightmares, I've started to ask myself, *am I dreaming, or am I remembering?*

The next dream was in slow motion, watching myself from the corner of the room as my little shape tiptoed through the darkness. I watched as I stretched, reaching for the lamp, and then, as though I finally remember where I am, what I'm watching, my focus turns to the bed. To what lies there. It's as if the fog of memory has shifted and I'm truly seeing it for the first time.

Waking up from that stupid dream, that stupid memory, something has changed. I think back to that darkened room, to the shapes in the bed. Dad had a beard, I'm sure of it. I remember it always scratching me whenever he'd tuck me into bed. And mum had jet-black hair, like me. The murkiness ebbs one more and I clearly see the bodies in the bed. This man is clean shaven… the woman, blonde.

Blinking past the sleep and the dust of this concrete prison, I notice a crumpled shape dropping over the bottom step of the stairs leading to the hatch above. Rubbing my eyes, I sit up and focus; a bag of dog kibble, slashed and scattered, spreads across the floor. My stomach growls – the kibble smells like dog farts and dirt, but I'm so hungry. A lone piece of the dried brown biscuit has rolled beside me. I pick it up and close my eyes. I'd pinch my nose, but it still hurts way too much. I'm certain my face is black and blue.

I crunch.

Individually, it's not so bad. It's like gnawing on a tiny brick of cardboard, if said brick was soaked in stale dog breath.

Scooping up a few stray pieces, I scoff them down. I'm just *that* starving that I honestly don't care.

The mounted wolf's head stares at me, and my heart aches, like a wound that won't stop bleeding, a raw and painful sting that refuses to go away. I've found myself talking to her. Is it really my mum? It can't be. My head is an absolute shit storm of thoughts; I can't gather them, can't corral the cats running around my brain.

"That newspaper article, the reports said…"

I shake my head, popping a few more pieces of dog biscuit in my mouth. How can I trust the news? How can I trust anything, or anyone? Did my parents OD? Were they murdered? Blonde hair, black hair… And if it wasn't Mum and Dad in the bed, who were they? And where were my parents? Was what I'd been told all these years true, that they'd run? Left me? Had they really been junkies, fleeing to save their own arses – too high to remember their own child, asleep in their bed? Alone?

I run my fingers through the knots in my hair, pulling at the roots, trying to get my thoughts in some kind of order. Writing helps. Writing always helps. But how the hell am I going to write in here?

Looking back over at the workbench, I notice a drawer towards the back. If I can just find a scrap of paper, a pen, pencil, something.

The sudden movement of standing shifts the silver collar around my next and I can't help but scream as the metal pops another blister.

Push through, Fred. I can feel the wolf's eyes on me, and my sinuses are on fire again, burning with tears aching to be free.

Rummaging through the drawer, I find an old receipt and the nub of a carpenter's pencil. Something inside me jumps. Maybe I have a little hope after all.

"What do you know, Fred…" my voice trails off, listening to the thoughts shouting in my head, each concept, each idea vying for my attention. Sitting on a pile of boxes, I lean against the bench, the pencil scribbling against the small piece of paper.

"My parents died when I was five," I add to the timeline on the paper. "Black hair, slash, blonde hair."

Then, like a crack of a thunderous storm, when light and sound converge, Ginny's words come rushing from my memory and onto the paper.

"Ginny's parents died when she was young, too. What did she say about them?" I squeeze my eyes shut, rocking back and forth, trying to focus.

"I don't remember Dad. Only through photos. I was only two. A hunting accident or something… Mum died when I was five. I don't really know what happened. I don't have much to remember her by, besides her name – my middle name."

"Malena." I swallow hard, ignoring the hiss of the silver,

ignoring my bruised face, ignoring the pain coursing through me. "Mal."

The great white wolf on the wall beside me seems to sigh, as if a weight has finally been lifted, as if a truth has finally been told.

Ginny found those files, gave them to me. She knows. She knows what Garamond did. And she's still there… with him. With that monster.

Any pain I felt, any semblance of fear, dries up, replaced with white-hot rage.

For so long I had been told half-truths and lies, and in turn, I had been alone.

Then Ginny had pranced into my life like some kind of pink apparition of hope.

There's that word again. *Hope.*

Then everything had gone to shit.

I'm not the problem. I'm not cursed.

A lone cricket hops across the concrete floor and into the bag of dried dog food, chirping happily.

I feel the anger inside me simmer. Staring down at my hands, I realise I've been clutching the runestones. I don't remember taking them out of my pocket. I feel the rage retreat. Not hiding. Waiting.

My fingers instinctively reach for my mouth. No weird wolf

teeth. They trail down my neck, over the sting of the collar, rubbing at the skin not yet scorched. No bristles of fur. I roll the stones in my hand and feel a warmth glow from them. Despite that boiling wrath, I didn't turn.

CHAPTER TWENTY-SEVEN

Dystopian world within my own mind

Yearning to be free of these

Shackles that have been

Placed upon me.

Heavy with the pain of not belonging,

Of not wanting to be in this form.

Righteous are those who try to tell me who

I am, yet know nothing of the

Anguish that swells within me.

CHAPTER TWENTY-EIGHT

The hatch above the stairs looms over me, a stubborn guardian that stands as my sole beacon of escape from this underground abyss. I've already tried picking the lock with some pliers I found down here, but they proved useless against its unyielding surface, the warped metal and wood sneering in defiance, as though mocking my attempts to break free.

Dread surges through my veins; even if I manage to break free, what chaotic mess awaits me on the surface? But underneath that fear, the simmering rage, the fire stoked by revelation still burns bright. The need to save Ginny, to protect her, is an ember burning, urging me to find a way out.

I have to keep her safe.

Staring at the hatch, I down the rest of the water, the plastic crumpling in my fingers as I squeeze the last drops onto my tongue. Water is getting low now. My eyes shift from the hatch to the old toilet behind a stack of boxes. I wonder if the water in the cistern is alright to drink? I cringe at the thought, but then again, I've been eating dog food for however long; I'm sure toilet water is the least of my problems.

"Going full dog." My voice mimics Mathusi's, and I laugh.

It's a sad sound, but I have to hold on to those moments.

Ginny's freckled face dances through my thoughts every time I close my eyes. I can hear Mathusi's laughter in the silence of this tomb. I'm almost certain I can hear his voice now, muffled, full of worry. I sigh. Maybe I'm going mad.

The hatch above the staircase creaks.

"Hello?" my voice rasps. I step back into the darkness, bumping the shelves of jars and boxes, a wooden crate falling to the ground. I watch as the wood snaps, dried herbs spreading across the floor.

"Shit…" I sneeze as the debris flicks up into my face.

The hatch rattles again, a thud, followed by a voice beyond. Scuttling across the concrete floor, I run for the far wall.

The guns.

Lunging for one of the mounted rifles bordering my mother's mane, I pull it down, my eyes pinned to the hatch, fingers haphazardly loading salt shells into the chamber. I drop the cartridge. And another – my fingers too eager, yet not knowing what to do. I've never loaded a bloody gun, let alone held or even been near one before. I pause – shit, I don't want this backfiring. Literally. I know it's only salt, but I like my fingers and face where they're at. Emptying the barrel, the final shell clatters to the floor.

Turning the rifle around and grabbing the long muzzle

instead, I swing the weapon through the air like a baseball bat.

"Yeah, this'll do. Blunt force kinda damage is more my style."

I flail the rifle in the air, eyes fixed on the stairs. Another creak, followed by the scaping of metal as the hatch opens, and something human-sized and heavy tumbles down the stairs. The hatch slams shut again, and the shape in front of me groans.

"Oi, fucker!" Stepping back, I grab a handful of shell casings and throw them at the moaning blob.

"Oi, stop it, ya goof."

Mathusi.

The rifle clunks to the floor, my knees skidding on the dusty concrete as I slide towards him, my hands rushing over him.

"Are you hurt; are you okay?"

Mathusi sits up, batting my hand away as I lift his shirt, inspecting him. No blood. That's good.

"Besides the wicked headache, I'm okay," he groans.

He's here. His hair's matted and frizzed, his face a little bruised, but he's here.

Every ache, every fear and worry, is shattered seeing this boy, my friend, my *family*, in front of me. My arms wrap around his neck. This is real. I stroke his matted curls, pulling out twigs, but I don't let go. Mathusi gasps.

"Less grippy, Fred," he chokes. "And what the hell is

burning me?"

I loosen my hug, my arms drop, but my fingers still tangle themselves with his, his hand in mine. He sighs heavily, looking at me through wet eyes. It's then his eyes widen, falling upon the silver collar around my neck.

"My admirer gifted me a lovely necklace." I grimace. Mathusi half laughs, tearing the sleeve of his T-shirt and gently sliding it between the silver collar and my blistering skin.

"I found you," he whispers.

"Took you long enough." I snort, a cough itching at my throat.

Mathusi rolls his eyes then pulls me closer, wincing against the hissing silver, and hugs me with everything he's got.

"I'm never letting go." My voice is barely a whisper in the crook of his neck. I can feel his cheeks rise, the smile on his face pressing against my own. The silver sizzles, but neither of us seems to care.

"Good."

We sit together like this for some time. I'm afraid to let go in case, well... in case I get torn away again, but the rumbling growl from Mathusi's stomach shatters the moment.

"Sorry. All this rescuing business makes a wolf hungry." Mathusi smirks, trying to lighten the mood.

"Okay, first off." I push myself away, folding my arms

against my chest. "Rescue?" I wrinkle my nose at him and look around the concrete cellar, raising a brow.

Mathusi stifles a laugh. "Fine. We *attempted* a rescue, then."

Rolling my eyes, I continue. "The hungry part, however." I stand, dragging the opened bag of dried dog food towards him. "I got you, Chuckles."

Mathusi's laughing face drops. "You gotta be kidding me."

"Oh, but wait, there's more!" I jog towards the darkened corner of the room, the ceramic scraping as I kick the bowl to him. "My own personalised drinking bowl!"

Mathusi turns the bowl over in his hands. "Winnifred," he reads. "That is all kinds of fucked up."

"Makes you wonder how long he's been planning this, huh?" I pause, uncertain if I want to know the answer to my next question. "How long have I been down here?"

Mathusi's shoulders sag. "Around a week." He takes my hand, pulling me down to my knees. He lifts my lip, counting my teeth. "Good. We were worried he'd pulled your canines out." His eyes skate over the collar again, at the blisters oozing on my skin. Mathusi reaches, his fingers searching for a way to release the silver shackle from my neck.

"I've tried. No use." I rub at the welting skin. "And as for your horrifying tooth fairy, no one's been down here to do anything."

"So, you've been here on your own this whole time?"

I glance over my shoulder. "Not entirely?" It comes out more like a question. I sigh through my nose. "Stand up."

"Why…?" Mathusi raises a brow.

"Just…" I stand myself, stepping forwards and taking his hand, dragging him to his feet.

I enter the darkness and find the familiar plastic switch, flicking it on. Mathusi squints at the sudden glow, and I watch him, unable to look behind me. His eyes widen, hands slowly edging to his mouth, covering it, as if making a noise will awaken the creature mounted in front of him. His eyes finally find mine. Stepping forward, Mathusi places a hand on my shoulder, squeezing it, his eyes drifting back to the lone wolf staring at us.

"Aasta MacTíre." He reads it again, frowning. "Wait. It can't be."

"Why not? Cover-ups and conspiracies seems to be the bread and butter of these Hunter creeps." I remember the diamante butterfly clip, and, sliding it from the workbench, toss it towards Mathusi. "Case in point."

Mathusi sniffs it.

"Dude!"

"It's Cassie's!" he exclaims.

"Yeah, I could've told you that, you grot. You don't have to sniff everything."

A smirk twitches at the corner of Mathusi's mouth, though it quickly falls as he places the butterfly back in my hand. "I'm sorry, Fred."

I exhale heavily "Yeah."

I stop, something Mathusi said before finally registering. "Wait. *We?*"

Mathusi stares blank-faced. "We? What?"

"You said before that *we* attempted a rescue…"

"Yeah, like, ten conversations ago," he laughs. Mathusi looks up at the great white wolf, then back to me, and sighs. "Ginny and I –"

"– I'm sorry? Ginny's here?" I run to the stairs, energy renewed, adrenaline pumping, my shoulder ramming the hatch. "Where is she?" I grunt as my should hits the wood. "She can't stay with him!" I yell over the sound of my body slamming against the hatch.

Mathusi grabs my arm. "You're gonna hurt yourself."

"You don't understand," I say, pushing him away, cupping my hands around my mouth, yelling Ginny's name through the cracks of the wood.

"I do understand, Fred, I do." Mathusi takes me hand, and his brown eyes, full of worry, find mine. "I looked over those files Ginny gave you, that day at the library." Mathusi reaches into his pocket and hands me a folded piece of paper.

My arms drop to my sides, and I turn, my backside falling heavily onto the top step. Mathusi squeezes himself next to me.

Staring down at the paper, I unfold it gently.

"A photo?"

"Trigger warning, it's a crime scene photo."

Air hisses through my teeth as I inhale sharply. "I don't know if I can do this –"

"– just. Look."

Unfolding the thick paper, I see my crochet mitten in the far corner, number cards dotted around the room. Then the bodies in the bed. A man, a woman. No beard. Blonde hair.

"It's not them," I breathe. "It's not my parents. It was never them." I look back up to the wolf mounted on the wall, then back at the creased photo in my hand, and I know. "Malena," I gasp. "That's Ginny's mum, isn't it?"

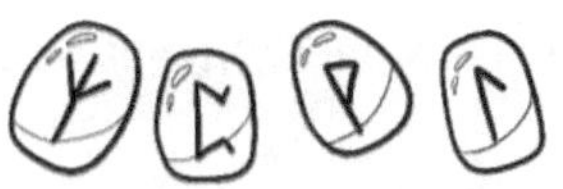

CHAPTER TWENTY-NINE

Mathusi shuffles on the step next to me and nods, his eyes downcast.

Pain fills me once more, a mixture of heartbreaking sadness and confusion, laced in anger. I wipe at a stray tear with the back of my hand.

"Alright, so… shit." I swallow, trying to collect my thoughts. I fold the photo and slide it into my back pocket. "Okay, one crisis at a time. How did you even find me?"

"Varg and Bett had been running circles trying to find you. Alma and Tosh even scouted this place midweek." He takes my hand in his, and I listen.

They'd searched all week. The cops had told Varg and Bett I'd done a runner, *typical foster brat shit*, the police had said. Apparently, there's not only a missing persons alert out for me, but an arrest warrant, too. Lovely.

"Then Ginny rocked up this morning," Mathusi continues. "She looked wrecked, said she hitchhiked from Outwash."

"She what?"

"I told her she was a nut for hitching, but she made it," Mathusi says, as if that makes the fact she hitched a good idea.

"And as she said," he continues, "it was better than being locked up."

My blood surges, frothing with a mix of anger and disbelief. "Garamond locked her up?"

Mathusi looks around. "I think her setup was a little more modern, and less –"

"Horror vibes," we both say. Laughter trickles past our lips despite the bleakness of it all. It feels good to have him here.

"How did you know I was here if Alma and Tosh had already sussed it out?"

"I had my suspicions, but it was Ginny."

"Little Miss Veronica Mars." I snort, the sound catching in my throat, and I cough.

"Pretty much. She found a map – "

I swallow hard, the irritation worsening.

"You alright?" he asks. I nod, trying to clear my throat, waving my hand for him to continue.

"Yeah, a map," he continues, raising a concerned brow. "A map that showed where all the old war tunnels were, and…" His voice trails off as the tickle in the back of my throat violently morphs into a suffocating grip on my chest.

"Fred…" Mathusi's eyes are wide, frantically searching me, trying to find the source. "Is it a panic attack?"

With each breath, my airways constrict like a tight coil.

"Take slow, deep breaths, try to stay calm," he urges, his voice steady and reassuring. "Focus on breathing in through your nose and out through your mouth. You've got this, just keep breathing with me."

He moves closer, one hand gently resting on my back, offering support as I struggle to control my breathing. I follow his guidance, attempting to mimic his rhythm. But I can't. It must be the dust, the grime, the filth down here.

Or…

"Herbs," I wheeze. I remember the wooden boxes on the shelves, amongst the jars and gross curiosities. A small crate falling. My hand haphazardly waves towards the shelves.

"Wolfsbane," Mathusi growls, seeing the remnants of the plant spilled on the floor.

My hands clutch at my chest, attempting to alleviate the pressure crushing my lungs. The sound of my wheezing coughs fills the stale air of the cellar. My eyes water, not only from the physical strain but also from the fear that this relentless onslaught might never cease.

Mathusi pulls his shirt up over his mouth and nose. "We've gotta get out of here."

Contorting into a coughing fit, thick mucus fills my throat, and I fall to the concrete ground, hacking, gagging, vomiting the viscous phlegm, the force pushing the slime through my nose. The claustrophobic nightmare wraps its suffocating grip around me once more, my airways constricting.

"This…" I wheeze, my voice struggling against the tightness in my chest. "Stupid…" The air feels so thin, each word a labour to utter. "Collar!"

Panicking, I claw at my neck, fingers scrabbling at the silver. It feels like it's tightening, crushing my windpipe. Pulling desperately at the metal, I can feel the skin scraping off my neck, gathering beneath my nails. My vision blurs, and my throat feels raw and ravaged.

"In through your nose, Fred. Out through your mouth," Mathusi orders, kicking the dried leaves and stems under the bookcase.

"What's…" I rasp. "…plan?"

Mathusi rummages through the shelves, jars clinking, before grabbing a small glass vial. Dragging me to the opposite end of the room, he pops the lid. "Open," he barks.

"Open…" I breathe. "What?" I push his hand away, the liquid in the bottle splashing.

"*Ipomoea alba,*" he offers again.

"Bless you?" I cough.

"Don't be a dick, Fred, just drink."

I take the vial. The liquid seems to shine in the small bottle, and I drink. I open my mouth and let the starry water wash the wolfsbane away.

"Ipomoea alba," Mathusi says again, as if I'm still meant to know what that means. A wry smile edges onto his face. "Guess listening to Mum natter on about flowers and herbs paid off. It means *moonflower*. The elixir is made by blending moonflower petals with water blessed by the full moon."

I feel the imaginary fist clenching my lungs ease, air freely coming and going, the darkness at the corners of my vision fading.

"Thank you."

Mathusi reaches out, squeezing my hand. "Always."

"Thank you will never feel like enough," I cough softly, still catching my breath. "You've saved me so many times. And here you are, again, in danger, because of me." I can feel the old familiar pang of guilt creep up my spine.

"Don't go there," Mathusi says, knowingly.

I nod, not wanting to delve into the abyss of guilt that threatens to consume me. I quickly regain composure, ensuring my emotions remain hidden, even as my heart overflows with appreciation for this fast friend who's been there for me, no matter the cost.

"So, what's the plan, how do we get out?" I try to stand, though my legs shake, the oxygen still finding its way to the rest of my body. "You mentioned tunnels? Ginny must have had some clue…"

"We didn't quite get that far into the, uh, plan. She just said the tunnels were our best chance," he sighs. "Then Sarge found us snooping around the fence line of the property and turned us in. He took Ginny to Garamond, and, well" – he spreads his arms – "here I am!"

I force a tight-lipped smile. "Right."

"I'm guessing in the time you've been stuck down here, you haven't been able to find a way to get out?" He looks around the room.

"Oh, yeah, totally. *So* many ways out. I just like it here. Horror chic," I say, deadpan. I point to the hatch. "Only way in or out."

"Hey…" Mathusi stands, walking back towards the white wolf on the far wall. "Do you see how one of the upper canines hangs lower than the other?" he asks, looking over his shoulder at me, then back to the wolf.

"Huh." After staring at her all this time, you'd think I'd have noticed. I move in front of the wolf, combing my fingers through the dense white fur bristling from her neck, when a memory dislodges. I see my hand – my tiny hand, with its tiny fingers – coursing through the same thick fur, my tiny pink nose nuzzling into it.

"Mum…" I whisper.

The clatter of a stone hitting the ground draws our attention. Mathusi picks up the round, flat moonstone, placing it in my hand. "That's how it landed."

"*Perthro*," I sigh, looking down at the rune, then back to Mathusi. "Guess we're taking a chance!"

Slipping the stone back in my pocket, I turn to face the wolf – to face my mother – and trace my finger along the length of the tooth, feeling the subtle ridges and contours from the gum to the pointed tip. The tooth wiggles, ever so slightly.

"It moved!" I look at Mathusi, eyes wide.

Mathusi nods eagerly, his eyes darting between me and the tooth.

With my finger on the sharpest point of the canine, I push upwards, the tooth retreating into the gum, followed by a metallic whir and clank behind the wall. The grating sound of rock on cement groans as the wall shifts forward, dust billowing from the opening.

Mathusi grabs the rifle that fell to the floor, filling his pockets with shells. "Not that it'll do much – thing's as old as time itself. But…" The rifle clicks as he slides the salt buckshot into the chamber, flakes of rust drifting down onto the ground. "It'll do. Just in case."

"Wait," I whisper. I remember seeing a torch among the grossness of wrinkly bits on the shelves. "Bingo!" The light flashes on.

Mathusi pulls the hidden door backwards, just enough for us to slide through. The tunnel ahead smells of dampness and soil.

"You first," I whisper to Mathusi.

"You have the torch." He tuts. "You light the way."

"Yeah, but, like, you have the gun."

Mathusi sighs. "Together?"

I shine the torch down the tunnel. "Looks wide enough."

We step over the threshold, hip to hip, and shuffle down the dark, dank, corridor.

CHAPTER THIRTY

Navigating the frigid, narrow tunnel, its eerie darkness pressing in, I'm beginning to second-guess our decision.

"You reckon we should've tried breaking the hatch first?" I mutter, my teeth chattering in the cold.

Mathusi shakes his head. "We couldn't stay in that room. Between the wolfsbane and who knows what else was on those shelves…" He adjusts his hold on the rifle. "Anyways, Ginny said our best bet were the tunnels, so, here we are."

The damp air clings to my skin, and the faint scent of mildew fills my nose. This never-ending corridor is starting to creep me out.

I've lost all concept of time – one week I'd been stuck in that room – so us walking down this musty old passageway – we could have been walking for five minutes, or five hours. This zombie hip shuffle we're doing doesn't help.

"We're walking at a snail's pace," I whisper to Mathusi.

He glances at me, his eyes reflecting the dim light. "Well, we can't exactly go running off into the darkness. Who knows what kind of traps are down here."

Valid. It'd be just our luck we find a possible way of escape, only to run off into a pit of spikes. Or get our leg caught in a bear trap. Or have some Indiana Jones dart get us in the jugular.

"Wait." I stop, sniffing. I inhale deeply, the cold air seeping into my lungs, carrying with it a scent I can't mistake, musky and wild. "I smell wolves."

"I know. I've smelt it since the last bend."

"Do you reckon it's your lot?"

Mathusi stops. I'm certain I can see his ears twitch in the shadows of the torchlight. He inhales through his nose.

"I can smell Rueth." Mathusi sniffs again. "I swear, she bathes in patchouli."

Resuming our slow, shuffling walk, listening to the scuff of our feet, my thoughts drift to Mathusi's cousins, my cousins, the other wolves. How long have they been missing, and why hasn't anyone heard anything? Usually, gossip spreads quickly through a small town like Acacia Hills, but there's been nothing about this.

"So, there's Aksel," I whisper, recollecting the pack. "And you mentioned Rueth just now."

Mathusi adjusts the butt of the rifle in his armpit. "Then there's Rex and Ema."

"And Sarge," I growl, remembering the man who betrayed us. "Where does Sarge fit into it all then?" I press. "And, dude, is his name really Luis Pine? Like, Lou Pine… *Lupine*?" I stifle a laugh, trying to keep the mood light despite our dire situation.

Mathusi's lips twitch. "That should have been a sign, right?"

"You think he was working with Garamond from the start?"

We shuffle in silence a few extra crabwalks.

"Probably," Mathusi sighs, confirming my suspicion.

I come to a sudden stop. "Wait."

Mathusi pulls the hammer back on the rifle with a loud *click* that echoes down the corridor. "What is it?"

"No…" I gently push the muzzle down, urging him to lower the weapon. Mathusi complies, adjusting the gun and returning the bolt with a *clunk*.

"So, there's Aksel…" I can sense Mathusi's exasperation building.

Mathusi groans. "Are you going mad? We literally *just* had this conversation."

I shush him and focus my thoughts. "Aksel. Then Rueth, Ema, and Rex. What's their pack name again?"

"Rustmane," Mathusi responds, his voice low and patient.

"The book Ginny sent me…" I begin, my voice trailing off as the pieces start to click into place. "There were initials, letters, and…" I pause, searching for the right word. "Some kind of measurement being tracked."

"What are you on about?" Mathusi rests on the rifle like a cane.

"The book, it had heaps-old writing in it; some of it looked French, maybe? Older. But the recent stuff. It was codes – AW, RUW, EW and REW… negative, neutral, positive, positive."

"It's official. You've gone mad." Mathusi laughs, the sound trailing off as the realisation dawns on his face. "Those initials…"

"Exactly! What if Garamond *was* working on a cure? AW was a negative. Does that mean it didn't take? EW and –"

"– Ema and Rex. EW is Ema, and you said REW after? That's gotta be Rex."

"Yeah, Ema and Rex had *positive* after their log entry."

"But the cure is a crock of shit," Mathusi scoffs. "It's just another means of controlling us." He picks up the rifle again and slides it under his arm. "Come on. This tunnel's gotta end soon. Or open somewhere."

I sniff the air once more. "I can smell the patchouli now, too."

Mathusi nods. "Then let's follow the smell of hippie and hope it's a way out."

I can't help but think of that book, of the list. It had gone on and on, the same codes, different measurements. Aksel's had come up negative every time, whatever that meant. If it's not a cure, then what is it?

A sudden cough echoes down the darkened hall, the sound

scuttling off the rocky walls. I dip the torch to our feet.

"Turn it off," Mathusi whispers. "Give it a bit, your eyes will adjust."

Adjust. Pfft. I close my eyes, opening them to darkness. I squint, then squeeze my eyelids shut, opening them again, expecting a world of vision.

"Wait for it…" Mathusi whispers.

Closing my eyes a third time, it's then I notice something I hadn't quite picked up before. There's a general dampness that anyone would notice down here, but this was almost like a separate note, like one musical note of a chord. I could smell the moss growing in the grooves of the rocks and bricks that line the corridor. Some held deeper notes of soil and dirt, while others were fresh and, well… green. *I can smell green?*

I open my eyes and the corridor is alight with sounds and scents. I watch as the shapes of water droplets, dripping from the roof, dribble down the cracks of the walls, lighting up each groove as they make their way to the floor below. The earthy scent of dirt is like a dark, brooding plum, whereas the moss and sprigs of weeds cast a forest green light, turning vibrant lime when a droplet of water spills onto them. The sounds and smells work in harmony to create a deep glow.

The cough pulses ahead. "I can see it!" my voice echoes down the passageway.

"Shhh!" Mathusi clamps his hand over my mouth. He adjusts the rifle, leading the way towards the sound.

Edging down the passageway towards the sweet, musky smell of patchouli, the dripping watery glow as our guide, we come to a sudden halt.

"Wait, what? The tunnel just ends?" Mathusi bangs the butt of the rifle against the muddied wall.

"But the smells. The cough…" I scratch at the mud, trying to find purchase. "Maybe there's another secret entry or something." I force my shoulder against the wall. Another cough sounds. Closer.

"It's right behind here!" I grab Mathusi. "This has gotta be an old door, or something. Come on. Help me!"

We take turns slamming our shoulders against the mud and muck, and there's a definite crack and creak of wood with each heavy bang. Mathusi and I stare at each other, and with one last heave, we slam both of our bodies against the wall, cracking through the mud and wood, tumbling through to the other side into a pile of debris and dust.

CHAPTER THIRTY-ONE

The woody scent of patchouli isn't the only smell to greet us as Mathusi and I tumble into the dimly lit room. The pungent, fetid stench of waste assaults my senses. I cover my mouth and nose, holding back the bile rising in my throat.

"What stinks?" I manage to mumble, my voice muffled behind my fingers. I open my mouth as little as possible. I don't know what's worse, the smell, or the fact I can taste it.

My eyes jerk around the room – the walls are all tiled, covered in grime and mould. A fluorescent bulb flickers further ahead. A smattering of rubbish and blankets are bundled in each far corner.

"Oh, no…" Mathusi's voice is barely a whisper, but he hurries ahead towards one of the piles of trash.

My eyes follow, and it's then I realise.

Not rubbish.

Not blankets.

People.

Wolves.

"It's Ema and Rueth." Mathusi's hands glide over their bodies, checking their wrists, their necks. He presses his ear to each of their chests. "They're alive… but barely."

I shuffle towards the pile in the opposite corner.

"Two more here!" I say, kneeling, pulling the neck of my shirt up over my nose, trying to stave away the smell of shit that's embedded itself into the walls, floor, and ceiling. Mathusi slides up next to me, his hands and face performing the same movements as before.

"They're alive."

A stare down at the dormant faces. "Who are they?"

"Rex and Aksel." Mathusi points to each man.

I stare at their emaciated faces, their limp ginger-and-grey peppered beards.

Mathusi's body tenses beside mine, his back rigid. "We have to get them out of here." His voice shakes, eyes staring at the closed door in front of us.

I place a hand on his shoulder. "We just can't go opening that. We have no idea what or who's behind it," I whisper.

His glistening eyes find mine. Mathusi purses his lips. "Fine."

Standing, I brush the dirt from my legs and hands, and move towards the door. "It's wood, so that's good, I guess. Maybe we could shoot through it?"

Mathusi, eyes still fixed on his cousins, says, "No. It's just salt buckshot in the rifle. They won't do shit. Plus, too loud, remember?"

I sigh, my fingers tracing over the grooves of the wood when I feel an indent, like a covered-up hole. I poke at it with my finger, and it cracks easily beneath my prodding.

"Mathusi." I wave him over, pointing to the coin-sized hole. "You listen. You're better at it than me."

Shuffling towards to the door, he presses his ear against the gap.

A shallow breath sounds behind me. A rustle.

"Pup…" the voice is raspy and barely a sound at all, more like the scratch of sandpaper.

Turning, I see a glassy eye staring at me. "Aksel…" I breathe. There's something familiar about the way he looks at me, the orange in his beard. "You're the beef jerky dog – or, uh, dingo," I stumble over my words. "And I saw you, at the campground."

A faint smile twitches at the corner of Aksel's mouth, and he nods. "You found us."

The silver collar is really starting to burn now, and I find myself tugging at the metal. I watch Aksel's eyes gloss over the shining choker around my neck.

"You're trapped…" Aksel breathes. "Like us." He coughs, the sound wet and thick.

"Aksel!" Mathusi's voice cuts through the murk of the room,

and he's kneeling next to the man, hands sweeping over him. "What has he done to you?" Mathusi's voice shakes.

"The cure…" Aksel coughs again, his words mumbled. "*Je wouj.*" He breathes heavily, his eyes flutter, and he's asleep again.

"Jay Wooj?" My face scrunches. Again with this name. "And what about the cure?" I stare back at the skeletal bodies. *Is this what the cure does?*

"I dunno," Mathusi grunts, standing. "But we have to get them out of here." He walks back to the door, tapping on the wood. "I think we could knock this down. I can't hear anyone on the other side, but I can hear water."

I look back down the darkened corridor from where we came, my eyes following the ceiling and the direction we walked. "It could be the river, or the creek?" I offer, thoughts racing. "Garamond's property backs onto the reserve and the campground."

"Which means a way out." Mathusi beams.

I nod emphatically, ignoring the sizzling skin at my neck.

"Alright, aim for that hole. The door's weakest there." Mathusi points at the dented wood, then thrusts his shoulder against it. The wood creaks beneath the force. I take a run at it too, my body connecting with the now-splintering door. My shoulder aches, my neck burns, my head is throbbing, but I keep going. I can hear the water, now, too. Up above and off in the distance. I know that sound. After nights of walking the campground, I know the sound of the trickling creek.

Mathusi pulls me back, his leg lifting, the sole of his boot slamming into the door with a deep snap, the door giving way.

The next room is a little brighter, and I shield my eyes, the dust settling over a table and chairs, an old refrigerator, and a makeshift stove. The walls are lined with shelves, filled with tins and jars and bottles. Reserves.

"This is a bunker," Mathusi says, just as the thought pops into my own mind.

Spying a giant plastic container, sealed and full of water, I drag it off the shelf.

"Of course Garamond has one in his own backyard," Mathusi growls, walking the length of the room towards a heavy cast-iron door.

I wrangle the jug of water, unscrewing the cap, the tepid liquid spilling all over me. Without a second thought, I lug the water towards Aksel, holding out the bottle to him before taking a sip for myself.

"Fred…" Mathusi looks over his shoulder, my eyes meeting his, and I follow his arm to the rusted handle in his hand.

"Is it…?" *open,* I think, afraid to finish the sentence out loud. I half stand, scurrying towards my friend and the metal door.

Please be open, please be open.

Mathusi exhales heavily through his nose, gripping the rusty door-handle, and pulls.

CHAPTER THIRTY-TWO

The sound of creaking metal grates in my ears, and I can't help but grit my teeth, bracing myself against the screeching onslaught. My eyes take a moment to adjust to the bright light streaming through the door.

Stepping out of the dark, damp bunker, Mathusi by my side, weapon at the ready, a sense of relief washes over me. After a week stuck in that horrid tomb, the warmth of the setting sun is like a shock to the system, and my eyes flutter closed, holding back the salty sting. The brightness, even of this late afternoon sun, glows against my eyelids, turning my world a mottled red.

With eyes still shut, I take in the sensation of the sun's rays on my skin and inhale the earthy smell of the bush around me, of eucalyptus in the air, and the crisp smell of the trickling creek. I've never felt so alive, and there's no holding back the ocean of tears I'm scrunching behind my eyelids. Tears stream down my face, falling over my chapped lips. It stings, but it's real. This is real. I'm real, and I'm alive.

Trees sway in the breeze, and a kookaburra laughs in the distance. It's all so beautiful, so perfect. I feel like I'm experiencing it all for the first time. I turn back to the bunker, and a shiver runs down my spine. The thought of going back in there fills me with dread, but…

"We need to get those people out."

Mathusi nods. "Agreed. We gotta find a way to get Aksel and the others out of there."

My thoughts race back to the pickled jars and cans on the shelves. "There was rope back there. Maybe if we broke the chairs and tied them together, we could make something to pull them along?" I run back inside, grabbing the rope. Mathusi follows, the rifle under his arm as he breaks one of the chairs inside, then drags two more out onto the path.

Tying the rope around the jagged edges of the splintered wood, the makeshift sled begins to take shape. Each knot tightens with a satisfying tug. With every pull and cinch, I can feel my hope renew. We're going to win.

"I'll see who we should move first," Mathusi says, when the crunch of footsteps startles us. The sound is uncomfortably close. Mathusi grows tense, and I see the fear in his eyes.

He takes my hand, and we quietly move, hiding behind a nearby tree, peering out to see a figure emerging from the bushes. It's a Hunter, that bastard from before, at the station. Constable Dale. My nose throbs at the memory. The glint of the afternoon sun pings off his holstered taser. We don't have any weapons other than the stupid rifle full of salt, and to be honest,

I don't want to engage in a fight unless it's absolutely necessary. We watch as he scans the area, looking for any signs of movement. For us.

"Come on, we can slip back inside. At least then, if he comes in, we can take him by surprise," Mathusi whispers.

We creep towards the bunker, stepping over the threshold, one of us on either side of the opened door. No point trying to close it; the noise will just draw attention. I spy a leg of a broken chair and grab it, wringing the wood in my hands, watching Dale in the distance.

"He's getting closer," my voice rasps.

"Just wait…" Mathusi croaks back.

His footsteps are growing louder, heavier, with each crunch on the dirt, making his way down the path to the open door. I watch as he unbuttons the taser from his belt, my eyes darting to Mathusi, then back to the approaching hunter.

"On the count of three," Mathusi mouths, the sounds coming out sticky. I nod.

Then footsteps, louder, and fast approaching, running towards us, but, from behind? I stand, spinning on my feet, as a fist connects with my jaw and I fall back against the wall.

Mathusi growls and yells, the thud of metal connecting as Mathusi swings the gun at the assailant. I shake my head, as if the motion will reset my spinning mind, and I lunge at Dale now running through the bunker door, grabbing onto his back, my hands latching on his face, fingers digging into his eyes and nose. His arms flail about, trying to grab me, but I bite. Hard. Tearing flesh from his collarbone. He screams, thrusting himself backwards against the wall, me taking the brunt of it. The wind leaves me as I fall, gasping for air.

"Enough!" the voice echoes from the other room.

Mathusi falls to the ground, clambering towards me, his arms around me. He's lost the gun. I've lost my stupid wooden leg. Through bleary eyes it's then I see him.

"You three have caused quite a fuss," Garamond sneers.

Three?

I blink hard, and notice Sarge holding Mathusi's rifle, his face bloodied. Sarge and Garamond must have come through the tunnels.

I notice a shape lingering behind Garamond, its pink joggers all muddy. A sob grips my heart, my throat.

"Ginny…" I gasp, fire racing through me, and I hurriedly kneel, kicking up dust and dirt, trying to gain purchase to crawl towards her, the pieces of my shattered heart pulsing with life.

Garamond charges, the heel of his boot finding my nose.

"Grandad, no!" Ginny's voice is wet with tears.

"They're monsters, Gin. And I'll prove it. Then you'll see," he laughs, the sound all black and twisted. "Then you'll know!"

Garamond grabs the rifle from Sarge. "Get the chains, dog!"

Sarge sulks to the back of the room and as he returns, the sound of scraping metal follows. I stare at the chains, at his sizzling hands. *Silver.*

"Tie 'em up, boys," Garamond smiles, stepping over Mathusi and out towards the growing dusk. "Full moon tonight. Let's get these beasts to show their true colours, hey?"

I can see Sarge's nostrils flare, the chains still in his hands.

"You don't have to do this…" Mathusi pleads.

"Yes, he does," Garamond growls.

Sarge grunts and wraps the chains around my ankles and wrists, hog-tying Mathusi and I, before stepping away. Garamond pats him on the back, slipping a small white tablet into his bloody hands. Sarge nods, popping it into his mouth.

The chains burn, and my already blistering skin sizzles even more. I try to pull my sleeves down under them, for some kind of relief, but it's pointless.

"Dale, drag 'em out to the posts and chain 'em up, good and tight."

I watch as he comes closer, his collarbone all red and purple with blood and bruising from where I took a chunk. I notice a tattoo amongst the carnage.

"I think the rest of your tatt is over there somewhere." I nod back to the entryway where we fought, a grin tugging at the corner of my mouth.

He grunts, tugging at my chains, pulling me face first onto the dusty floor, and dragging me out into the approaching night.

I don't kick. I don't fight. Instead, I make myself a heavy, dead weight. *Reserve your strength, Fred.* Through my one good eye, I catch sight of those pink shoes again, and I muster what I hope is a reassuring smile for the girl at the other end of them – for Ginny.

"It'll be okay," I whisper, my swollen eyes finding hers, wet and sparkling with tears.

"I'm sorry." Her mouth curls around the words, not letting a sound escape.

CHAPTER THIRTY-THREE

The night is crisp. The last few days of rain have cooled the stagnant air, making it feel fresh and new. The moon hangs low on the horizon, behind the grey gumtrees, yet her glow lights up the clearing.

And here we are, Mathusi and I, like apparitions from a forgotten chapter in history, bound together by silver chains beneath this silver moon. However, unlike the moon, which can wax and wane as she pleases, we are prisoners. Victims of a world which fears those who dare to defy the norm. The restraints chafe our wrists and ankles, tethering us to the obelisk of petrified wood, which stands like a grim reminder of our imminent demise – condemned, like so many before us, amidst the muck and mire.

I feel the desperation sinking in, and I can't help but wonder if we were to shout, would the sound even carry across this place of death, reach someone who could help? But it's then I look up at the night sky once more and find my bearings. We're too far out from any roads, any houses, even campsites. We are truly alone.

Garamond drags up one of the wooden chairs Mathusi had

pulled out of the bunker, a smarmy leer on his face. "Thanks for taking these out, mate. It's as if you knew what was going to happen." He smirks.

"I hope it breaks and impales you," Mathusi spits.

Garamond tuts. "Save your energy, lad." He nods to the rising moon. "Won't be long now."

Sarge drags another chair behind him, Ginny stumbling along, Dale shoving her. I feel the heat rising in me.

"The shoving isn't necessary, Dale," Garamond hisses, then pats the chair next to him. "Come sit, Gin. Enjoy the show!" he adds, nodding his head to Dale. "Shall you do us the honour, young constable?" Garamond grins.

Dale smirks, unbuttoning his taser, his glowering eyes pinned to mine. "With pleasure, sir."

Prick.

The moon edges up over the trees, and I can feel her beams pulling me. It doesn't hurt, but I can feel it beckon, calling me, like an old friend, asking me to join her, to dance and frolic with her in the starry night. But the chains burn harder, yanking me back to the now, to my human form. I squeeze my eyes and groan.

Dale ignites the taser, the blue electricity crackling.

Sarge coughs. "Sir, we may not even need to harm them. They're young. They'll most likely turn on their own without our…" – he pauses, his eyes shifting to the taser in Dale's hand – "…influence."

Garamond scoffs. "Where's the fun in that?" The old man turns to face the sergeant, rummaging through his pocket and retrieving something small. "Here. Take another one. Can't have you wolfing out on me."

Sarge rolls the tablet in the palm of his hand. Another pill. He took something similar before, didn't he?

Garamond turns back to face us, sneering, and I notice Sarge's scowl and watch him toss the small white pill behind him. His eyes lock with mine, though he quickly shifts his gaze, his dull eyes staring at the dull ground.

"Go on then," Garamond says, laughing, waving his hand for Dale to proceed. "Let's have some fun."

Ginny squirms in her seat, her knees drawn up to her chest, her face buried in between them. I yank at the chains, the metal burning deeper.

"She shouldn't be here; she shouldn't be seeing this!"

Ginny doesn't deserve this. Her blonde hair sticks to her face, all wet, as she looks up at me, her face contorting, her eyes wide in fear as Dale plunges the taser into my neck. A searing eruption of pain explodes within me, the stench of burnt flesh and ozone filling the air. My vision momentarily whites out as electric currents surge through me, my body writhing involuntarily. I clench my teeth so hard they could shatter, a cacophony of shivers coursing through me as my skin sizzles and smokes. The moon's influence sharpens as I convulse, and I can feel every cell in my body awaken, the pull of the moon heightened. The hairs on my arms bristle and thicken.

"No…" I whimper, my eyes swollen and bruised, though I look for her, for Ginny. She's cowering. Garamond has her. He's grabbing her, making her stay, making her watch.

Dale ruthlessly plunges the taser into my ribs, his malicious laughter ringing through the air. His eyes shift to Mathusi, and the taser follows his gaze. My scream mingles with Mathusi's wild roar, our howls piercing the night. And then, I feel it. The primal growl rising within me, the luminous moonlight filling me with an almost unbearable intensity.

Mathusi grunts. "Force it down, Fred. We turn on our own. We can't be forced!"

"Look at them, Gin!" Garamond grabs her jaw, thrusting her face towards us. Her eyes are glowing, but not in fear. Not with terror. With something else.

"Look at these monsters!" Garamond howls.

Ginny squirms from her grandad's hold, ducking away from his lunging grasp, and grabs the old rifle.

"They're not the monster." Her hands shake, the click of the weapon sounds, and Sarge steps to the side, away from Ginny and Garamond, edging closer to us on the pole.

"I've seen the files. I know the truth!" her voice bellows.

Rage. Those sparkling eyes were full of rage.

Garamond sighs, unbothered. "What *truth*?" He tuts.

Ginny shoves her hand into her pocket and pulls out a crumpling piece of paper, flicking it angrily in Garamond's face. He unfolds it.

I hold back a snarl, Dale thrusting the taser into my side again, smirking, jabbing the weapon into my hip. But he's a little too eager, a little too close, and I lunge. Teeth bared, I grab his forearm, the force of my bite tearing flesh from the bone. He staggers back, falling. Wailing, crying, reaching for his gun.

"No!" Sarge growls, kicking the pistol from Dale's hands. "Get up, coward."

"The bitch bit me," Dale sobs angrily, a snot bubble popping from his nose.

"They could've done far worse," Sarge snaps, his eyes finding mine. *His* amber *eyes.*

"You killed my mum!" Ginny's voice echoes through the field, our collective gaze moving to her.

Garamond's stare widens, his nostrils flaring like a wild beast's. "I don't know what you're talking about, Genevieve. You must have misunderstood something." His lips barely move, his jaw clenching tight.

"How could you?" Ginny whimpers, rubbing her nose on the sleeve of her jacket, the rifle still aiming true. She reaches into her pocket again, another piece of scrunched-up paper that she flicks at her grandfather. "It's all here in black and white."

"Enough!" Garamond's face twists with anger as he snatches the weapon from Ginny's grasp. "You're being fed lies by this, this…" Garamond's eyes find mine. "This filth."

Ginny steps forward, her eyes blazing with fury. "The only filth I see are your lies."

Garamond's eyes flash, the rage building, the tang of monstrous anger oozing from him.

"No…" my voice croaks. I lurch, trying to make it to Ginny. The silver burns; I can feel my skin peeling away at my wrists. And something else. A pulsating throb, a heat, on my thigh. My pocket? I shake my head, my eyes focusing on Ginny. She's not safe.

"At least I'm not like you," Ginny spits. "You're the monster."

The moon is above us now, the night as bright as day, and the hairs on my arms are thick.

Mathusi groans, his ears shifting, pointing, but the silver is holding back the turn.

"I said *enough!*" Garamond roars, grabbing Ginny by the hood of her jacket, pulling her towards us. "I'm just trying to keep you safe from this bitch!" Garamond's words are like acid, burning and corroding everything in their path. He throws Ginny hard into the dirt in front of me. "But if you're so hellbent on being a dog's toy, be my guest. Just like your damn mother!"

My teeth loosen as a surge of anger courses through me. I clench my jaw, the silver chains suppressing the raging wolf within. The warmth in my pocket pulses again – the runestones. *Not now, you stupid rocks, I need to help Ginny.*

Ginny looks up at Garamond through tears and sobs. "So, you admit it…"

I lunge again, and she's close enough, my fingers latch on to her arm, and I pull her into me, holding her, her body shaking, quivering with rage and sorrow.

Garamond towers over us, the creases on his brow glistening with sweat, his face twisted into a mask of unbridled rage. His chest heaves with each angry, laboured breath. "Shoot the boy," he sneers. "Get it done, Sarge. That's a good dog," and pats the sergeant on the head before turning to leave.

"Garamond?" Sarge asks.

"You're talking, dog. I didn't ask you to talk. Kill." He shoos the Sarge away like an errant fly.

"Just one thing."

A low growl rumbles from Garamond's direction. "What?"

"The cure," Sarge continues. "It's nearly ready, right? The

pills, they calm it, but, it's not a cure. The real deal, it's done, yeah?"

Garamond laughs, a deep, throaty sound. "Soon, dog," he says, and stomps over the hill.

Sarge turns back, facing us. His lips purse, his eyes wide. The amber shine has subsided now, but the look on his face… *is the cure real?*

"Unshackle the kid." Sarge points from Dale to Mathusi.

"Fuck that, you do it, dog," Dale laughs.

Sarge unholsters his weapon, pointing it at Dale. "Get in there and do it." His eyes flash yellow.

Dale's back goes rigid. "Righto, fine," he mumbles, and walks behind us, unhooking Mathusi from the chain of silver attached to the pole.

I hold Ginny closer, stroking her hair. I think of the runes in my pocket, the trident of protection. I remember the shape, the curves of *Algiz*. Not like a trident, but like a person standing tall, their arms raised, asking for protection. Protection that we need now. I close my eyes, imagining the symbol, drawing it in the stars. When I can see it, as clear as if it were right in front of me, I open my eyes and let the rune's protection wash over us. A warm, gentle wind sweeps through the underbrush, and I begin to wonder if these rocks have a power of their own. Is this the legacy my mum has left me?

Ginny nuzzles into my bloody, sweaty shirt, and my swollen eyes are now on Sarge as he paces the dirt in front of us, scratching his head with the butt of his pistol.

Dale yanks on the chain. "Come on, dog." Mathusi stumbles, falling to the dirt.

"Up there, over the hill." Sarge flicks the gun in his hand in the direction Garamond left. Dale drags Mathusi on his knees up and over the hill.

"Sarge," my voice rasps. "Please…"

"Soon? What…" Sarge prowls back and forth. "What's 'soon'? Does he even have a cure?"

"He's lying," I manage, hoping my words hold meaning.

Sarge continues to pace, eyes wild. "I gave them up. Gave up my damn pack. And for what?" His eyes meet mine, full of anger.

Ginny trembles in my arms.

"FUCK!" Sarge's voice cracks like thunder through the night, and like lightning, he bounds over the hill, firing a shot. Another, then another. The sounds echo through the field, deep in my bones.

Mathusi…

Ginny burrows herself deeper into my chest, screaming, sobbing, rocking. I can't feel the silver burning anymore. I can't feel anything. I stare out at the moon-covered hill, waiting.

Waiting for Mathusi to come back. Waiting to see his curly hair bouncing over the crest, running towards us, safe. But time has forgotten us as I rock back and forth, Ginny nestled between my legs, wrapped in my arms. I rock. As if the motion will lull us to sleep, where dreams are far better than this fucked-up reality.

"I'm sorry…" the wet whisper sounds from inside the Ginny cocoon.

I find her face amongst the hair and the tears, my puffy eyes meeting hers. The glow of the moon shines on her perfect face.

"You have nothing to be sorry for," I breathe, stroking her tear-stained cheek.

Despite the glittering sky above, she's still the fairest of all the stars that shine.

CHAPTER THIRTY-FOUR

"What did you do?" My voice is harsh and scratchy, tired and angry. The moon above us shines strong, her light filling me. I growl again, "Where's Mathusi!" It's not so much a question as a command, thrown at the coward sergeant walking back over the mound towards us.

Sarge's knuckles, bloodied and bruised, glisten in the moonlight. His eyes flicker yellow. "He's gone."

The already shattered pieces of my heart grow heavy with betrayal.

I can feel the wolf inside howling to be free, its presence a throbbing tension in my muscles. It demands release, so it can devour this double-crossing pig where he stands. "Traitor!"

Sarge scoffs, tossing something small and metal towards me. It strikes the side of my face before falling to the ground. Sarge's yellow eyes find mine before he turns and walks back over the crest towards the bunker, leaving me in the shadow of his treachery.

"Hey…" My voice scratches, barely audible. I cough, attempting to push the harshness away.

"Hey!" I try to stand, to shuffle forward. "Where are you

going? You can't…"

My mind races. Is he really leaving us here? Abandoning Ginny? I try to uncurl the Ginny knot in front of me, hoping she might follow him, but she remains in my arms, her shoulders shuddering with each whimpering sob.

I let her sink into me, shielding her from the uncertainty, and watch as Sarge's silhouette dips below the crest of the hill.

A glint in the dirt catches my eye, and I stretch my fingers towards it. It's the metal object that Sarge had thrown, now a tiny beacon of hope, like a star in the darkest night.

The key.

I shuffle forward, doing my best to rouse the trembling figure in front of me.

"Ginny, it's okay," I whisper, my voice barely louder than a breath.

I reach for the key once more, the metal brushing my fingertips with a cold, unforgiving hiss. The key's silver. Of course it's fucking silver.

Ginny stirs, her eyes shift from mine to the glint of silver in the dirt.

"Please, Ginny," I continue, my hands outstretched, pleading, the cuffs leaving angry, red welts on my wrists. "He's gone. They've both gone. But I'm sure they'll be back…"

Ginny nods, unwrapping herself, life breathing into her

limbs as she frantically grabs the key, fumbling with the lock, missing the latch and hole every time. She worries at her lip, teething a chapped bit of skin, and I rest my forehead against hers, my breath slowing, trying to ease her to do the same. Ginny's shoulders rise with a deep inhale, her breath hot against my face as she looks at me. I nod, gently, placing my bound hands in hers.

The cuffs snap open, the sound resonating in the still night air, and they tumble to the earth with a heavy thud. Relief courses through me like a wave, the burden of one restraint finally lifted.

"My ankles, please."

Ginny crawls through the dirt to the cuffs on my ankles, and the rattle of the chain's release sends goosebumps up my thighs, my back.

Staring at my wrists, the silver's cruel touch has etched its memory into my skin. The pain is unrelenting; a torrent of agony shoots up my arms, my flesh still feeling the silver's icy grip. Stretching my legs out in front of me, I wince; a red, raw circle of blisters bubbles and bursts, the pain splintering up my shins, only to recede. Like a relentless tide, its searing fire coursing through my veins, and I can feel my flesh weave itself back together. Muscles and sinew, subdermal layers of skin stitching itself back into place, each thread igniting with a white-hot intensity. The pain is unyielding, a constant throbbing that pulses with every beat of my heart.

Ginny kneels beside me, her face streaked with tears and dirt. She nods to the thick silver collar around my neck, and I exhale, bracing myself for the peeling pain.

Leaning in closer, her breath against my cheek, she searches for the lock. Her hands shake. "I can't find it."

"Other side," I croak, and Ginny shifts her weight, shuffling one leg over mine, a knee on either side of my thighs. Despite the pain, despite this entirely morbid shit-show – Ginny Chase is straddling me. A fresh agony rolls through me.

Ginny's fingers trace over the silver, searching for the lock, her eyes shining bright as she finds her mark, the key slipping in with a soft *click*.

I shudder as the latch snaps open, my head falling against Ginny's shoulder.

"Gently…" I rasp as Ginny peels the metal away. All over, my flesh prickles, and I can feel the hair, the fur, bristle, then sigh, retreating beneath my skin. It's almost as though the moon above sighs with me. I can feel the pull of the wolf, but it's calmer now, subdued, not fighting to be free. Not frightened. Not hurt. It can come or go as it chooses. And it's as if knowing that, it retreats, and waits.

Slowly, the pain begins to fade. It's not a sudden release, but a gradual ebbing of agony, like a tide receding. And as the pain lessens, I become aware of something new, something strange… and wondrous.

My body is changing.

The wounds have sealed shut, no longer oozing and blistering, revealing instead a patch of tender, pink skin that appears almost freshly born.

Looking up at Ginny, her eyes glow with the same gentle radiance as the moon. Her fingers trail across my neck, sending shivers down my spine, her hand tracing up to my cheek, and I lean into her touch, desperate for her warmth. For her.

"I thought I'd lost you." Her voice is soft, barely above a whisper, but it carries a world of emotion, her eyes brimming with tears. "You disappeared. You were gone."

The lump in my throat threatens to choke me, and I struggle to find my voice. "I'm here," I manage, my heart pounding in my chest. "You found me."

Ginny inches closer, and the gap between us vanishes. Our lips hover just a breath apart, and I feel her warmth against my skin. Amidst the whirlwind of emotions, amidst the scent of earth, the tang of sweat and blood, her presence lingers – honey-sweet and intoxicating. I surrender to the moment, lost in the sensation. My fingers intertwine with hers, and I gently press her fingertips against my lips, my hungry eyes tracing every contour of her face. I long for more. More of her. Her lips, her touch. Ginny draws nearer, our chests pressed together, breaths synchronised, sharing the same air. She is my reason for living, and I'm certain I would do anything for her.

Time stands still as we share this fragile, unspoken moment. The world around us fades away, and there's only her and I, drawn together by a magnetic force that defies reason.

"Can I…" I shudder, the tension electric, the desire palpable.

I watch as the skin on Ginny's neck shivers with goose-bumps, her cherry lips parting softly, the one word whispering past, full of want and desire and need.

"Yes," she breathes, her eyes moving to my lips.

My breath quickens, and I can't hold back anymore. I never want to be alone. I never want to live in solitude again, but instead, live in this moment, with her. Forever.

My hands slide up to cup Ginny's face, the world holding its breath as our mouths finally meet.

Her lips are soft, warm, and taste of hope and promise. It's a kiss that speaks of everything we've endured and everything we hope to be. A kiss that ignites a fire within me, a fire that burns away the darkness that once threatened to consume us.

A soft moan escapes Ginny's lips as our kiss deepens. Our bodies press closer, and I can feel the rapid beat of her heart, matching the frantic rhythm of my own.

Ginny's fingers tangle in my hair, pulling me closer, and I respond with a hunger that matches her own.

As our lips part, I breathe for what feels like the first time, and I lean forward, our foreheads resting against each other. Our eyes meet, and in that moment, we know that we've found our way back to each. We are no longer alone. We have each other, and that is enough to face whatever challenges lie ahead.

CHAPTER THIRTY-FIVE

The taste of Ginny's kiss still lingers on my lips, a sweet memory that warms my heart as we stand together in the quiet embrace of the night. But even as the echoes of our kiss resonate in my mind, a faint rustle of leaves stirs the air, and my heart quickens. Fear slams into me, pushing the butterflies to the pit of my stomach. My gaze flickers towards the woods, searching for any signs of movement, any indication of danger. But nothing moves. Only the whispering of leaves in the breeze, Ginny's warm breath on my cheek, and the lingering memory of that kiss.

Yet, as if on cue, heavy and deliberate footsteps crunch in the mud and grass over the crest, breaking the stillness.

"I can't leave you alone for five fucking minutes, you worthless dog."

Garamond.

"Ginny," I whisper urgently, my fingers tightening around hers. "We have to go."

My eyes dart to Garamond cursing over the hill, dragging someone along. Sarge, his face bloodied and bruised. Garamond's eyes settle upon me. On us. His wild gaze darts to the silver chains and cuffs discarded in the mud.

"Run," I gasp, the single word torn from my throat like a prayer.

In that heartbeat, we bolt, our footsteps a frantic drumbeat on the forest floor. My heart, a wild beast in my chest, syncs its rhythm with Ginny's as we sprint through the dark woods. The wind howls, tearing at our clothes, and the scent of eucalyptus and earth mingles in the cold night air.

Ginny's hand, warm and soft, is a lifeline in the chaos, and I clutch it desperately, as if it's the only connection to reality. Each step is a gamble, our lives hanging by a thread, and the forest closes in around us, a labyrinth of shadows.

Crack! The rifle shot reverberates through the trees, a deafening explosion that propels us forwards with newfound urgency. My blood runs cold as I hear it, and the birds above, startled by the gunshot, burst into chaos. Cockatoos screech and flee their roosts, taking to the night sky like a ghostly exodus.

Our breaths come in ragged bursts, fear and adrenaline flooding our veins. Every step is a promise of survival, a plea for escape from the nightmare chasing us. In the darkness, Garamond is a faceless spectre, a hunter in pursuit, and we are the prey. The forest offers no solace, only a maze of uncertainty, and the sound of his rifle echoes in our souls.

"Get back here, bitch!"

Garamond's bellowing cuts through the scrub, straight to us.

We bound between trees, leap over fallen branches, and stumble over rocks. Every breath is ragged, every muscle in our bodies aching from the strain, I can feel the effort in Ginny to keep up. I look back over my shoulder, my heart thudding in my chest.

Garamond's close behind, his footsteps getting louder and more menacing with each passing moment. Ginny and I push ourselves harder, running as fast as we can, but it feels like we're barely moving.

I glance at Ginny, fear etched on her face, but her eyes burn with a fierce determination. We can make it. We keep running, and then I see it: a small clearing ahead, the campground. A sliver of hope. Someone can help us, someone has to be here. We sprint towards it, our legs pumping furiously, our hearts racing. Ginny and I reach the clearing; a lone tent tucked beneath a drooping wattle tree opens, the zipper sliding, two faces peering out.

"What're you dykes doing here?" Steven's voice is disgusting and crass, as always, but it's *someone*.

"Was that a fucking gun going off?" another voice sounds from within the tent. A familiar voice.

My stomach drops. It can't be. Garamond said… but she…

I can feel my skin tighten, my stomach churn.

Her ginger hair pokes out first, then her freckled face.

"Shit, Fred!"

I watch as Cassie stumbles from the tent, eyes wide with concern, taking me in.

"Are you okay?" Her eyes move between me and Ginny. The mud, the blood.

Steven's eyes are on us, too. "What the fuck… are you guys alright?"

Genuine. He's being genuine. And Cassie. Cassie's alive!

Ginny and I are both in shock, staring at Cassie as she fumbles with my jacket, searching me, making sure I'm okay. Even Steven looks concerned, his phone out and in the air, trying to get reception in this forsaken bushland.

My hands finally have life in them as I take Cassie's face, pulling her towards me, arms wrapping around her.

"I thought you were dead…" I shudder. "I thought I… Garamond said I'd killed you…"

Cassie half laughs. "Shit. You're serious," she adds, her voice growing concerned again. "Freddy, look." She takes my hand in hers. "I'm very much alive. I don't know what he said, but, yeah." She flicks her braid over her shoulder. "I think he's gone a bit mad. He said you were arrested, but no one knew why."

"Maybe if you guys'd answered my bloody texts," Ginny

scoffs.

Cassie and Steven look to one another. "I thought your gran-dad told you?"

"Told her what…?" I ask, my voice low.

"We just thought it was everyone," Steven adds.

"Garamond took all our phones," Cassie continues. "Said it was part of the investigation about Randy."

"He was really fucking weird about it," Steven snorts. "Even gave us some cash to keep it quiet. Said to go to Outwash."

"But fuck Outwash. With the amount of money he gave us, we thought we'd have ourselves a bush bash out here at the campground. Especially since the dingo thing is a crock of shit," Cassie laughs, though her face falls, her eyes on me again. "Freddy, are you okay?"

I can't quite wrap my head around the fact Cassie is alive. I take in every frizz jutting from her dishevelled braid, her crooked front tooth, the *new* sweat-stained jacket hanging over her shoulders, and I can't help but laugh. Laugh with relief. She's alive. As much as I pushed her away in the past, she was always a sister to me – even if I never admitted it. She was the first person to offer me something that could have been more… and even though I ignored her, pushed back… she was worried about me. *Is* worried.

She's alive.

"I'm fine," I answer, rubbing the wet from my nose. "Who else is out here?" I finally say, forcing my mouth and brain to work together.

"Tyson and some others, maybe seven of us?" Cassie looks back to the tents.

Ginny's face drops, eyes wild, staring behind us. It's then I hear it.

"You fucking kids just can't take orders. I'm trying to keep you little shits safe!" Garamond's voice chides from the edge of the clearing, the darkness of him creeping through the trees. The leaves rustle as his shadowy figure emerges. "Can *no one* do what they're fucking *told*?"

"Go," I grunt, urgency in my voice. "Get everyone out of here."

I can feel my eyes shift, adjusting to the gloom as the dark night lights up. My head turns to Steven. My eyes must be shining now, by the look of absolute terror on his face. "Keep her safe," I growl.

Steven's wide-eyed stare moves between the three of us, to the man at the edge of the clearing, and he nods. Without hesitation, he takes Cassie by the hand, and they run past the clearing, their feet crunching on the gravel as they make their escape.

I turn back to the figure lumbering out into the glow of the night.

Ginny slides her hand into mine, her blue eyes and freckles as bright as any sun. My sun. And me, her moon.

I squeeze her hand. "Thank you. For coming to rescue me. For believing in me."

Ginny's smile shatters through the horror of the night, filling me. "Always."

"This is really sweet and all," Garamond mocks, his voice strained. "But I have a whole mess to clean up."

I watch Garamond struggle, pulling something behind him, his back hunched, his muscles straining against. It's then I see it – realise what's he's dragging as Sarge's bloodied and bruised form comes into view.

"You know what?" Garamond continues, a sardonic grin plastered on his face, "I'm getting a bit of déjà vu here."

"Shut up, old man." My heart pounds in my chest, knowing what callous words are coming next. I try to maintain my composure, taking a deep breath to steady myself. "I reckon you just like the sound of your own monstrous voice."

He lets out a small grumble of laughter, lip curling. "It was a night much like this," he continues, stepping forward, dragging Sarge along in one swift pull of the chain. "Yeah, a night *exactly* like this." Another step forward, closing the gap. "I hadn't intended on hunting down two wolves, but when opportunity arises." He pauses, his unblinking eyes firmly fixed to mine.

I meet his cold gaze with determination, refusing to break. "Oh? You hadn't intended on slaughtering a mother while she slept in her bed?"

I can feel Ginny tremble beside me.

"Bed?" Garamond pauses, tilting his head slightly, his eyes squinting, confused. "You said something similar a week ago, and silver nitrate." He adjusts his hold on Sarge's chains. "I slaughtered your dear mummy and daddy at the lake…" A grin, all teeth, creeps across his face. "I believe you saw *mother dearest* down in my den."

My knees buckle slightly. "…and Dad?" I ask, voice shaking.

Garamond pauses, and something like sorrow flashes on his face, so quickly I almost miss it – a flicker of his eyelashes, a minute twitch of his ragged beard. His grizzly snarl returns as he speaks. "I shot that dog before he turned."

Ginny pushes past me, lunging forward. "You pig!"

"Ginny…" the darkness of Garamond's eyes subsides.

"Fred's parents weren't the only people you killed that night," Ginny seethes.

"– Gin, no, I –"

The blonde hair from my memory, from the crime scene photo in my pocket. I slide the crumpled photo from my jeans.

"Mal." The name passes my lips before I realise. "Malena." I hold the picture out for Ginny, her shaking hand clasping at the torn edges.

"This!" Ginny hisses, throwing the photo towards her grandad, tears freshly falling from over her cheeks.

Garamond's nostrils flare, his eyes moving from the photo in the dirt, to us. "Why can't you see I'm trying to protect you, Ginny!" He drags Sarge in front of him, the limp body falling between us. "Sarge is proof!" Garamond bends down, the sergeant's muddy face in his hand, his fingers folding back Sarge's bloodied lips. "He's cured, see?"

Plain old human teeth. No protruding wolfish canines. No, it can't be true…

"The cure's a lie, just to make us all your little lapdogs," I snap.

Sarge falls back to the dirt, his entire body shivering.

Garamond glares at me, his focus drawn back to Ginny. "If you're so adamant, like your mother, to fall for a pathetic *dog*," he snarls, "at least let me vaccinate the mutt." He takes a vial from his pocket, a pointed needle at the end.

Watching Sarge writhe in the dirt, I notice something different. A smell… that's gone.

He is *cured…*

"My mum?" Ginny whispers, her fists clenching. "Don't you

dare talk about her. You killed her!" The words burst from her, tinged with pain.

Sarge tries to push himself up, but Garamond offers him a boot to his jaw. "Don't get any ideas, *sergeant*. You've given me enough grief. I need to show Gin the truth –"

"– what, that you murder innocent people?" I growl.

Darkness fills Garamond's face once more. "There's nothing innocent about monsters." He pauses, looking at Ginny. "I'm just trying to protect you, Gin. That's all I've ever been trying to do."

Amidst the bitter eucalypt of the bush, and the odious rage wafting from Garamond, there's another smell. A familiar smell. I close my eyes, sniffing again, and find myself back at the bunker. The smell of filth, of death and decay. And blood. Wolf blood.

My eyes fling open, and I see. I see the smell on the breeze, drifting in the air. And it's coming from Garamond! From his pocket. From that syringe. From his mouth. From his skin, seeping from every pore.

"You…" My voice is guttural, primal, as I sniff again, taking a longer stride towards the monster before me.

Garamond's eye twitches, his snarling lips hidden beneath his stained beard. "Me?" He stares, unblinking.

I sniff again. "Bloodbags." I recall the word Garamond used

back at the police station. "You were bleeding them… Aksel, his pack," I growl, tilting my head, following the smell.

"Their blood held the cure," Garamond sneers.

"But why are *you* taking it?" I can feel my canines edging over my lips. The wolf within, scratching, clawing to be free.

Garamond scoffs. "Two monsters, one stone. A cure for one, and the power to defeat another."

Another?

The wolf within me snarls and circles, the smell overpowering now, the moon edging closer to its apex. "And by *defeat another*, do you mean helpless people? Like Randy?"

Garamond charges forward, his huge square hand on my throat, nails growing, extending, digging into flesh. "I think you're mistaking me for a monster."

I squirm in his grasp, the coppery stench of death swirling around my face. "So, microdosing wolf blood gets you jacked, huh," I laugh, the sound barely making it past his squeezing fingers. "You're the only monster here."

"There are worse things out there than you mangy dogs." Garamond's voice wavers, and that same noxious smell, all stale onions, the smell of fear, seeps from his skin. His breath is sour on my face.

"You're afraid," I rasp, the realisation hitting me. What would make Garamond afraid?

Garamond's eyes flicker momentarily before his hold on me tightens. "I never hurt your mum, Gin," he says over my shoulder. "I was trying to save her, just as I've been trying to save you."

I can feel Ginny behind me. I can feel her anger, her pain. "Save me," she scoffs. "And what about Dad, huh? Was *his* death a lie, too?"

Garamond's eyes, full of bloodlust and fury, flash again, finding Ginny's. "That's who I'm trying to protect you from, you stupid girl!"

Ginny stands, frozen, and I can feel Garamond's grip loosen. The old man's shoulders slump, his whole body shifting, defeated.

"Gin… there's so much you just don't know."

"Then tell me!"

Garamond's jaw clenches, his eyes locked on a figure emerging from the bracken. His back and shoulders stiffen, and, as I follow his gaze, I spot Varg, a dark silhouette in the dim light, his amber eyes piercing the shadows.

"Talking to your own kin like that, Garamond," Varg's voice echoes from the woods behind us.

Stepping forward, an obsidian wolf, shining, walks beside him, and another two grey wolves prowl behind.

Garamond growls, pushing me to the ground, turning to face

Varg and the pack.

"I have to agree with Fred on this one," Varg says, picking at a fleck of dirt on the sleeve of his shirt. "I think you're the only monster here."

CHAPTER THIRTY-SIX

The trees grow eerily silent, save for the faint buzz of cicadas in the warm summer night. Shadows lengthen, and an unexplainable tension hangs in the air. A chilling coolness descends upon the clearing, as if the night itself has embraced an ageless touch, and all warmth retreats. The cicadas fall silent.

"Monster is such a vile word."

The voice seems to come from all around us, from the trees, on the wind, from the dark recesses of my very thoughts.

"No. Not now. I'm not ready." Garamond's face turns ashen, his voice trembling.

"What *not now*?" I watch, my heart pounding, as Garamond fumbles with a small vial, its contents a disturbing shade of red.

"Get Ginny out of here. Now!" With wide, desperate eyes, he steadies his shaking hand and swiftly stabs the dart of crimson liquid into his neck. Another vial slips from his pocket, its contents spilling onto the ground. Reaching for a third, Garamond gulps down the elixir. The veins in his neck throb. The muscles in his arms pulse and ripple. And yet, as his gaze meets Ginny's, I witness a flicker of hesitation amidst the predatory glint in his eyes.

He's not a wolf, but a strange human hybrid, muscles writhing, teeth gnashing.

"Go!" Garamond snarls, shoving Ginny too hard, and she falls to the ground.

The rage within me floods, a torrent of emotion fuelled by my love for Ginny… for Randy, for Garamond's demented lies about Cassie. It's a fiery anger, like a blaze that burns within me, consuming everything in its path. For my mum, my dad. For Mathusi. Their deaths, the sorrow, the fury, drives me. A guttural scream, like a primal howl, bursts from my throat as I launch myself forward, clenched fists swinging to strike at Garamond. He dodges effortlessly and hits back, his claws raking across my side. Pain sears through me, like a branding iron against my skin, but I refuse to let it slow me down.

We circle each other, stalking, waiting. My eyes narrow, their focus intense, scanning Garamond's in the dim moonlight, waiting for his next move. It's then I realise I haven't wolfed out. I'm standing on two legs, just like Garamond, somehow between shifts. I can feel the celestial pull, but I rein in the wolf, tugging on its leash. Its growl reverberates through my chest.

"I'm not your enemy!" Garamond snarls, the words grating past his jagged teeth. "Not now."

"You kidnapped me!" I lunge, claws at the ready. "You accused me of murdering innocent people!"

Garamond blocks the swipe with his forearm, pushing me back. I know I must be careful; Garamond is bigger and stronger than me. But my pain is driving me forward, my muscles aching against the full moon.

"Mathusi," I whimper, his name powering me as I barge Garamond, nails grabbing, my knee finding the soft spot between his legs. "You killed my parents!"

Garamond howls, his eyes wide with fury and pain. He charges me, and I brace myself, ready to meet his attack head-on. Our bodies collide, and we tumble to the ground, rolling and snarling as we fight for dominance.

"Your cowardly parents deserved what they got! They left Malena there to die!"

Cowardly?

Garamond might be stronger, but I'm faster. With lightning reflexes, I swiftly evade Garamond's grasp, effortlessly slipping through his fingers like a fleeting shadow. My body becomes a symphony of graceful movements, a dance of evasion, as I twist, spin, and duck, defying his attempts to hold me captive until I manage to pin him to the ground.

"You killed Mal!" My nails dig into Garamond's shoulders, the memories rushing back. "I remember her dirty blonde hair, her bloodshot eyes hanging open, staring at me, her vomit stuck between my toes!"

Garamond slows, panting, his breath ragged as his chest heaves for air. In a crescendo of agony and fury, he unleashes a primal roar that cuts through the air, before shoving me to the dirt. Varg and the other wolves move in closer, ready to attack, and I can feel the electric surge of the pack's energy course through me, enveloping me in a wave of heightened awareness and anticipation.

"I never meant to kill Aasta and Connor." Garamond's eyes look to mine, searching. The anger that flared up like a blazing firework moments before, bursting with fierce intensity, now reduced to faint wisps of anguish. Buckling over, Garamond clutches his chest, his eyes wet with tears. "I told Mal to leave. I warned her he was coming."

What's happening? I can feel the wolf in me subside. *Is he… crying?* I look down to my bloodied hands, my body shuddering with the residue of adrenaline.

Ginny runs to her grandad's side.

Garamond attempts to stand, though he falls to his knees, wheezing. Ginny clutches his shoulder and rubs his back.

"Grandad, breathe. Follow me: in through your nose, out through your mouth –"

A low and gentle whine sounds behind me as the obsidian wolf shifts. "He's having a panic attack," Bett interrupts, fur still bristling along her arms as she rushes towards us, moving closer to Garamond. She reaches into a satchel tied around her bare waist, removing a small glass jar. She dabs the ointment on Garamond's temples.

The other wolves, once poised to attack, watch the scene with a mix of uncertainty and empathy. Their growls soften, replaced by hushed whispers.

"I never meant to kill them," Garamond chokes, his giant form now crumbled on the sodden ground. "And I never killed Mal. Malena. My sweet girl…" Garamond's voice trembles with genuine remorse as he speaks, his words barely audible through his sobs. "You have to believe me."

Ginny nods, her own cheeks wet with tears.

Garamond's hands reach for mine, but I flinch, repulsed and confused. He falls, his face in the muck, hands reaching for my knees, my feet, tears still falling between his fractured breaths.

"I never meant to kill them…"

The air crackles with tension. "Oh, but you decided to mount my mother's head on your wall?" My fists clench at the memories of the devastation Garamond has caused, the lives he has taken. Hatred surges within me, battling against the weariness that has settled deep into my bones. He wanted to change wolves, change me. I don't need or want a cure. I'm not broken. The weight of vengeance pulls at my heart, urging me to strike him down. But as I gaze into Ginny's tear-stained face, the strength in her eyes, a glimmer of compassion begins to spark within me.

Garamond's hands reach for my own once more, his grip weak but desperate. He rises, supported by Ginny. His tears still flow, his face contorted with a mix of grief, regret, and relief.

"What happened, Grandad… that night?" Ginny swallows, and I can smell the unease, like the distant scent of burning embers, wisps of worry clinging to her very words.

"I was meant to visit your mum the day after… after…" Garamond's voice wavers. "I had to warn her. I'd been following him, and he'd found where she was." He stops, wiping his face. "You were safe, Gin. I had you somewhere safe, but your mum…" he scoffs, pain filling his eyes. "Just as stubborn as you." A faint smile creases his lips.

Ginny squeezes her grandad's hand, lost in the moment, but I need answers, need them now.

"Who's *him*?" I interrupt.

Garamond's smile falls, his eyes glazing over with memory. "I was tracking *him*." Garamond points to the distant gums. "I was only trying to protect Malena, and I thought…" He stops, the words silent in his mouth as his eyes slowly move to find my own. "I thought they were part of his nest. I was after him. I didn't know."

Nest?

"I hate to break up such a fun little gathering," the voice from before jests once more, "but I'm getting tired of this back-and-forth."

A crimson flash, faster than anything I've ever seen, shoots through the trees, a sinister laugh following.

I look over at the pack, their teeth bared, eyes scanning the line of paperbarks and gums.

"I didn't know they were wolves," Garamond continues, his voice shaking.

"That didn't stop you from decapitating my mum and mounting her fucking head on your wall!" I growl.

Garamond flinches, eyes dart along the tree line, following the red blur, frantically searching. "I thought –" Garamond's voice gurgles and splutters; his body stills, eyes wide and wild.

The world is suddenly a blur of snarling fur and meaty thuds, the wolves attacking the invisible foe, an overwhelming storm of violent chaos. A heavy silence descends, and then I see him, standing behind Garamond, his arm plunging through the old man's chest, heart still beating in his fist, blood dripping through his fingers, over his ring – *an opulent golden ring with a hunk of green rock nestled in the middle.*

"Can't let you wolves have all the fun."

Time slows to a crawl as I take in the carnage around me. The werewolves, once formidable and proud, now lie prone on the ground. They're alive, but their bodies bear the marks of a merciless beating. Their mangled forms, covered in torn flesh and matted fur, create a grotesque tapestry of agony that assaults my senses. How could one person possess such speed, such strength?

Amidst the turmoil, amidst the fighting and rage, the fallen bodies of my new family, lying breathless on the ground, I forget about Ginny until I hear her voice.

"Dad?"

…what?

"Ginny, darling. Just the person I'm looking for." Garamond's heart falls to the floor with a wet thud, the blonde-haired man stepping over the old man's now slumping body.

Dad? But Ginny's dad died… a hunting accident.

"Yes, yes, *hunting accident*. The same rubbish Garamond always spews." The man flashes me a fanged smile, his eyes glowing red.

"And yes, this one *can* read minds." He grins. "Well, to an extent. I find blind rage leaves the mind *wide* open."

"Je Wouj…" Bett's voice snarls behind us, the pack's wolf form dulled by the clouds filling the sky, their human forms returning.

"Mm, yes. Never quite liked that name," he snaps. "I prefer Samuel." His eyes fall to Ginny. "Not quite your *dad* anymore,

Gin. Daddy took a little bite from a vampire some time ago, and, well, Mumsie was *not* impressed. Said she couldn't be with a *monster* like me, kicked me to the curb," he scoffs, standing in front of his daughter.

I try to move, to step closer to Ginny, to take her hand, to pull her away, but I can't.

Samuel smiles, a knowing smirk, his elongated finger pressing against his lips. "Shush, puppy. *Sit.*"

My legs give way and I fall to the ground.

Varg snarls behind me, stepping closer.

"Uh, uh. I may not be able to control your old mind, Vargus, but I can certainly have fun with this pup of yours." Samuel's grin fades, his eyes flashing red. *"Don't push me."*

With a painted smile, Samuel continues. "You see, Grandaddy over there, he truly was just trying to protect you, Gin." He pauses, a laugh dancing on his lips. "He was even willing to forgive and forget about the whole *werewolf* love interest. He'd devoted his life to a cure, you know, ever since his own daughter fell in love with a wretched mutt!" The words spit from his mouth. "Looks like Fred was right about *apples and trees*, just not in the way they thought."

I can feel the pack spreading out, Varg and Tosh moving to the left, Bett and Alma, the right. Without looking, I can feel their steps, as if we're moving as one.

A strange warmth radiates from my pocket, and I feel the familiar lumps of Mum's runes. I slide one into the palm of my hand, Samuel still nattering on, oblivious. I feel the stone's warmth permeate through me, and I know instantly which rune it is.

"*I could never love a monster*, Malena had said," Samuel mocks.

I roll the stone in my hand, my eyes closing, and the memory of song, a prayer, washes over me, the words a distant memory of my life before. Of my family before. Of mum.

Shield me from harm, shield me from fear,
and with your strength, keep danger clear.
Keep me safe, and keep me sound,
for in your warm embrace, I'm bound.

I whisper the words, the chant becoming stronger with each recital, and I feel Samuel's control lifting.

"And then what does that bitch do?" Samuel continues. "Shacks up with a pack of dogs. Even invites one into her fucking bed." Samuel takes a breath, closing his eyes. He tugs at the sleeve of his jacket, adjusting his lapel.

I shift my legs, moving into a crouch as the power of Algiz fills me, my attention, every fibre of my being focused now on

Samuel.

"You see, it wasn't your grandfather who killed your mum, Gin." Samuel's eyes flare with wild, feral delight. "It was me."

CHAPTER THIRTY-SEVEN

Ginny's scream is all-consuming. The pain in her voice cuts through the night, carrying the weight of a truth too terrible to bear. In that heart-wrenching moment, I see her soul unravel, the shock in her eyes.

"And Randy, I guess I should own up to that one, too. Got a bit carried away. Stalking a daughter and her paramour can make one quite famished," Samuel laughs.

That mocking sound ignites a fire within me, and I feel the change coming.

"And I guess I should own up to Aunty Sofia." Samuel raises his hands in the air, joining his wrists together, turning to Garamond's lifeless form. "Book me, Daddy," he laughs. "Those dull Donaldsons, too. That horrid woman with the limp. I couldn't quite finish off that chap with the comb-over, he was far too bitter."

Shock and rage hit me. He's been there. Every time. Following me. Ruining me. Waves of power wash over me, the moon at its apex. My bones start to ache. A shiver from deep within erupts and my entire body trembles, flesh tightening with goosebumps. My breath becomes laboured as I try to resist the shift. I focus on Ginny, my grounding force, her face a contorted mixture of shock and anger, her eyes darting between her ravaged grandfather and the murderous man she once called *Dad*.

If I focus on Ginny, maybe I can stop it. Focus on her, on making sure she's safe.

But the pull's too strong, the wolf within me too insistent.

I let out a growl of frustration, and my muscles begin to bulge and contort.

No…

It's as though a thousand needles are piercing my flesh from the inside. I can feel the fur pushing through my pores like sharp blades breaking free.

I double over in agony, my spine cracking, the pressure building in my face, the weight of a snout pushing forth, my mouth metallic as my teeth lengthen, sharpening further.

The runes fall from the pockets of my shredding clothes, and I see the familiar shapes in the dirt. Wunjo. Laguz. I grab the smooth stones, one in each morphing fist, my eyes flashing to Ginny, watching as Samuel circles her, his movements a languid dance of power.

"No!" the word barks, and I stand, the warmth of the runes running through my hands, a surge of adrenaline pulsing through my veins. The pack senses it, their instincts heightened, their curiosity piqued. I feel their collective gaze upon me, like a wave of energy washing over my skin.

Samuel turns, slowly, his red eyes meeting mine. A flicker of rage sparks on his once composed face. "I said sit!"

The word hits me, and I feel the force of it, but my will is stronger. My power is stronger.

"No…" I growl, stepping forward, my heart pounding in rhythm with the pack's growing excitement. The moon, a silver sentinel above us, casts our shadows long and fierce. Varg and Bett, their eyes alight with anticipation, close in, their breaths synchronising with mine.

The air crackles with tension as the pack senses the undiluted power coursing through me, a power that defies Samuel's command and his dominance. In this moment, I am not just one of them; I am their protector, their beacon of hope. The pack's unity and my newfound control over my transformation create a symphony of exhilaration that reverberates through the night, as if the very earth beneath us is trembling in response to our collective strength.

"Don't make this worse than it needs to be, *pup*," Samuel spits, eyes wild.

"Too late." I smile, my grin turning predatory, sharp teeth catching the moonlight. With the swiftness of lightning striking earth, I lunge at Samuel, a blur of fur and fury. His surprise registers for a split second before my claws find their mark, tearing through his defences. The pack erupts in a chorus of howls and snarls, joining the fray with a surge of ferocity that matches my own.

A vicious hiss escapes Samuel's lips, drowned out by the pack's thunderous assault. We're a whirlwind of motion and rage. Teeth snap, claws slash. I stay relentless, my human form melding with the wolf, giving me strength beyond words, my movements fluid and precise, pressing my advantage against Samuel. The pack's collective strength surges around us, lending us the power of the wild.

But something cold and undead resides in Samuel, and I can feel it with every assault of his own. Tosh falls first, retreating to the underbrush, with Alma soon following.

Bett retreats, transforming in the shade of the gumtrees, tending to the wounds of her pack.

"He's stronger than I thought," I snarl, Varg's bristling white mane shaking in agreement, and I feel a moment of panic. Not for me. Not for us.

"Where's Ginny?" My eyes search the field, and I see her quivering body lying in the dirt.

Without a word, Varg bounds to her, nuzzling, pulling her up onto his body before bounding off to the underbrush with the rest of the pack.

"And that's your weakness," Samuel laughs, spitting

blackened blood to the dirt. "You have a heart."

Samuel charges again, but this time, I'm ready. I leap over him, spinning in midair like a shadow unfurling in the moonlight, my transformation a seamless dance with the night. Unlike the agonising pain of before, the wolf within me is a willing partner, slipping through my consciousness like silk through a loom. I'm not bound by the usual confines of my kind; I am the master of my own transformation, a symphony conductor directing every note of my existence.

With each stride, I embrace the duality of my being, the human mind harmonising with the wild heart. My leap carries me over Samuel's charge, and as I land, my form is not a beastly caricature but a manifestation of power and control. The moon bathes me in its silver glow, and I pounce, clamping my jaws around Samuel's neck and collarbone, twisting and tugging until I hear a sickening snap.

Samuel's anguished cry echoes through the air, but I don't let go. My heart, the very thing he mocked as weakness, beats steadily within my chest, guiding me with a purpose beyond mere survival. It's the heart that connects me to the pack, to Ginny, and to the unwavering conviction that we fight for something greater than ourselves.

As Samuel's struggles grow weaker, his taunts turn into desperate pleas. "Let go, damn you!"

With one final twist, I wrench my jaws from Samuel's neck, releasing him. He crumples to the ground, gasping for air, clutching his shredded throat. I step back, my gaze never leaving him as the wolf subsides and Fred returns.

"You see, Samuel," I say, my tone unwavering, "you were right. I do have a heart. And it's that very heart that makes me stronger than you could ever be."

Samuel gasps for breath, his eyes darting wildly between me and Ginny. Before I can react, he disappears in a blur of motion, vampire speed taking him towards Ginny, his cruel laughter piercing the night.

"But hearts are such fragile things, aren't they?" Samuel sneers, shoving Varg to the dirt before clasping Ginny by the throat, his other hand hovering above her chest, fingers long and poised as needles.

My heart races. "Don't hurt her!"

Movement through the dense scrub catches my eye as a strange fog seeps through the logs and leaves.

Suddenly, a flash of golden fur streaks from the shadows, a sleek but mighty wolf charging with incredible speed. In one fluid, breathtaking motion, the wolf leaps towards Samuel, teeth bared and jaws wide, aiming for his taloned hand. In one deft motion, the golden wolf seizes Samuel's hand, swiftly dragging him to the ground and disappearing into the bracken. The underbrush rustles and shivers as the confrontation vanishes from sight.

Ginny, freed from Samuel's grasp, collapses to the ground, gasping for breath and clutching her throat.

Growls and yelps fill the air. Then, as if summoned by an unspoken call to arms, Varg and the other wolves launch themselves into the dense foliage, their powerful forms converging on the undead fiend.

Amid this tumult, a lone wolf comes hurtling from the dense bushes, landing with a resounding thud.

Bett.

Undaunted, the obsidian wolf quickly regains her footing, muscles coiled with renewed determination. With a fierce snarl, her fur matted with dirt and leaves, Bett lunges back into the throng of battle.

I hold Ginny close in my arms, enveloping her in a desperate shield from the horror that unfurls before us. Her body trembles against mine, and I can feel the rhythm of her fear. I pull her closer, covering her ears with my arms as the air vibrates with Samuel's blood-curdling scream, slicing through the night like a serrated blade. The wolves' primal howls reverberate, a cacophony of raw, untamed fury cut short by a sickening, wet tearing that rips through the chaos.

The shivering of leaves and branches subsides. The wolves,

drenched in filth and gore, limp from the bushes retreating to the shadows to mend to their wounds.

And that's when I see him, his fur a deep, lustrous black with subtle golden highlights that shimmer in the moonlight, triumphant. The gruesome trophy in his mouth drops to the ground as his body morphs, his gleaming fur retreating, leaving golden brown skin.

It can't be.

My heart twists, relief flooding through me like a tidal wave. With burning eyes and a tightening throat, my vision blurs as tears well up, uncontrollable and fierce. Every fibre of my being succumbs to the overwhelming rush of emotions. I watch in awe as Mathusi, alive and unharmed, walks towards me, Samuel's gnarled head now clutched in his hand like a gruesome relic of victory.

"But... You... Sarge..." I stutter, the words bubbling past the tears.

Mathusi falls to the ground in front of me. "Sarge had a change of heart."

"But the gunshot..."

"*Cunt*stable Dale won't be bad-mouthing any more wolves any time soon. And besides. Couldn't let you have all the fun, ya goof." His eyes shimmer as he wraps his arms around me, pulling Ginny and me close.

"Is it over?" Ginny's voice whispers from between us.

Tears stream down my cheeks as my laughter bubbles up, a strange and beautiful fusion of joy and sorrow. "It fucking better be."

Sarge bounds over the crest, a group of wolves following, their howls echoing through the forest.

"Aksel…" Varg's voice quivers. "Cousin!"

In the shadows of a blossoming bottlebrush, the two men limp and stumble towards each other, laughing, crying, embracing. The rest of the Rustmane pack follow, their ginger coats transforming away from the moon's glow.

I look to Mathusi, eyes wide. "Sarge was a crumpled mess on the ground. The beating he took… then the cure! How did he…"

"While you lot were carrying on, he crawled away. Came back to help me with them." Mathusi nods to the Rustmane pack. "Sarge ain't so bad after all." He shrugs. "Being human suits him."

Staring down at Ginny in my arms, her chest rising and falling with each laboured breath, and Mathusi by my side, I can't help but feel that this moment is a turning point. The bonds of family forged, the unity of the pack, and the power of our love have carried us through this darkness.

I lean down and press my lips to Ginny's forehead, a gentle, tender kiss that speaks of emotions too overwhelming to put into words. Then I look to Mathusi, my friend, my family, offering him a grateful smile.

"How about a little less hugging and a whole lot more clothes, hm?"

EPILOGUE

ONE YEAR LATER

As I reflect on the moon's ever-changing phases and my own evolution, I'm reminded that the journey of self-discovery is ongoing. Just as the moon continues to wax and wane, so too does my understanding of myself and my place in the world. Each phase brings new insights, new challenges, and new opportunities for growth.

In the quiet moments of our lives, as we rebuild ourselves from the wreckage of the past, there are also stories of new beginnings and fresh horizons.

I've been accepted into the creative writing program at Outwash's Capitol University, fulfilling a long-held dream. The world of words and storytelling has truly become my refuge, a place where I can channel the extraordinary experiences of our journey into tales of wonder and magic. It's a path of self-discovery, and every word I pen is a step towards understanding myself and the world around me.

Ginny, too, despite the past year, has found solace in her work and her studies. Her hard work has paid off, the veterinary scholarship she had worked so tirelessly to achieve now a reality. Her love for animals and her determination to heal and protect them shine brightly in her chosen path. As she delves into her studies, her once-muted spirit begins to thrive once more, and she's become a beacon of hope and resilience.

Reflecting on the year that has passed, amidst the achievements and newfound paths we've embarked on, there's a particular light shining on the revelation of a cure for lycanthropy. While I've come to embrace my own lycanthropy as a part of my identity, I can't help but feel a sense of relief knowing that others like me now have a choice. The Hunter's Guild's careful approach, with thorough assessments and regulations in place, ensures that the decision to undergo the cure remains deeply personal and consensual. Witnessing the Rustmane pack, now a united family, opt for the cure after enduring so much, fills me with a sense of solidarity and understanding. It's not about rejecting one's nature, but rather embracing the freedom to choose one's path, whether human or lycanthrope. As they settle into their new human lives in Acacia Hills, I'm reminded of the importance of agency and acceptance in shaping our own narratives, both as individuals and as a community.

Community. Home. Something I thought I'd never have, yet here I am, my life moving in ways I could never have predicted. Ginny and I are now living together, sharing a small apartment in the heart of Outwash. Our days are filled with the simple joys of domesticity, like cooking meals together and cuddling on the couch with a book or a movie.

And then there's Mathusi, the unexpected addition to our household. His knowledge of plants and herbs has taken him on an interesting path, resulting in a love of baking, his interest blossoming after a chance encounter with Nina's nephew, Dan, at the bakery in Outwash. Dan introduced Mathusi to the art of the knead, and it's become a passion he can't resist. Our kitchen is often filled with the delightful aroma of freshly baked breads and cakes, infused with his mother's teachings of the power of plants. Mathusi's creations are nothing short of spectacular.

But there's more to Mathusi's story. He and Dan have formed a deep connection, one that transcends friendship. They are both navigating the complexities of their identities, exploring what queer asexual dating looks like, and supporting each other every step of the way. It's a beautiful and profound journey of self-discovery and love, and I can't help but be inspired by their courage and openness.

As I look around our cosy apartment, filled with books, the scent of Mathusi's latest baking experiment wafting through the air, I realise that life has a way of surprising us. We have faced the darkness together, and now we are embracing the light, one day at a time.

Our journey is far from over, and the road ahead holds its own share of challenges and adventures. But we are bound by the threads of love and friendship, and together, we continue to write the stories of our lives, one beautiful chapter at a time.

I look up from the typed words on my laptop just as a knock comes from the front door of our little apartment. Ginny's at the veterinary clinic today, and both Mathusi and Dan left to catch a movie.

What's the bet Mathusi forgot his keys.

The knock rattles again.

"Yeah, yeah, I'm coming, keep your pants on," I laugh, picking up my scattered rune stones and sliding them into my pocket before unlatching the door. My smile soon fades. "You're not Mathusi."

The man at the door blinks. "Uh. Delivery for Fred McTire?" The courier smiles.

"That'd be me."

He hands me an international express envelope. I turn the envelope over in my hand, idly scribbling my signature against the courier's digital display. "Thanks," I mumble, closing the door to his receding footsteps.

Pulling on the red tab, the heavy cardboard opens, a smaller envelope inside slipping out. My fingers trace over the embossed golden seal pressed against the back of the letter. I scrunch my face, trying to read the emblem. "The Luna Fidelis Society?"

Bett's words come rushing into my mind, *sometimes, the past catches up with us…*

"*No matter how hard we try to escape it.*" My shoulders involuntarily shiver. "Ominous much?"

Turning the envelope over in my hand, I shrug, and place it on the kitchen table atop the bowl of fruit. "That's something for future Fred to worry about."

The apartment suddenly feels very quiet, and very small, the glint of the embossed gold seal glinting menacingly next to an overripe banana.

"It's just a dumb letter," I mumble. Just as I consider making some coffee and trying my hardest to forget that goldleaf envelope doesn't exist, keys jingle outside the apartment door, the latch clicking open, Ginny's cheerful voice eradicating the ick that was settling into the space.

"Fred, I'm back!" she yells, her keys clinking into the bowl by the door. "It was quiet at the clinic, so I got to finish early."

"Coffee?"

Padding into the kitchen, Ginny hums happily in reply, her arms around my waist, her kiss on my shoulder.

"Oh. What's that?" she asks, her hands sliding out from the

hug.

"They're oranges, sweety," I tease.

Even with my back turned, busying myself with the kettle, I can sense her little tongue poking out at me.

"I meant the envelope wedged *inside* the bowl of oranges."

Glancing at the envelope, I'm still unsure if I want to know. "Dunno." I shrug.

Ginny's fingers trace the golden sigil on the back, and she lets out a low whistle. "Fancy."

I let out a wry chuckle, knowing I should probably open it and find out what this *Luna Fidelis Society* wants. "Maybe it's an invitation to an exclusive club," I joke, though my tone doesn't mask the unease that lingers in the room.

Ginny narrows her eyes at the envelope. "Well, it doesn't look like the kinda club I'd wanna join."

Soon the kitchen fills with the rich, earthy scent of freshly poured coffee, a comforting fragrance that reminds me of countless mornings shared with Ginny, and I feel my mind ease.

With a click, the apartment door opens again, Mathusi and Dan stepping inside. Their laughter melds seamlessly with the scents and sounds of the kitchen, transforming the space into a cosy haven where the worries of the world momentarily dissipate.

"Hey, we're back!" Mathusi calls out, his voice carrying a

note of excitement.

Dan grins and adds, "Yeah, we caught that new indie flick. It was awesome."

I smile as they enter the kitchen, always in awe at Dan and the way he dresses. I've learned so much from him, watching his approach to life, the way he manifests confidence around himself, evident today by his skintight corduroy leggings, bright purple to match his bright purple eyeliner.

I wonder if he knew Ms Robinson?

His carefree energy fills the room, and it's these moments with my friends, the warmth of Ginny's presence, and the smell of coffee brewing that make me cherish the simple joys of life. I hold off on mentioning the envelope and the unease it brings.

"Mmm, yes please!" Mathusi sings, taking the coffee from my hands.

"Rude," I jest.

Mathusi smiles, his eyes falling on the envelope, and a look of recognition crosses his face. "The Luna Fidelis Society," he mutters, pausing before adding, "You should open it."

"Yeah, but, who are they?" I ask, taking the envelope, my finger sliding under the lip of the seal.

"They're the Werewolf Guild," Mathusi says, sitting at the kitchen table.

Curiosity and anxiety swirl in my chest. "What would they

want with me?"

"Come on, open it," Ginny says, patting the chair next to her. "Might be important."

Sitting down, I carefully tear past the gold sigil, removing a neatly folded piece of paper. I can feel Mathusi and Ginny's eyes on me. Dan, however… I watch from the corner of my eye as he paces the doorway to the kitchen, his teeth picking at the wick of his thumb.

"What does it say?" Ginny asks, almost bursting out of her seat.

"Dunno." I look back down at the paper, turning it over in my hand, the letters written in a language I can't make heads nor tails of. "I can't read it."

"Do you need glasses or something?" Mathusi grins, and I swat him with my free hand.

"My eyesight's just fine, thanks. I mean it's not in English." I stare down at the curling words.

"It's *Laramaic*," Dan says, still pacing the entry to the kitchen. He's not looking too good, his face sickly pale.

"Dan, you alright?" I ask.

Mathusi turns in his seat. "Babe?"

"And what's *Laramaic*?" Ginny asks.

"An ancient hybrid language. Latin and Aramaic." His voice quivers as he stops.

I want to laugh and make a joke about how many languages he thinks he knows, but something in his eyes holds me back. He's not looking at me, but at the letter in my hands, as though it might explode.

"Let me see," Dan breathes, his voice a harsh whisper.

I nod. Holding out the letter, Dan cautiously approaches the table, reaching out a hesitant hand. After a brief pause, he gently pinches the corner, peering at the scrawling words inside, his eyes widening, nostrils flaring.

"This isn't from the Luna Fidelis Society." Dan's voice trembles, and I wonder if the paper is actually going to self-combust as Dan inhales a sharp breath. That's when I see it. We all do. Dan's eyes. No longer gentle brown, the eyes staring back at us shift to an eerie shade of crimson.

Only one other person had eyes like that. Samuel. A vampire.

Mathusi's face turns ashen, and Ginny's already at the kitchen sink, knife in hand. I can feel the hairs on my neck bristle, the wolf within growling.

Dan steps back, palms open, hands out as he slumps against the wall, sliding down to the tiles below. "No, no, it's okay, please, please, just…" Dan rubs his eyes, the red subsiding, but when he looks back at us, his features seem softer, and his eyes…

"Please," Dan begs, his eyes no longer red. They aren't even brown, but instead sparkle like twin sapphires bathed in celestial light, mirroring the boundless expanse of the open sky on a cloudless summer day. The rune stones in my pocket seem to chitter with excitement.

"What's going on, Dan?" I ask, poised, ready to strike if this all goes horribly wrong… but something makes me think otherwise. I can feel the warmth of the stones against my thigh.

Mathusi slowly steps closer, crouching next to the trembling ball of Dan.

"That letter… it's not from the Werewolf Guild," Dan whispers, his shimmering eyes darting between the three of us. "And I'm not a vampire, please believe me."

"I believe you," I whisper, taking the knife from Ginny's hand, guiding us to the open floor in front of the fridge. "*We* believe you."

Ginny's eyes find mine, questioning, though I squeeze her fingers back in reassurance, patting the runes in my pocket, and Ginny's face softens. I look down at the letter on the floor between us. "Who's it from?"

Dan takes the paper once more, turning it over in his hands. He closes his eyes, his mouth moving, whispering words even I can't hear, then places it back down in front of us. The paper seems to writhe and slither, as if it were alive. The letters coil across the page, the words moving, transforming, converging to form one, bold statement.

"It's from The Sanguine Order," Dan says, absolute. "The Vampire Guild."

Ginny clutches my thigh, squeezing.

"Fred…" Mathusi's voice is low and laced with concern.

I stare down at the paper, at the jumble of blood-red words.

"Winnifred Mac Tíre Must Die."